Beneath the Wild Fig Tree

Fiona Preston

Wild Mind Publishing

First published in 2024

Wild Mind Publishing acknowledges the Traditional Owners and their custodianship of the unceded lands on which this novel takes place and was written, and pays respect to their Ancestors and their descendants, and their continued cultural and spiritual connections to Country.

Wild Mind Publishing
Gumbaynggirr Country
NSW, Australia
Email: wildmindpublishing@gmail.com
Web: www.wildmindpublishing.com.au

Cover design by Andy Banks. Moonbird on the Wing
Typeset in 11/20 pt Minion Pro by Post Pre-press Group

 A catalogue record for this book is available from the National Library of Australia

ISBN 978-1-7635886-0-8 (paperback)
ISBN 978-1-7635886-1-5 (hardback)
ISBN 978-1-7635886-2-2 (e-book)

FOR HANNAH

Contents

1

Continental Drift, 1984

I WAS BORN BENEATH a wild fig tree one humid afternoon. My arrival cut short my parents' camping trip and within minutes a hard rain baptised me. Rivers burst their banks. Drought transformed into flood, but the van, inclined to falter in the slightest drizzle, staggered up a collapsing pass, and carried us home to Armidale.

My birth is a family legend. The story has been repeated so many times, with so many details thrown in, that it's not clear where truth ends and fantasy begins. Dad said the afterbirth was seized by ravens. Mum said it was left to nourish the tree. He said my hair was wild and orange, she said I was bald and calm, but neither of them told me I'd been born into a web of deceit that contributed to the endless years of our continental drift.

They said I learned to walk on the dunes of K'gari, that I first spoke on Bama Country near Cairns, and that my first attempt at swimming was on the Great Barrier Reef. I began school in the sweaty heat of Darwin, and in Top End towns like Kununurra Dad found work on cattle stations. The years we lived near Albany were my happiest. There, on the Great Southern Ocean's coastline, forests seemed endless and small granite islands basked in a turquoise ocean. I made my first friend when I was ten, but my parents insisted on moving on.

Dad played guitar in Coorong pubs and we lived in a houseboat on the Murray River. He took to carpentry and boatbuilding and plied these skills as we moved slowly across Victoria. Back in New South Wales, he helped friends build a mud brick house in the Snowy Mountains. But whatever he did and wherever we went, he had poetry in his rucksack and his guitar on the back seat.

Mum's archaeology textbooks sat in neat stacks while she worried daily about our bank balance. In the gaps between casual work and studying long distance, she sometimes home-schooled me. And as for me? I knew nothing yet of the promise in my past or the island in my future.

Our aimless wandering coincided with Mum's earth mother phase and although our unsteady lifestyle tired her, when I got anxious about starting at new schools, she said it would give me backbone. It didn't. I longed for stability. My parents yearned for the next place along the scenic route.

In Bermagui, when I was twelve, Dad and his workmates formed a syndicate and won big on TattsLotto, so we visited his family in Scotland, then went to Aotearoa, to the skinny South Island, Te Waipounamu, with its ridge of snowy mountains, where we camped in their shadow, beside a glacial river.

One impeccable morning, with the sun lighting up the long, wet grass, we went for a walk. Foxgloves splashed purple along the path that ran beside the riverbank and up to the clifftop, high enough to alarm my mum. I tried to join Dad at the edge, but I didn't anticipate the giddiness that would overcome me. As I lurched against him, Mum whipped me back. Transfixed with terror, we watched as in slow motion Dad teetered against the big blue sky then with an anguished yell, vanished over the edge.

That elongated moment haunts me still. Whenever I hear a sound like pebbles tumbling or a large splash, or encounter purple foxgloves, I'm back there at that river.

Moment as ghost, is what Nan called it.

'Wheeler!' Mum screamed.

'I've killed him,' I howled, as we watched him being swept away, and, panicking, rushed down that path, to where we could help him out. He collapsed on the grass, blue-skinned, teeth chattering, grazed all over. Blood spurted from a gash on his leg.

Back at the van, I sat beside him sobbing and apologising. Mum bandaged him and covered him in all the clothes and blankets we had to prevent hypothermia. She gave him whisky and insisted he sleep, then she and I lay in the sunshine discussing the debacle. I believed we were both thinking about how in that one elongated moment we had realised how important we were to each other, but she had our lifestyle on her mind.

'I'm going to assert myself, Nicky. It's time.'

The next day we left the campsite. Dad had cracked some ribs, so Mum drove. We followed the river past rapids he was lucky he hadn't gone over. *I* was lucky too, because then I'd have been a murderer.

Downstream that river became a loose, liquid plait, all silvery along the wide valley floor. I was thinking how serene it seemed here when I heard Mum having a serious conversation with Dad.

'We're going to settle down in Hobart and live like a conventional family. Going home is hard for me, but I want stability and Nicky *needs* it.' She looked across at him. 'This adventuring life hasn't always been fun. It's been difficult, *especially* for Nicky,' and she smiled at me in the rear-view mirror. 'Sweetheart, we'll find you a good school. And here's my promise – we will *never* move again. And Wheeler,' she added, 'you're wasting your talents and your degree. You must start teaching.'

That is exactly what she said. She was a new person.

My throat felt too tight for speech. Yesterday I'd cried because of what I'd done. Now I was crying with relief because our travelling days were ending, even though more than once during that long conversation, Dad said through gritted teeth that the way she'd gone about it wasn't fair. We were driving slowly, the road was winding. He said, 'Maybe for a year or two, Freya,' and we both said, 'No, forever!'

'Talk about getting stuck into a bloke when he's down,' and he winced as we went over another bump.

Mum smiled at me conspiratorially. 'The girls finally get a win,' she said, and I leaned back and started dreaming about making real friends and finally getting to know my nan.

The fact is, if we hadn't gone to Aotearoa, Dad wouldn't have fallen in the river, and we wouldn't have come to Hobart, and without that happening our story wouldn't have unfolded in the way it did. For instance, after crossing Bass Strait on the overnight ferry, we met a lost dog running beside the Midlands Highway, where, on either side of the road the hills looked bare for miles and the trees were shattered and dead. We picked him up and he certainly seemed relieved to have found us.

'Probably out on the scrounge for a new life,' said Dad. 'Like you two.'

The dog sat beside me, gazing out the window. His feathery tail waved, and whenever he opened his mouth, he broke into a smile. Mum wanted to drop him off at a pound. She thought his owner might be looking for him and worse, he might infect us with hydatids.

Dad and I agreed he was a little bit collie, a wee bit kelpie, perhaps a sheepdog gone AWOL, and Dad said his snoz was distinctly Afghan, lending him a certain aristocratic air. The dog kept looking out that window, then glancing quickly back at me as though he wanted to share a joke and as we'd been taking turns reading *Kes* by Barry Hines, and as this hitchhiker had a kestrel's eye for the sky, his name was decided.

Mum insisted on silence as we swooped down to the bridge. Across that wide and beautiful estuary with Storm Bay beyond it, I saw the city nestled in the foothills of the purple mountain.

'Home,' she sighed, touching a finger to her eye.

Dad sadly hummed 'Goodbye Yellow Brick Road'. I hugged Kes, bursting with happiness. The city was exquisite.

At first we stayed with Nan and then we rented a house. Dad found temporary teaching jobs and charmed his way into a band, and Mum was excited she could study archaeology on campus. Home was sunlit and warm and full of music, with Dad bashing about on his guitar and Mum happy to go exploring with me and Kes, up and down the mountain she knew so well and along the river. I made friends. Nan was wonderful. I even learned to sail on the river with my best friend, Sally, who lived down the road.

After a year or two, tiny tensions began to grow. Mum said that by staying in one place, we were simply finding a new balance, and I believed her.

I hadn't yet learned that parents should never be trusted.

2

Gadigal Country (Paddington, Sydney) 2000

Cool Enigma

I DIDN'T WANT THE phone call, and it couldn't have been more poorly timed. Sydney was sweltering. The air conditioner had failed again in the offices of Riley & Blair Corporate Lawyers. Moods were brittle, the pressure intense, and the most impatient man in the firm was at my door, jabbing his finger at his watch.

'One moment, Max.'

'We're late, goddammit!'

'It's Sally Jones,' said the caller. 'It's been a while! I told Freya you'd be thrown, but I'd love to catch up and she's given me a parcel for you.'

We made hasty arrangements to meet on Friday evening, but after putting down the phone, I realised she didn't mean next Friday, she meant this Friday, as in two days from now, exactly when Arno was getting back from Italy. I'd struggle to make the airport in time.

'Damn,' I muttered.

'Damn bloody hurry,' said Max, striding off ahead of me.

He marched me to the lift, briefing me all the way up to the board-room. The more miserable I feel the straighter I hold myself.

'Good afternoon, gentlemen,' I said and took my seat, posture perfect.

~

At home, I tried phoning Arno at his parents' place in Rome, but the call rang out. Instead, over a glass of wine, I reviewed the day.

The meeting had been tense, had resulted in yet another contract to write while other matters compounded on my desk. The new senior partner had been patronising each time he interrupted me, and at the end of the meeting the boys' club closed ranks. The year 2000 was disappointing me. *Time to move on*, whispered the voice in my head.

Right now, there were more pressing matters, like Sally's visit. I regretted suggesting we meet at my place, but as I didn't have her number, I couldn't reschedule. Today my poise, so carefully cultivated, had given way to distractibility and I hated not living up to my own expectations.

I knew Arno would return with perfume. It had become a thing after he'd once bought me a fragrance called Cool Enigma. Lying on my bed with his arms behind his head he'd watched me spray it on my wrists.

'The name suits you, Nicky.'

He saw me wince and reassured me. The next time he went away he bought me Coco, but that comment lingered.

Later, I stood on my balcony, anxiously planning how to reach the airport on time after seeing Sally. Across the road neighbours moved like shadows behind their blinds and in the dark sky overhead I saw the lights of a plane. Arno's absence felt endless. I desperately wanted him back.

~

Sally stood on my doorstep, a bottle of wine in one hand and a bouquet of irises in the other. Her dress picked up their colour and the bracelet on her arm matched their lime stalks, yet she looked as though she'd got ready in a rush, her long blonde hair wild, and her sandals scuffed.

'Nicky!' She moved to embrace me. 'Love this Victorian terrace. A pity there aren't any trees on your street, though.'

'Lovely to see you, Sally.' I accepted the flowers and ushered her in.

'I so enjoyed my walk here. Love Sydney – all those avenues of wild figs and paperbarks.'

'And jacarandas,' I said, searching for a vase while she studied my living room. 'Don't be harsh. It's a short-term rental snapped up in a hurry.'

'I remember how much you loved the ocean. I imagined you'd be on the edge of the harbour.'

I live on a narrow Paddington road congested with traffic during the week – the lifeblood of Sydney rushing through this small, constricted capillary. My house is like a cell down in the guts of a shape-shifting monster. Inconsequential it and I may be, but we are a part of a greater thing, the city, that moves and breathes, spreading in all directions simultaneously. It's true there are no trees on my street and it's easy to believe it's on no bird's flight path. In fact, the only thing that isn't man-made is the sky, and increasingly that wears a human stain.

'I happen to like the inner city.' *And time is a trickster; I'd forgotten how effusive yet blunt you can be*, I thought, putting the vase on the kitchen counter.

Sally studied me. 'I guess we're typical Tasmanians, heading off to the mainland or overseas in search of different experiences. My share house isn't nearly as tidy as this, but it's fun. We're a bunch of musos and a few of us have green fingers, so we harvest a good vegie crop. We're in the Adelaide Hills, not far from your mother. It's more like you and I were used to. The bush, you know.'

I poured the wine. 'Tell me about your music.'

She settled herself on a stool and chatted while I prepped the food, then set the table. Apart from two recordings, her musical career was not unfolding the way she'd hoped, but the landscaping business she'd started, hoping to bring in some extra cash, was thriving; the problem was that it ate into the time she had to focus on songwriting.

She got up to investigate my music collection. 'I've got a thing for Van Morrison,' she said. 'Do you mind?' And she swapped the reggae I'd put on for one of his albums.

'When did we last see each other?' I wondered, wine glass in my hand.

'Honestly?' She adjusted the volume. 'Towards the end of those years you spent at your grandmother's home, when you barely left your room, and everyone was concerned about your depression and your behaviour.'

Enough! said the voice inside my head.

'It was awkward because often you didn't seem to want to see me. And it was sad, because I missed the old you, Nicky, I really did, and I know our paths parted ways but I guess because our parents were good friends, it did feel like something precious was broken.'

'We might have mixed in different circles, Sal, but I depended on your friendship more than I let on. You'd been on the island. You knew what was eating me.'

She leaned back to regard me, and I hastily served up the pasta I'd thrown together, remembering how back when we'd declared ourselves sisters, Sally always, annoyingly, seemed to know more about my life than I did.

'Just so you know, I have to leave for the airport in an hour,' I said, and refilled her glass.

My comment went unacknowledged as she asked about my work.

'You're *that* kind of lawyer? I'd never have imagined.'

'I'm beginning to question the choice. This year's been tough.' And randomly I mentioned the put-downs, a co-worker's unwanted advances and then the aggravating issue of unequal pay.

'Hah! Tough being the token woman. Yay for the patriarchy, driving us ever on towards the abyss. Anyway, Nicky, I'm sure you once told me that you wanted to be involved in environmental law or human rights, something like that?'

I deflected the conversation back to music, but soon the focus returned to me.

'Please tell me you're still writing?'

'Why would I be?'

'You were *always* writing, Nicky. In fact, you and Wheeler both. That study of his, in the lighthouse, remember? Honestly, your father was a big influence on my life, the whole music thing, you know.' She was on a roll. She dazzled me with stories. Her world did, in fact, seem gourmet to my buffet.

I relaxed. Talking to Sally, that old friendship seemed to settle tenuously back into place. I hinted at my whirlwind romance with Arno and how, after much uncertainty on my part and encouragement on his, I'd decided to move in with him.

'You've had huge trust issues to overcome.'

I straightened my back.

'You're afraid of betrayal, of being hurt. It's that simple.'

She was smashing through boundaries, and I needed her gone.

She wanted to see a photo of Arno. Reluctantly I fetched the one I'd framed.

She held it thoughtfully. 'Love the dimple. Italian? He has warm eyes.'

I reclaimed it. He was worth so much more than that brief comment.

'Nicky,' she said, and then after a small pause, 'I'm sorry. I can see I've hurt your feelings.' She reached her hand across the table.

'Don't be silly.' I moved to refill her water.

For the next half hour I kept the conversation firmly in a musical domain. But she nibbled her lip as she piled up our plates and as I took them, she said, 'Nearly forgot,' and fetched the package from her bag. 'Do you know what it is?'

'No idea. Not sure I care.' I dumped it on the counter and glanced at my watch. 'I'll need to leave for the airport in fifteen.' My anxiety was mounting.

'Ouch,' she said. Then returned to reminiscing about our childhood. I allowed a silence to develop.

'Freya sends her love, but she looked *so* tired. I'm worried about her. She'd absolutely love you to visit.'

I breathed in, slid my hands down my spine.

'You know, there was a time when I envied the relationship you had with your mother.'

I tapped my fingers on the side of my chair.

'It's not irretrievable.' She closed her eyes, her face so beautiful, as, briefly, she sang along with the music, reminding me of a night on the island when we'd all sat around a fire together, the Milky Way drifting down the night sky, the full moon and the Seven Sisters above us.

'It was a long time ago and I know how much you suffered. I know I don't have the right to presume, but you'll always be important to me, Nicky, a sister really, although I understand if the feeling isn't mutual.'

Time to get her big feet walking out that door. I looked at my watch and began getting ready to leave.

'Let's not lose touch again,' she said, smothering me in a hug. 'And I'll let Freya know you send your love.'

I closed the door and leaned against it, breathing a mistaken sigh of relief. I didn't know it at the time, but Sally bursting out of my past was the first indication that my tomorrows were about to smash into my yesterdays.

3

Gadigal and Bidjigal Country (Coogee, Sydney) 2000

L'Heure Exquise

LUCK WASN'T ON MY side. I got mired in a traffic jam and panic had replaced anxiety as I rushed through the terminal unsuccessfully seeking Arno. Devastated, I returned to my darkened home and tried to ring him. Ten times my calls rang out.

Eventually he picked up. 'So jetlagged, Nicky. I'm going to sleep in tomorrow.'

'You sound exhausted,' and my words tripped over each other as I explained my debacle of an evening.

The silence on the other end of the phone wasn't promising, but he agreed to meet me at L'Heure Exquise, our favourite Coogee restaurant, for lunch. My shout, I decided, putting the receiver down slowly.

The arrangement gave me time the next morning to drive to McIver's Ladies Pool. A moment to linger and look out to sea, a filigree of surf lacing Wedding Cake Island, and below me to the north, sun umbrellas up on the beach and the lure of the languorous surf had a couple of hopefuls sitting on their boards waiting for a break. Hot sun on my back, the merest tickle of a breeze against my skin, I descended the rock steps and soon I was into the first of twenty laps, close to the periwinkled rock edge, small waves occasionally breaking into the pool, the ocean stretching away beside me, north, east, and down south to embrace Tasmania.

At times my strokes felt energised by a sense of anticipation over what the day would bring, but Freya's parcel was also on my mind. When I'd opened it, an old letter from a high school teacher had fallen out, commending me on my writing, expressing concern about my well-being and asking for a meeting. It accompanied a version of my island journal, redrafted several times during the lost years Sally had referred to. It had been meant to tame distressing memories and help develop a carapace for my protection. Sometimes I think it had the opposite effect.

Now, immersed in seawater, I found myself thinking about my parents, exhaling hard to push the past away. I'd slip into breaststroke and feel irritated with Sally – her fault, the past rushing in. Her fault I hadn't made the airport. I hoped Arno would be over his jetlag and back to his usual amicable self by lunch time. I rolled into backstroke and thought about our first meeting, at a friend's wedding, a year ago. Inviting him back to my flat had seemed the most natural thing in the world to do – and the most compelling. He'd stayed that night and then the next and so our life fell into a routine of nights at mine followed by a gap and then weekends at his.

We arrived at the restaurant at much the same time. I dashed through traffic, and into his arms.

'I am so sorry about last night! I stuffed up big time.'

'Old acquaintance over love of your life?' He smiled at me quizzically. 'Forgive me?'

His kiss was reassuring. He squeezed my hand as he ushered me through the door. Soon we were at a table and ordering. *Perfect company, perfect food, perfect music*, I was thinking as we chatted about his trip, and all the time I was waiting for the right moment to tell him that having missed him intensely, and with my lease up, I was finally ready to move in.

But when we got to dessert our conversation took an unexpected turn. He reached across the table for my hand.

'Being in Italy, I had time to think. You and me, almost exactly twelve months now.'

My heart lurched at the gravity in his voice, the look in his eyes.

'But still, after all this time, Nicky, you keep so much to yourself I don't always feel the connection. I like that you're so independent. I also wish sometimes you'd rely on me more.'

'What do you mean, Arno?'

'I never feel needed.'

'But I do need you! And I wanted to tell you that I've decided—'

'And family. I'm always talking about mine. You're the opposite. Like I've said before, there is some problem here. This is something we've talked about, not so? It's a fact; I bring more commitment, more effort to this relationship.'

'But I love you, Arno. The whole time you were away – the whole time – I can't tell you how much I missed you.' I faltered, my voice unsteady.

The hiss of the espresso machine and the voices around us created a wall of sound enclosing the tension of our silence.

He reached into his pocket and put a small gift on the table. 'I've been thinking about this with a most heavy heart.' He took my hand and placed it on his chest while he went on talking, then moved our hands down so that they covered the gift.

'Arno, wait! I've been thinking too! I wanted to tell you, I'm ready to move in, I understand what you're saying, but I was planning to tell you, I'm not making this up, I've been so looking forward to seeing you, to telling you …'

He smiled at me with an awful kindness and stroked my hand. 'There's a lot between us that is good.' He said 'good' carefully as though it was made of fragile stuff. 'But no you at the airport? No you at my place?' He shook his head. 'I mean so little that you prioritise someone you've never mentioned?'

'Honestly, I tried *so* hard to get there. You know I hate being late.'

He spread his hands. 'Try seeing it from my point of view,' and he gave me the dimpled smile that kills me every time. 'I've made money fast; you know that by the time I'm forty, I want to be doing something more meaningful, I want to be in the right relationship, I want a big family, Nicky, like the one I come from. I want to be back in Italy.'

I stared out the window, my body rigid. A small headache started up in my right temple. Not for the first time, my heart felt like it was breaking.

He squeezed my hands, little furrows crinkling his forehead.

'Nicky, wake up! You're not really living.' He gave my hands a small shake. 'We need to get a clearer perspective on this, maybe you need some counselling?' And he let my hands go.

I reached for my glass of water. Water in a glass is tame. It's small in there, captured and vulnerable, as opposed to wild water – wilful, determined, accepting no boundaries. Looking up, I shrank him to a tiny dot, so far away his words blurred.

And then, 'I met someone in Italy. Talking to this person clarified my thoughts.'

The world shifted on its axis.

I gazed at him. He gazed at me. That old familiar feeling of loss and betrayal overwhelmed me again. Time slowed. Sound faded. I stood up and slowly drank that glass of water. Then I reached for my bag, slung it over my shoulder, carefully smoothed down my dress.

'It's over,' I said. And wobbling slightly on my heels, I strode out through that drift of music and voices.

Outside an elderly man was playing something poignant on a saxophone. Noticing me, he gave a small bow and segued into a Leonard Cohen number. The traffic had the sound of the river in it. The song he'd chosen was one of Wheeler's favourites – something about a book, diamonds, and junk. I stood on the edge of the pavement, flooded by the moment.

'Abscond, thoughts!' I said out loud. A pedestrian raised an eyebrow and moved aside.

I focussed on numbing my feelings, on closing down longing, because here was the thing about Arno – he had too much charisma. Every time we went out I'd be hypervigilant. It left me feeling diminished.

I'd been stupid to think this issue would fade away once we were living together. And as if I'd ever move to Italy.

Arno had been a big waste of time. 'Hate you, hate you,' I muttered, unlocking my car. Then I reached into my bag for a tissue, unable to stem my tears.

At home all I had was a half-finished bottle of wine. Not enough, unfortunately.

4

Gadigal Country (Paddington, Sydney) 2000

In the Bunker

I LAY IN BED, curtains drawn, not drunk enough for stupor. At some point the phone rang. It was Freya.

'Have I got you at a bad time?' she asked. 'Nicky, are you all right?' She started asking about work and then paused. 'Are you sure you're all right?'

'I'm slightly feverish, that's all.'

She suggested chicken soup, wondered if Sally had given me the parcel, said she and Steve were thinking about a weekend away at Port Fairy, but that she, too, had not been feeling well.

Steve. The awful second husband. 'Right,' I said.

'I wish you had someone to look after you.'

I listened to her struggle to keep up a one-sided conversation. Then came the dreaded invitation, as usual.

'Will you think about visiting? You know, when you're feeling better?'

Sensing from my silence that my position held, she began talking about her cellar needing spring-cleaning. She was teary and the topic was ridiculous.

I cut her off. The disappointment in her voice as she squeezed in her goodbye left me unmoved. My mother always managed to bring out the worst in me.

That night insomnia shattered my sleep into slivers of dark emotion, and as though he was standing at the bottom of my bed, I'd hear Arno talking without being able to decipher the words.

Waking early, I eyed that old journal suspiciously. Back in 1984, my teacher, Mrs Porter, had made me keep a journal while I was on the island, and Nan had later given me leather-bound notebooks she'd bought in Paris, where she'd grown up. During the time my world contracted to her house, she'd urged me to rewrite that island journal, teasing me that she was being for me what she had always wanted for herself: a patron, cultivating the talent she believed I had. She told me that writing weaves magic into memories. Her white hair, when she said this, was caught up in the light, and her blue eyes shone. She had the warmest smile. If you'd asked me what she was like, I would have said she was like a candle.

She brought out the worn map that once steered Wheeler, Freya, and me around the continent. She put the bird-girl sculpture she'd made me on my desk. Quietly, I added my banded pebble, to act as a paperweight.

'Your touchstone,' Nan said, her hands on my shoulders. She kissed my head. 'Now find your heart, lay down your troubles and transform them.'

It was 1986. I was sixteen. I started redrafting my journal but it wasn't the curative Nan thought it would be. I was riddled with vulnerabilities. The past wrapped itself around me and I couldn't break free.

5

Gayamaygal Country (Reef Beach, Sydney) 2000

Mouheneenner Country (Hobart) 1984

Pink Fish and a Eucalypt Leaf

NAN'S PRESENCE FELT PALPABLE as I dragged myself out of bed that hot Sydney morning, made a strong coffee and hesitantly opened the journal. 'Continental Drift,' I read. 'I was born beneath a wild fig tree one humid afternoon …'

Contractual clauses are my language now and with work hours like mine, I barely get time for reading. Yet books had saved me from those 'lost years' of drinking, drugs, and a wasted boyfriend. I often failed to make it to class, but in my last year of school I'd pulled off a last-minute pivot and my final marks stunned everyone.

I'd loved the memoirs of writers like Anne Frank, Anaïs Nin, and Vera Brittain. My teacher stressed narrative and dialogue, and these were the influences I'd used to craft my 1984 journal. I was fourteen and regarded as ahead of my peers in English at least, when those events took place that shaped me forever.

I was subdued when I returned to the office; the pain and shame of Arno's betrayal was acute. The practice is a large one and it can seem impersonal, hostile even, when you're one of a handful of women and the patriarchy rules with a heavy hand. I placed a large vase of flowers on my desk and held my head high, my disposition dispassionate. Max can be a tyrant. That week his temper jarred everyone, causing tension to ripple through the firm. When he wasn't muttering about the large client we'd lost, he was uptight about missed deadlines and financially weak clients with large outstanding payments. During case acceptance meetings, desperate to expunge Arno from my mind, I drifted into childhood memories, present in body, my mind on the island.

The week was endless. No evenings with Arno. No calls, no email. I worked until nine, came home and fell into bed. I still had things at his place, but I didn't feel ready to fetch them.

On the weekend I packed my daypack and, after a moment's hesitation, picked up the journal. We'd been a family of scribes. Dad kept his 'writer's notebooks' in a series of ledgers and even though he swore my scribbling came from him, Freya's letters were a form of creative expression that went unacknowledged. She wrote regularly to her sister, Anneke, but as she had no fixed address, many letters were either never sent or came back 'return to sender'. I'd once found a pile of them at the back of a cupboard and had nicked them, carrying them with me, unread, through various share houses. Now, putting my scruples aside, I plonked them in my daypack before walking out the door.

I headed for small, secluded, Reef Beach at Dobroyd Head, wandering down the bush path, dappled by eucalypt shade, the understory a peacefulness of grass trees, grevillea, and casuarina, listening to the thump of a wallaby, kookaburra laughter, and the small grunts of bush turkeys picking through the undergrowth.

My good luck – the beach was occupied by a heron on the southern reef, but no people. It was low tide. Small, translucent waves broke with a quiet swish. I spread my towel in the fig's generous shade, then listened for a moment to the magpie perched above me. Banyan. Moreton Bay fig. *Ficus macrophylla*. Tree with many Indigenous names. The magpie flew off and I wandered down to the water's edge, seeking the breeze with my cheek, the water's temperature with my toe, paying respect to the communities of oysters, nerites and limpets inhabiting the pocked and patterned sandstone reefs. There were yachts moored off Forty Baskets beach and at Manly, where the ferry was about to berth. I could see Arno's apartment block, perched above the water. I took a moment to feel the discomfort of its presence, but soon the beach's serenity flowed through me. Behind me, bush. Before me, the tranquillity of North Harbour. In the kind shade of that generous tree, I reached for the journal and started reading about the hours Freya used to spend on campus when she was doing her PhD or away on field trips, and how much Wheeler had grumbled.

'She might as well bivouac up there,' he'd complain. He'd ask if I knew her plans or the people she was going on this or that field trip with. I evaded his questions because I felt uneasy too. Once, at Sally's, when we were practising applying mascara, she'd said, 'Why do you sometimes call your parents by their first names?'

'You know, when they're being aggravating. Freya often calls my nan Celeste, actually.'

She considered herself in the mirror. 'I'm going to call my parents Mr and Mrs Jones.'

'That's so old fashioned, Sal. Call them Marti and Janet.'

'Well, they are old-fashioned! They're way too strict.'

But I'd stopped listening to her. I could hear my mother telling Janet how great campus was, how much she liked a particular group of students, and then in a lower voice, she said something about it being such good luck, getting a supervisor she'd clicked with immediately.

Dad was teaching, finally using his degree. He prided himself on speaking his mind, but it had put him at odds with the principal. 'There the staff sit,' he'd tell me. 'The enthused but meek, the frustrated and the overworked, and then the rest of them. Nicky, always stand up for your principles.'

We'd take Kes for walks, out across Knocklofty or along the mountain trails. We'd discuss the books we were reading or go to the State Cinema. Sometimes we'd simply sprawl around at home, me with my head in a book and him playing his guitar or writing a song, or we'd watch TV, or go down the road so he could catch up with his best mate Marti and I could catch up with Sally. It was better going to her house because she'd always bring her guitar when she came to see me, and if Dad was home, she'd beg him for lessons.

An essay I wrote about the Greek philosophers had been chosen for a national competition, even though, prompted by Dad, I'd questioned why we looked to Greece when this country had a long-enduring philosophy of its own. Mrs Porter could hardly contain her delight. She called me 'outstanding'. Sam Doody took no notice, but he brushed against me as we left the classroom, maybe on purpose. *Even if I don't win*, I'd written, *perhaps I can be a writer one day.* I wasn't sure what kind. I didn't think I had much imagination.

I liked my school. I had friends. My teachers loved my marks. I'd gone to a couple of parties with Sally and Sam had sought me out at one and kissed me on a jetty below Battery Point. That was the day after my mother returned from a field trip, so happy she was dancing around the house, singing in her horrifying voice. Instead of going out to practise with The Crazed Desert Gophers, the band he was playing lead guitar with, Dad had cooked a special curry, put Ry Cooder on the turntable and danced her around the lounge to 'Little Sister', Kes prancing around them, making us all laugh. We'd sliced up oranges and Mum had poured Cointreau over them, and we'd had them for dessert. It was the first time she'd let me taste alcohol.

I slowly took Freya's letters out of my bag and checked for 1984. And then I paused. I felt exceedingly queasy reading them without permission. I watched the heron, surveyed North Harbour, and then eased the pages from an envelope marked 'Return to Sender.'

Monday, 26 March 1984

Dear Anneke,

Here's a letter because it's easier than writing my thesis, and also because lately I've been wishing you were back in Tassie too. I've been exploring the mountain and beaches with Nicky – it's always nostalgic because it reminds me of doing the same with you.

Remember how you loved messing about on Marti's yacht, the cruises you did with his family down the D'Entrecasteaux Channel and up the east coast – like the one to the Furneaux Islands? You were so hooked on the sea! You never realised how awed I was by my big sister's creativity and independence.

FYI, Wheeler and Nicky have got into sailing with Marti too. Patterns repeating. Isn't life strange that the Marti who seemed so grown-up to me when he was your boyfriend is now Wheeler's friend, and mine too?

This afternoon was stunning. I took Nicky to campus with me, Kes scouting out ahead of us as we walked along Mount Stuart Road, looking down the river to Betsy Island and Storm Bay. I was remembering that day you and I went swimming at Short Beach …

She'd told me about that day so often we'd come to call it The Blue Cloud Day. They'd stood in clear water, bathed in sunlight and there wasn't a wisp of white above the mountain, just a rainbow suspended above the estuary and a blue cloud weeping over Droughty Point. Their towels lay on the sand behind them, and small silver fish wove between their legs. It was a Wednesday morning. Everyone was at school, but Nan had chosen bed over her studio; they didn't know why, and they'd shirked lessons in favour of the beach.

When they got home that bright morning, she told them their father had left with the suitcase that to his daughters symbolised surprises and mystery, exotic places, and the warmth of return. He'd left for good, and everything disintegrated.

As we'd walked along, Kes's tail making happy loops, she'd said that Nan's distress played out in a way that hurt Anneke in particular. She believed Anneke had known about his affair and had withheld this information out of loyalty to her father. They argued. Artworks were smashed.

Anneke stopped painting. She locked herself in her room, seldom came out, and as she told me this Freya stopped in the middle of the pavement, touched her finger to my chin and made me look into her brown eyes, promising me she'd *never, ever* let me go through that sort of pain.

'It's how we lost her. And no matter how great our efforts to reach her were after that – barely a word.'

As we walked down the sheer slope of Mellifont Street, she told me that when Anneke was deeply distressed, she'd painted pink fish all over the school oval, horrifying everyone. A spiralling aftermath had followed. She understood why Anneke took to dreaming of foreign countries, the ocean and the pleasures of anonymity, but she lost her sister to more than just geography.

We walked along Lansdowne Crescent (the shady trees, the weatherboard and sandstone houses) then down the decline of Cavell Street to Goulburn Street, and alongside the primary school Sally had gone to, the one with the big spreading oak tree and below it the old sandstone church, wedged in the confluence of two roads.

In Barrack Street we dropped a note off at The Doghouse, a pub where Wheeler's band played, then stopped to contemplate the unloved rivulet. She told me how she used to tag along after Anneke and

Marti, exploring its upper reaches as far as O'Grady's Falls, sometimes catching yabbies or spotting a platypus. Here it was caged in cement and restrained in the dark beneath buildings. We gave it flowers, watching them float away from us, and wished for its liberty.

Freya was talking about her field trip later that month, an archaeological survey at Port Davey, in the remote South West. She said she felt sad about leaving us alone for so long. But I'd also heard her enthusing about the trip with Janet. It made me uneasy.

We idled through Sandy Bay, laughing and chatting, and then raced each other across the playing fields to the uni.

When we got to the faculty her supervisor came out of his office. He didn't notice me. He greeted her with startling warmth and when I looked up, the reciprocity in her eyes shocked me. Outside the big window, the eucalypts were washed in light, long teal leaves floating soundlessly around their white limbs. The breeze gathered a little strength and a single leaf twirled slowly away across my field of vision, marking the start of the great unravelling.

6

Gayamaygal Country (Reef Beach, Sydney) 2000

Mouheneenner Country (Hobart) 1984

Complicated Relationships

I SLOWLY TORE FREYA's letter into tiny pieces, caught up in that uneasy moment on campus. Better to remember how exhilarated the three of us used to be, watching, from various vantage points, the mountain gathering the wind, the sun, and the clouds, choreographing lyrical sequences of weather for us, its devoted audience. But after the teal leaf fell, it seemed the mountain's choreography grew darker, and infiltrated home.

I reached for the next letter, also returned unread. Once I'd asked Dad why my mother wrote to Anneke when she hardly ever responded.

'Anneke means a lot to Freya,' he'd replied. 'She'd love her to visit so they can sort out their issues – although you didn't hear that from me, Nicky.'

Boring grown-up stuff. It silenced my questions, but here on Reef Beach, they were on my mind, and so I opened it.

Friday, 8 June 1984

… It's been almost a year with no word from you. Seriously, these letters are becoming more like a conversation with myself. Celeste is so concerned and we wish you could get to know Nicky. Think about a family reunion, Anneke. Please!

My news – having finally completed several pages of my thesis (to be called 'Changing with the Climate: Environmental Trends and Human Occupation in Tasmania'), I was interrupted by my supervisor, Steve, and two of the other postgraduate students, Tracey and Mark. I'm sure I've mentioned them – they also came to Port Davey.

We went to the Alighieri Gallery at Salamanca Place and Celeste was there, minding the desk. I told her that Nicky and I would visit her on Saturday and then I escaped. But that meeting threw me off balance because you know how she jumps to irrational conclusions. Not that I've anything to be guilty about, but the way she looked at my friends, and the fact that they didn't come over to meet her, left me feeling both they and I had been harshly judged.

By the time we reached the Illusion Café rain was falling and the mountain was lost from view. We spent so long discussing fieldwork that it wasn't worth returning to uni and so I went to Steve's place to talk about some difficulties I'm having with my thesis. It meant I was late home again and walked in to find Wheeler miserable about his job and none too happy with me either. Nicky succumbed to his wretched mood and flung herself about the house complaining that we ignore her. I stood in the doorway watching the unhappy scene unfold. I know he feels I've trapped him, but I think we're simply taking longer than expected to transition into a more settled life-style. Still, Anneke, in those moments when everything begins to feel too much, I'm sorry I made the promise, wish I didn't owe Wheeler everything, wish I didn't feel so compromised. I perpetually feel as though I'm pushing back chaos.

Anyway, the next day I was feeling ill, bloody endometriosis, and stayed at home and I was making lunch when Wheeler walked in – home early.

Home for good, he told me.

When I asked about the promised extension of his contract he said it had never been likely. Now I'm wondering how much reorgan-ising of our lives we'll have to do this time Honestly, Anneke, I felt so distressed I just had to get out of the house.

I ended up at the faculty, and Steve took one look at me and invited me back to his place. He listens, Anneke. We laugh. He's calm and understanding, and then – he made me a hot water bottle because the pain was killing me!!

But he's not going to be my supervisor for much longer. There's no conflict of interest in us being friends, but as he says, people some-times develop unfounded perceptions, as I was about to discover.

We hadn't been there long when there were loud bangs on his front door. Wheeler had been to campus, spoken to Mark and reached certain conclusions. I retrieved what dignity I could and mouthed apologies as Wheeler marched ahead of me to the car. The worn tyres spun. All I could think as we tore up the road was the shame, the shame!

We fought about Steve and we fought about the lost job and I made him drop me on Davey Street. I spent what was left of the afternoon walking aimlessly around town clutching my stomach, so it was late when I got home. He had disappeared, leaving empty beer bottles lying on the table. The house was freezing, All I wanted to do was climb into bed, but there was Nicky.

Fortunately, he didn't return until the early hours and she's a heavy sleeper. Because that night I risked phoning Steve to apologise before pain overwhelmed me.

I went and cooled off in the water, childhood memories manipulating my mood. Treading water, I watched a couple and their child leave the path and settle beneath the eucalypt at the eastern end of the beach. My thoughts turned to Arno and the vanishing dreams of my future.

7

Lyluequonny Country (Recherche Bay) 1984

Hope

I MOVED MY TOWEL to some shaded sand and lay down, flipping through pages while my memories sharpened. That afternoon in June 1984, Sally and I were in her bedroom talking about bras, Kes snoozing on the floor beside us. She'd been the first of my friends to get one, I'd written, and now everyone wore one, even me, although I didn't need to. I was secretly convinced I was growing inwards, because of the sensation of roots burying into my chest. I constantly ached. Meanwhile, Sally kept bounding through sizes and I never came close to catching up.

In the middle of our conversation, I remembered my new Split Enz *Time and Tide* cassette and went home alone to get it, down the steps and along the side then through my rickety bedroom window, so light-footed that nothing creaked. That's when I heard Dad in the kitchen. At first I couldn't identify the sound; then I realised he was crying.

I sat on my bed. My heart was thumping; I'd never heard him so distressed. It scared me.

He poured a drink. It was a bad sign.

The clouds swallowed up the sun and my room darkened and cooled. I reached for my cassette then slipped out the window and ran back to Sally's place, feeling alarmed.

It was late when Mum came looking for me. Janet was already laying the table and I strained to hear what they were saying through the bedroom wall. Sally was at her dressing table trying on a bunch of lipsticks her grandmother had given her and singing along sporadically to 'Six Months in a Leaky Boat'.

'What's the matter?' she asked, wiping a plum smear off her lips. My despondency was annoying her. She ejected my cassette in favour of Joan Armatrading, pausing for a moment to listen to our mothers, their voices low and confidential. 'Mrs Jones is probably complaining because my dad spent a couple of extra days on Verloren Island,' she said. 'I wish he'd take me there.' And she turned up 'Me Myself and I' and sang into her hairbrush as though it was a mic, while I stroked Kes, who sat beside me on the floor, occasionally turning his head to lick my hand.

Mum and I didn't talk as we hurried up the road, Kes out ahead of us. The wind had strengthened. Stars came and went behind huge banks of cloud. She hunched her shoulders. I angled my face up to the southwesterly so that it sliced away on either side of it. The gate was swinging against the post. The porch light was off, and she struggled in the dark to find the front door key.

'Your dad's sick,' she whispered, quietly opening the door.

So that's why he was groaning!

'And I'm not feeling great either,' she added.

I squeezed her hand. Her endo could be excruciating.

'Can I go and say goodnight?

'No, sweetheart. He doesn't want to be disturbed.'

My heart began racing and I called Kes over to lie on the bed beside me, while Mum warmed a pizza, which we ate at the kitchen table. I finally plucked up the courage to ask, 'Is he very sick?'

'It's just, you know, a touch of flu and a lousy day at school. We'll talk more tomorrow when I'm thinking a little straighter. But really, you don't need to worry.' And she took my hand and kissed it.

Afterwards, I offered to do the washing-up so she could have a bath. As I walked past her to the kitchen sink, she reached out an arm to hug me and briefly leaned her head against me. I stopped and closed my eyes. Mum had been forgetting to hug me and had even stopped kissing me goodnight. I supposed it was because I'm fourteen, but sometimes I wondered whether it was because of her thesis and her campus friends.

'I love you Nicky. Best daughter ever.'

'I love you too. Best mother.'

Later, I lay listening to the wind's small howls as it rushed around the corners of the house, wondering what the matter really was with my dad.

I heard her go into their room. The door shut with a click and then a while later she tiptoed back down the passage and made a quiet phone call.

She's phoning Nan, I thought. To tell her he's dying.

Her voice was soft. Occasionally she murmured in a warm, sleepy sort of way. In between blowing her nose she even managed a few gentle laughs, which was soothing.

I heard her checking doors and saying goodnight to Kes. She switched off the lights. There was still no sound from Dad and every now and then my heart started racing.

Kes left his basket. His nails clicked on the wooden floors as he made his way to my room and jumped on the bed. I reached for him, then closed my eyes and watched the eucalypt leaf falling again.

The next morning I walked into the kitchen for breakfast and they stopped talking. Mum was pouring a coffee. Dad, spreading Vegemite on his toast, told me that he was going to drive down the D'Entrecasteaux Channel.

'But you're sick!'

He raised his eyebrows and gave me a puzzled look.

'Want to come with me, Nicky?'

Mum put her mug down so hard coffee slopped on the counter.

'Ah well, I'll just have to enjoy my first day of freedom alone,' he said.

Mum gave him a bitter look as she strode out of the room and my stomach tightened. She came back moments later to feed Kes, who looked like I felt, tail tightly curled between his legs and his eyes anxious. I went back to my bedroom and made busy noises, but as soon as Mum left, I told Dad that I'd go with him. It meant missing a test, but he really needed company.

That day Dad, Kes and I drove through a landscape of paddocks and water and plump-clouded skies. We drove past white goats and black cows with huge bellies, and yachts and fingers of land, hills and valleys, islands and bays, and we drove through shifting sunlight and little showers of rain. When we got hungry, we stopped and bought Coke and chips and greasy food Freya wouldn't have approved of, and we put on country and western music and sang along. Dad, Kes and I, shoulder to shoulder on the front seat.

Dad's eyes were glittery. He didn't look well. We didn't talk about his job. We talked about the tracks we were listening to and the things we were seeing and with the map on my knees I navigated us across the Huon River south to Recherche Bay. We bumped along the pot-holed track, the car knocking its belly on the ground. We drove over the creek that glinted like topaz, through the trees and out again into cleared land and the sight of the frisky ocean.

There were sandy coves and a creek at Recherche, and a handful of shacks. We had it to ourselves. Dad turned off the ignition. We listened to the car ticking over. A yacht, at anchor, looked abandoned. The wind, the bush and the cold sea made the place feel desolate. I tried imagining what it was like with huts along the bay. In the empty silence, the people who belonged to it, who had spoken its language, haunted the place, owning it still.

Kes was whimpering and kneading his front paws on the seat, nudging us with his wet nose. Dad kicked open his creaky door and Kes flew out and raced for the sand, where he whirled in happy circles before sprinting up and down. We laughed, the past evaporated, and Dad reached beneath the seat to get the tinnie that had been rolling around there. I opened the door, breathing in the beach, then I walked down to the sand with my notebook.

'Tasmania reminds me of Scotland, Nicky. I wanted warm, yet here I am. Back in the cold. Might as well have stayed in Edinburgh,' Dad said, sitting down beside me.

'Maybe you should have stayed in Greece, since you loved it so much.'

I liked his stories about the house on Samos, the artists and musicians who came and went, including Anneke.

'Tell me about her again.'

He knocked back his beer. 'Quirky, arty, big personality, warm and funny, but ridiculously over-sensitive. Great voice. A real adventurer. A bunch of us rode motorbikes to Istanbul. I'll tell you what, Nicky – she was a good mechanic.'

'And then?'

'The others wanted to continue overland to Australia. I chose to fly to Brisbane. The rest is history.'

Then he went bellowing into the Southern Ocean. The sea was an icy turquoise way out. Gusts of wind were licking up a filigree of white spume. Closer in, the water was crystal clear with a white lip of foam left by the tiny waves breaking on the shore. Kelp lay along the wrack line.

Mum had recently told me about the D'Entrecasteaux expedition – how the *Recherche* and the *Espérance*, damaged by storms, sailed into this bay in 1792 and again in 1793. A woman, Louise Girardin, was on board, disguised as a man. And so, instead of the lone yacht at anchor in the bay, I imagined these ships, with Louise leaning against the rails, saw long boats lowered, sailors rowing towards the shore, a worried clan observing from the shadows as the bizarrely clad trespassers examined their baskets of shellfish, used their hearths, inspected their homes and fished their sea. They'd have watched the strangers build kilns, usurp their space and dirty their water. But Mum said when the expeditioners returned in 1793, that clan was hospitable – were described by the French as kind and humorous. This didn't save them. It was the beginning of the end of their world.

Dad was swimming backstroke. Kes had found a dead fish. I leapt up and yelled. He cocked his head, disappointed, and galloped half-heartedly back towards me.

'That water's invigorating. You don't know what you're missing,' Dad said, running towards me. He dried himself with his jumper, his brown hair messy, his green eyes gleaming, then we raced each other back to the car. I felt lit up inside by the brisk sea running and the South West stretching away behind us, all soggy, boggy buttongrass plain and hummocky hills and mountains.

'Imagine, Nicky, if we'd chosen to sail the world rather than stick to the road.' He was looking at the yacht with a dreamy expression on his face.

I decided to risk talking to him about his 'freedom'. He reached across and ruffled my hair.

'Well,' he said. 'A boy I taught was emphatic he was Aboriginal. Proud of his heritage. Wouldn't back down on this, so he was being taunted. His father had recently died. None of the staff acknowledged his death. His grades had plummeted and the quieter he got, the more these two boys goaded him. I'd chatted to them all, tried to defuse things, but yesterday he lost the plot. Threw a chair out a window, yelled at his history teacher. Glass everywhere. Instant expulsion. No attempt by the staff or the principal to understand his situation.

'I had it out with the headmaster then handed in my notice before I got given my marching orders. Your mother wishes I'd discussed this with her first, had been hoping I'd get an extension. Between the two of us, sweetheart, it's the last thing I wanted. I don't want to sell my soul to the system. I prefer acquiring new skills I can bring together one day, somehow.'

I thought how different that school sounded to mine, but I didn't think this was why he'd been so unhappy yesterday.

I took a deep breath and said, 'Do you have cancer?'

'What?' He was genuinely surprised. 'My health is great.' He reached out and squeezed my leg. 'It's not a big deal, but I'd be happier if Freya was more understanding. I wish she'd spend more time with us – but you've got to learn how to shape the bad to your advantage.'

'Are you worried about money?'

'No. I've got shares. Compounding is a beautiful thing – TattsLotto keeps on giving. Besides, there's a river of cash out there, Nicky. I'll find a way to divert a little more our way. I've no desire to be financially obese but I'll always make sure there's enough to keep us happy, and enough to give away.'

The small waves bowed their heads and spread their skirts along the shore, then drew back again. He shoved our rubbish into a bag then gave me a hug. I felt proud of him for standing up for that boy, but something niggled, and when I said that I also thought he should discuss these things with us first, he gave a non-committal sort of shrug.

He watched Kes walk stiff legged and suspicious around a stranded jellyfish, and then he said, 'Life's an adventure and I've got a swag of ideas, don't you worry, Nicky.'

Mum used to say that if we got paid for all his ideas, we'd be living in Point Piper and driving a Porsche, and we wouldn't have to scrounge in op shops either.

8

Mouheneenner Country (Mount Stuart, Hobart) 1984

Fast, Dark River

CO-CONSPIRATORS, INTENT ON CONJURING up happiness, we'd driven home singing along to Dylan, and planning the evening to come. 'We'll put candles on the table. We'll write her a song,' said Dad. By the time we got home we'd written lyrics and had a melody. They were rough but would at least show we had tried.

I made chocolate brownies and Dad found a Moroccan recipe for the main course. Mum's pain was worse. She was exhausted from her walk up the hill and ready for bed, but when she saw the effort we'd gone to, she rose to the occasion, and as we ate, we talked about places we'd been to and Dad made us laugh, making comedic the hilarious predicaments we'd sometimes found ourselves in.

Later, he sat on the floor beside the fire, Kes beside him, and tuned his guitar. Mum and I were on the couch and she was telling us about a new project she might get involved in – an archaeological survey of the Bass Strait islands.

Dad began strumming and then, lifting his head and smiling at her, he started to sing the corny love song we'd written. I thought it would take forever before she said anything. When she finally spoke, she said, 'I get it. I've got to do better around here.' She leaned over and gave me a kiss, then blew one over to Dad. 'Things have been a bit tough for all of us,' she acknowledged.

On the mantelpiece, next to a photograph of me when I was tiny, there was a photograph of the two of them taken during their time in Armidale together, and I thought it would be good timing to ask Dad to repeat the story of how they'd met.

He played a few lines from Van Morrison's 'Brown Eyed Girl', then said, 'In Tamworth. At a music festival. I met a beautiful lass,' and they shared a smile.

'But here's the amazing coincidence, Nicky. All the time, on a sliver of twisted paper at the bottom of my pocket, your mum's name was written in Anneke's crazy writing.'

'But you missed out the beginning,' I complained. 'About how you met Anneke on Samos.'

'Down at the harbour, drinking ouzo with friends.'

'And because he was coming to Australia and because Armidale was on his "maybe" route she gave him my address,' said Mum, holding her wine glass in front of her as though it were a posy. 'He was a gift from my sister.'

He put his guitar down. 'Girls, things haven't been as stable as we'd hoped since moving here. I know you're worried about what happens next, but I'm going to make a plan that works for us all. Do you trust me?'

'Yes,' I said.

'We need to talk about that,' said Mum.

'Nicky,' said Dad. 'Bedtime.'

~

I lay in bed trying to hear what they were saying. I picked up words like 'options', 'skills', and 'direction'. I heard him mention family cohesion and she talked money, then her PhD, and later it sounded like he was teasing her because I heard her giggling.

They went into the kitchen. There was the clink of dishes. Dad was talking about possibly renovating houses and then I heard him mention the word 'yacht'.

'Get real, Wheeler,' she said, and I could picture her sighing and staring out the window at the city lights like the starry sky inverted. Kes was with them, and in the darkness I felt the weight again, pressing down on my chest, stopping my breath, and when I slept, I dreamed it was night and I was standing outside a lonely mansion beside a fast, dark river. Freya came striding out the front door – you could hear her footsteps ringing down the path, and she climbed into a road train festooned with tiny glittering lanterns. Doe-eyed cattle were squashed in the back. Their breath looked like small ghosts rising, then they morphed into people.

Beneath a thin peel of moon, she ground the gears and started careering down the empty road, and the only sounds as it receded were my sobbing breath and the slap of my feet running behind it, with the river water rising.

9

Gayamaygal Country (North Harbour) 2000

Mouheneenner Country (Hobart) 1984

Geographic Rights

SULPHUR-CRESTED COCKATOOS FLEW ACROSS the cobalt sky. White sails cupped the breeze. The heron was long gone and another group had arrived on the beach. I considered the long afternoon and empty evening stretching out ahead of me. A walk, perhaps, but for now, another letter, describing a visit to Nan, who was gardening. Snow had fallen on the mountain overnight, the wind had a glacial edge and tiny fairy-wrens were flitting among the fallen leaves.

... Anneke, you should see her hands! They're absolutely wrecked! The whole time I was there she kept moisturising them, complaining that just the smell of clay and they go berserk, so now she's painting instead.

I'd brought her a Debussy recording I'd found in an op shop. We were quiet for a while, listening, and it seemed to me (speaking to you as an artist) that Debussy would have loved the garden that day with its goldfish and the reflections on water. A few weeks ago, leaves still clung to the birch trees like clusters of yellow butterflies. I'd watched them take flight, swirling away over the roofs. Now those trees are bare and their papery limbs, etched with black scribbles, are elegantly gaunt against the tumultuous colours of the winter sky. And that's what she's been painting. In gouache.

When I told her Wheeler had handed in his notice she was concerned. She said she'd always be there for us, as, you need to know, she'd like to be there for you, too. Obviously we'd try not to impose and he really is trying – he's out looking for jobs even as I write this, but they're not teaching jobs. He wants to write, focus on music and work with his hands. Musical instruments, he says. Boats, he muses. Seriously, Anneke, it gets exhausting ...

~

Feeling defiance towards Arno and his Manly domain across the water, I asserted my geographic rights by walking the track from Reef Beach around the harbour to Little Manly Cove near his apartment.

I walked beneath a eucalypt canopy, enjoying springs and lichened boulders, crossed a creek, stepped carefully along rocky platforms to avoid the tiny blue periwinkles, passed worm-hunting magpies, seagulls and yacht moorings, then gardens of clivias and bougainvillea, frangipani and oleanders, and kayaks and dinghies drawn up on grassy verges.

There were kayakers off Forty Baskets Bay, but Arno wasn't among them. 'Better off without you,' I said out loud, and decided to make this the mantra for my exercise.

At Fairlight I did several laps of the ocean pool. The water was warm, the rockpool sunlit and I relaxed at the far end, enjoying the view of Sydney Heads, more peaceful than the Manly Swimming Enclosure, bright with rowdy children. But as I sloshed along through ankle-deep water, I considered how my journal had shaped me, how the past influenced me still, and about the gaps the letters were filling. I couldn't read my journal without a pen in my hand. If I were to collate everything into a memoir how helpful would that be?

I walked on towards the ferry, where the crowds began to grow. There was every chance I might bump into Arno here … and there he was, on his bicycle. My heart lurched, even after I realised it was not him at all. I increased my pace, scanning the crowd as if I had some sort of optical tic and was relieved to reach Little Manly Cove without an encounter. Losing patience with pools, children, and drifting plastic, I headed over the hill to the ocean by way of Shelly Beach for a decent swim in the surf and a late lunch.

Then another evening wasted with a bottle of wine.

~

One evening, I dug around in my filing cabinet for my father's ledgers. This is the thing about being an Only – you are the wrack line along which parental flotsam gathers. And so here I was, exploring unnamed folders and misplaced files, the disorderly sea upon which my minimalist existence floats.

I found the 1984 documents and climbed into bed with a whisky sour. His scribblings included broken lines of poetry and lyrics, ideas for novels, and disconnected thoughts about physics, philosophy and the natural world, as well as dated entries and quotations.

When we'd arrived in Hobart, he'd complained that the demand for a tradie's skills was as flat as the wildlife spread-eagled on the roads, and playing guitar on the weekends wasn't enough money for lentils, which is why he'd submitted to dusting off his degree and gone teaching. Maths and science had fired his imagination as much as a good poem or a song, but he was self-deprecating about his abilities.

On 18 June 1984, he wrote about telling Freya he'd quit his job and records his growing suspicions about Steve because of her 'expression of unconcealed horror when she saw me at his door.' (So it was relationship agony I'd heard from my room all those many years ago! I knew that feeling well!)

And then—

Friday night at the pub with mates. Dreich weather, even by Scottish standards. Rain out of the southwest and puddles so deep the gulls were bathing in them. Kes mournfully waiting at the door. Every time I caught his eye, shivers shimmied up his sodden spine.

The lads and I settled in around the fire and I told them I'm between jobs. Tiny, the boat builder, said no problem, he needs an offsider. Seems I start on Monday.

Marti looked concerned, but I sidelined the issue until the others left and it was just the two of us knocking back a Guinness.

He bought another round and showed me photos of his recent cruise to a Bass Strait island called Verloren. Said he sailed there twice with his father and Anneke when they were kids and that he tries to get there whenever he can, although that's only every other year, given its remoteness. His Uncle Arthur holds the lease and gets annoyed with locals visiting. Mentioned a boy who tends to treat it as if it's his own and a woman called Yolla. Marti said he and his mates did a bit of fishing. Said it was hard to leave. His uncle still runs a few cattle but doesn't often visit because the arthritis in his hip is getting to him.

Marti says it's a beaut island. Looking at the photos, I couldn't help agreeing.

I was still thinking about Verloren when I got home. Freya turned away when I fell into bed, but when I slept, I dreamed of islands.

The next day had a sparkle. White gulls and a dazzling sky. Freya and Nicky went shopping. Gave the house a flick with the duster, fixed a cupboard door and after lunch I went around to Marti's to watch footy.

Had successfully guided our banter to the topic of the island when Janet appeared with mugs of coffee and Maynard scored a goal. Then the siren went.

Now about that island, I began.

Freya had been hanging out with Steve, Tracey, and Mark that afternoon, talking archaeology. Mark had suggested they go to a movie at the State Cinema. She'd said she couldn't, then felt hurt by Mark's response – he accused her of playing with Steve's feelings, and so she headed home, brooding over why so small an event had knocked her so profoundly. She wanted space from them all, because doubt had begun to unfurl its tiny leaves in the loam of her depression.

Doubt was shaking its leaves at me too. The more I read, the more the past confused me and I was losing confidence in my ability to interpret what lay unstated in the gaps between Freya's words, but what was clear was that Wheeler held on to his plan for a week, finessing the details. His job at the boatyard was the perfect place for sorting out technicalities, like who to get to take us to Verloren Island. His ledger records that Arthur Mahoney gave us a three-month minimum stay in the lighthousekeeper's cottage he'd bought off the government.

Freya spent that week at home, curled up in bed cradling a hot water bottle and enduring pain. She wasn't in a talking mood. Stacked up high on her bedside table was a pile of journal articles and she was working her way through them as fast as she could.

What I now know but didn't at the time was that on the Friday night, when I was with friends and the two of them had the house to themselves, Wheeler moved into persuasive mode, adorning his plan with sparkles and possibilities, and presenting it to Freya like a gift.

When you can sing and play guitar, when you know your partner's favourite wine, most loved meal and most cherished dessert and can toss a Gaelic word or two into your conversation for good measure, your arsenal is complete. He lit the fire. The candles glowed. He tucked her up on the couch. He let Leonard Cohen help him woo her while he finished up in the kitchen, Kes beside him, waiting for the crumbs to fall.

Rain drummed on the windows while he did the usual – a little bit on the guitar and a whole lot of chat about the island and its archaeology, the seabirds, and its landforms. He coloured up its sealing history, shipwrecks, historic buildings, and its lighthouse – all the things that Anneke had once told Freya about, when she'd returned home from sailing there with Marti. He left space for her own recognition – that it would be a perfect spot to search for hints in sand and soil of human life lived there during the Ice Age.

I was both the final obstacle and the ammunition. When Freya expressed concern that I would miss my friends, that it would affect my schooling and that he'd promised our gypsy days were done, he said he'd plan with the school and Distance Ed, because he was happy to be my teacher and, most importantly, it would enable them to rekindle their relationship.

'Because,' he reminded her, 'You promised you'd never put Nicky through your experience.'

Freya was ambivalent. She thought it was the wrong time and too expensive. Much as she wanted to visit, she didn't want to stay.

'I'm talking about saving our relationship, Frey. Nicky is the price of that.'

'A couple of weeks,' she conceded.

'A couple of months.'

'The idea is madness.'

'The idea is amazing.'

'You go, we'll stay.'

'We all go.'

'It's not fair on Nicky. Not at this age, not when she's finally enjoying stability.'

'She'll love it. Just three months, Frey, no longer.'

'Wheeler—'

'Is that a yes?'

'I don't have a choice in this, do I?'

'Yes?'

'Okay. But Wheeler, this is make or break.'

The most solid thing in the world is Freya's 'yes', he wrote. *She never goes back on her word.*

For my mother, the meal, the music, the falling rain, and his charisma – it had all possessed a dangerously intimate quality coming when her endo and Mark's comment had laid her low. His capacity to charm undid her resolve. In that moment, it represented an escape she could take to stop herself being pulled towards something she was struggling to resist – her feelings for Steve.

Ultimately (or so she wanted Anneke to believe) it was one of those moments when life felt too hard, and she was aware she was sliding into a lethal mood of compliance.

But how wrong he was about her keeping her word when they were both carelessly discarding their promise to me.

10

Mouheneenner Country (Sandy Bay, Hobart) 1984

Sanctuary

I TURNED TO MY journal to clarify my memories of that period, and as though it were yesterday my teenage self declared that *they* should have told me the news. But instead, it was Sally who grabbed me as I was walking up the road. She wanted to know if I was excited, and when I said, 'About what?' she said, 'About going to live on Uncle Arthur's island.'

I kept saying, 'I'm not going to live on an *island!*' and she kept saying I was, her parents had said so. In fact, what she actually said was, 'They said you're going to live on the island and there are reasons and then there are reasons.'

Mum and Dad were in the backyard when I got home. He was reading the paper in the shade cast by the pepper tree. She was doing stretching exercises. She was sweaty and her body shone damply in the winter sunlight.

What happened next went something like this:

I said, 'Here's the milk. I'll put the change on the table,' and Dad said, 'Good-oh,' and turned to the sports page. 'Essendon beat Richmond.'

Mum and I hate footy. 'Great,' we drawled. 'Go boys!'

I stopped on the steps and turned around. I looked at her leaning against the tree with her eyes shut, and Wheeler reading, shaking his head, and giving disbelieving little whistles. A deep peace filled the garden. It was there in the cool sunshine and the pooled shade, in the tree with its leaves swaying sleepily, in Kes dozing in the sun. It was there in the sound of birdsong and a small plane droning over the mountain. Sunday. Corpulent and sweet tempered.

I breathed in crisp air. Just for that moment the world seemed perfect.

'You won't believe this,' I began. 'Sally has a dumb idea that we're going to live on an *island*.' And I started to laugh because it was so stupid.

Mum didn't move.

Dad folded the newspaper.

'She's weird!' But my voice was off balance and the words I had spoken swept away that big, billowy peacefulness.

Dad opened his arms, and as I walked into them, he said into my hair, 'We are, love, we are,' and Mum opened her eyes and told me they'd *only just heard,* which was a complete lie.

When I started demanding how come Sally knew before me, she said, 'It's her uncle's island. We were waiting for the right moment to tell you.'

I screamed at them. I screamed that it wasn't fair, I screamed insults. I screamed out all my frustration and my sense of betrayal and despair and then I ran inside, dropping the milk on the steps, not caring that the carton broke or that a small white river flowed into the dandelions and oxalis even though I'd walked all the way down, then back up the hill to get it for them.

And then I discovered that I hadn't got rid of those feelings at all. I felt hurt and excluded and foolish, and a thin pain was drilling up the side of my head. I yelled loud enough for the whole of Mount Stuart to hear that I was not going to that island, *not ever.*

Without telling them where I was going, I rode my bike to Sandy Bay, to ask Nan if I could stay with her while they went off to their rotten little island.

She made us some tea and we sat in her sunroom, and she allowed me to rail against the unfair world and horrible parents, then she fetched a box of tissues and smoothed my hair as I cried.

But she said that I couldn't stay with her, much as she'd have liked that, because she was going to France, hadn't I remembered? Then my mother phoned to ask if I was there, and I said to tell her I wasn't coming home.

That night at Nan's place, and in my own bed when I returned a few days later, I wept because Sam Doody would fall for someone else and while my friends were going to parties I'd be alone on a rock, banished from the life I'd started to create for myself. No more Sam, no more Sally, no more friends, or netball team, or sailing. No more anything.

I complained about my parents to my friends, but I couldn't describe the feeling underlying our departure. It had to do with the eucalypt leaf falling, and the dark weight that pressed down on me at night. I'd lie completely still, shallow breathing, wanting to fall asleep, but trying not to because of the nightmares I kept having.

I also noticed that although it was my father's idea, my mother was organising it. As for me, I escaped by taking Kes for long walks, sometimes to Nan's house, which was way too many hills away for my liking.

At her house the smell of cooking, the way wood fell in the wood heater, the water-swollen back door – these were the little things that made me feel safe when I sensed darkness hovering. I loved the sound of her voice when she sang, the perfumed warmth of her hugs and how her eyes always met mine so tenderly. She cherished me, and in return, I cherished her.

~

My father wanted to leave immediately, before anything could disrupt his crazy plan, but the boatbuilding work tied him down, and my mother insisted there was still too much to arrange. Even so, it was happening in a rush – the date was set for early August. What organising he was doing was largely centred on working out my curriculum with the school and the people at Distance Education.

Dad said schools don't teach you anything you can't learn for yourself, so his idea was for me to be dropped into a 'rich natural environment' and to be largely 'self-directed', with him as my guide. I hoped my parents knew more than I thought they did, otherwise it would be a disaster.

After school one day, Mrs Porter, my favourite teacher, took me aside for a 'little chat'. She said that although she'd prefer that I wasn't going to the island, she saw it as an opportunity for me to write something of real interest. We had a long talk about how I might do this and then she said she'd put our ideas together and outline the plan in a letter. For the first time I felt slightly keen about the island.

Then one day, towards the end of July, Mum and I went to the Illusion Café, wallpapered with sheet music, and everything in it black and white except for the fluorescent sculptures that colour shift. The sun slid through the big glass windows, softening everything, making patterns, and slowing down time. Hobart in the late afternoon, one or two people we knew on the street. I wondered if the light would play over the island the same way it did here.

Mum was rabbiting on about packing, but she said that if I really hated the island I could stay with Nan once she'd returned from France. She said not everyone gets such an opportunity, that the really hard thing is choosing between two good opportunities, or how to deal with opportunities that get in the way of responsibilities, but that ultimately, we are people who never turn down adventure. I was thinking about broken promises and about her friends – her supervisor in particular – and how, months earlier, in the bookshop, someone said, 'guess who?' and when I looked around, there he stood with his hands over her eyes, and she'd turned red and mortified. He was alarmed when he noticed me, or maybe because everyone in the shop had looked up and was staring at them, this man literally hugging my mother from behind. After they regained their composure, we swapped advice on different authors. We were both mad about Chekhov. When we left, Mum said in an irritable voice, 'My friends aren't usually so silly.'

I didn't respond. He was tall with dark hair and his clothes were immaculate and looked expensive, not op shop clothes like ours. Dad distrusted wealth, but Mum liked to daydream over those magazines full of beautiful homes we'd never be able to afford.

~

At the bottom of Sally's garden there's an old shed. A huntsman spider lives in it and it's damp and stale smelling, but we were sitting there while a short shower of rain splashed down on the roof. She started talking about her birthday, and I felt little cactus prickles at the back of my nose, because I love Hobart and my friends, our house and the river, the mountain, and the little suffering rivulets. I'd never thought about this before, so deeply. It's my home. I'm a part of it. It's part of me. This seemed an astonishing thing, to belong to a place so completely. I had a sudden understanding that there were powerful, invisible threads connecting the whole city together, as real as electrical wires or the plumbing system. Then, inside my head, *Home is where the heart is* boomed like a gong.

People say clichés should be avoided, but Nan says they're only hollow if you've never had an epiphany. When a cliché is powered by an epiphany, understanding drops from your head into your heart. That's when it becomes a great metaphor again and dazzles, just for a moment and just for you.

Down in Sally's shed that cliché, briefly, became magnificent again.

I got teary when I realised I wouldn't be there for the party. She hugged me and promised she'd visit me on the island, nothing would stop her, and then I ran home beneath sullen clouds in my flimsy T-shirt and cotton skirt, the wind blowing through me.

In bed that night I wondered if we were leaving Hobart for good and knew I wouldn't get a straight answer and then I slid into a dream, and I was in a tree house. Sam Doody climbed up to visit me. He brought me *The Iliad* and a bouquet of dandelions. I tossed the dandelions everywhere and strewed pages across the floor. Sam Doody was so upset he ran away.

In the days leading up to our departure, life felt dark until Mrs Porter gave me this letter:

Dear Nicky,

We must be positive and regard your island adventure as a writing opportunity. To most people such a lifestyle would seem exotic, and from what I've heard, it's a diverse island that will appeal to your enquiring mind.

Here is your project. You will need a notebook, a tape recorder and lots of journals for the many drafts I want you to complete. You'll need to exercise your memory, hone your eye for detail and develop loads of determination.

Noting facts and practising dialogue in your notebook, record your life regularly. Try to see each entry as a miniature story.

Although a great distance will separate you, the storyteller, from your teachers and friends, we have no intention of forgetting you.

Bon voyage,

Mrs Porter

I thought she was the best teacher in the world and I began my journal immediately.

That weekend I stayed with Nan and she said we'd make it a special occasion. It was comforting being there in her old weatherboard house and her big old garden, stroking Holly, her Burmese cat, looking at the trees and the clouds and simply being with her, my lovely Nan.

I lay on my stomach and watched goldfish drift beneath the lily pads. Together we planted winter seedlings and I realised that when you're about to lose the things you take for granted – every object, from a flower to a spade, acquires a magical, shimmering aliveness.

Nan wanted to know everything that had been happening, even though I'd already told her a hundred times on the phone, but chatting in the sunroom was *kinder* somehow. It looks out on to the cherry trees and down to the river and what she calls 'the grand march of precipitory megafauna across the heavens'. (Dad says she's a romantic. 'Clouds' is much simpler terminology.)

When I'm on the island missing Nan, I will be thinking of her skinny hands cracked by clay, her laugh and her accent, and especially her clear blue eyes. She has one sad eye that looks in and one warm eye that looks out. I think everyone has an 'inward' and an 'outward' eye, but with Nan it's obvious, at least to me.

Also, she nearly always wears a black hat. Sometimes the band around it changes, but it's always the same black hat, a patch of clay here, a bit of glaze there. And she likes to sing along to operatic arias. It makes Mum clench her jaw, but I don't mind at all.

Once, when I complained about my hair, she told me that orange is the colour of fire, of soul and spirit.

'The way you think about your hair, Nicky, and the way you think about things like the island, will shape your life because your thoughts create who you become.'

Once her hair was orange too. She said it's our special bond. That's when I started to love my hair.

We sat at the kitchen table and listened to the frogs and the boobook owl. She doesn't have television because she's 'rebelling against the modern age'.

'It will be even quieter on "*l'isle joyeuse*", *ma chérie*,' she said, spooning out the soufflé. (Nan is mad about Debussy.) 'Your parents are converts to my cause. They, too, are rebelling against superficiality.'

I said maybe that's what Janet was talking about when she said that 'there are reasons and then there are reasons' for us going to the island. But Nan simply looked at the ceiling and sighed. She said she didn't have the time to think about what Janet might be on about. The ceiling creaked. I could hear my teeth chewing the raw julienne carrot, but after I'd swallowed, I said, 'They've agreed that if I don't like it on the island, I can stay here,' and she said, 'You *will* like it, Nicky. You're the type of person who rises to a challenge.'

'And if I can't?'

'Then of course.'

Everyone keeps saying that beacuse I'm so clever (I wish) missing school won't matter, but there's a principle involved: *they* promised we'd never move. It shows they don't care about me at all.

~

After supper Nan lit the candle on the mantelpiece (to remind her of Anneke) and put on Strauss – the 'Blue Danube'. As the music unfurled, she reached for my hands and we waltzed down the hall, into the garden and across to her studio, giggling.

The studio door is made of recycled wood, and a blue convolvulus creeper trails down beside it. It's a simple room with long wooden benches smeared with clay and cluttered with jars, brushes, and sculpture. There's a kiln at the far end and the air has a cool, earthy fragrance. You can see the river through the big wooden windows and at night, the Milky Way. Nan's studio is the safest, most peaceful place I know.

She led me over to a shape hidden beneath a blue cloth. 'For you, sweetheart. To take to the island.'

I lifted the cloth and caught my breath. She had made a creature half bird, half girl out of silver wire, clay, ceramic shards, and sky-blue feathers. I stroked it lightly with my fingers, then turned and hugged her – but I didn't let her see my tears. This work must have made her hands sore, but she did it for me.

Outside, beneath the constellations, I held my gift carefully while she locked the door, and later, lying in bed listening to the *keh keh keh* of plovers shouting to each other in the dark, I realised that Nan's home is my sanctuary.

11

Gadigal and Birrabirragal Country (Parsley Bay, Sydney) 2000

Mouheneenner Country (Hobart) 1984

Constitution Dock

MY WEEK HAD INVOLVED so much self-initiated overtime that I felt mentally and emotionally drained, collapsing into bed as soon as I got home and getting up early to plough through work while the office was empty. Seeking solitude, that Saturday I went to Parsley Bay on the southeastern side of the harbour, with a packed lunch and our scribblings. I planned to begin collating this memoir.

I startled a water dragon off the warm bush path as I walked down to the cove, and found a spot on the lawn, beneath the trees. This tiny, narrow inlet is separated from the homes of the well-heeled by a sandstone cliff, over which a small stream falls, making its way across the beach and into the harbour. Children splashed, someone was snorkelling, and walkers heading south towards Watsons Bay thumped across the footbridge overhead. On the reef, a child crouched over a rockpool. I stood in sunshine, looking at the tidal pools, then, trying not to startle the white ibis listening for giveaway sounds beneath the wet soil close by, I settled down to read, starting with a letter dated 26 June 1984. It was two in the morning, the river black, the lights along the eastern shore a spangled galaxy. It was in the witching hours that my mother agonised about the island venture, particularly because after returning to campus she'd encountered Steve in a corridor of students. The distance between them felt contrived – they feigned a casual greeting. Later he dropped by her study. He'd heard about the island from Tracey.

… Another coffee back on his couch. Arguments with Wheeler are explosive. With Steve, the more I protest, the more considered he becomes. He told me that 'everyone' assumes we're having an affair!! I was mortified but decided to be frank about my increasingly confused feelings and in the silence that followed, an awareness came that we were in this predicament together.

I know. You're horrified. Anneke, more than anyone else, you're the person who's shaped my life. I haven't forgotten your difficulties after Dad abandoned us. I can't repeat the pattern! Steve believes comparing the two situations is 'unhelpful' but really, what would he know?

I find my mind ceaselessly grappling with this issue. It's not been that long since events first conspired to draw us closer – damn field-work! Damn yachts! He asked me not to go to the island but it's a done deal. That said, the finality underlying our parting felt momen-tous and arriving home late again I was greeted more generously than I deserved.

My spirit of adventure says a muted 'yes' to the island but my head and my heart aren't convinced. I hope you care that I chose this course, because, I know this is silly, but I sort of think that if everyone thinks we're having an affair, then what's the point of not?

Promises. That's what.

And Nicky …

~

Dad's mates loaded up a rusty ute and we drove our stuff down to Constitution Dock in a light drizzle. The skipper watched the gear build up on the wharf and shook his head.

'He thinks we're nuts,' said Mum. We were watching the activity, neither of us inclined to help.

All those adults in their blue jeans and boots clustered beside the boat and only Freya with her hair twisted up, her big loop earrings and her long red dress standing out from the crowd. Wheeler was lifting boxes, spinning yarns, and winning over the reticent skipper.

He can win over anyone. Mum says it's the way he treats everyone the same and his charm and generosity. I think it's also his voice. It's big and deep in the middle with a warm gravelly edge. Nan says it's pure Pavarotti but he doesn't care for opera. He'd rather sing like Johnny Cash.

I went and stood on the edge of the wharf with Kes beside me. I looked at the *Rosy Wrasse* and then at the weather and hoped for blue skies. She was a ketch-rigged cray boat, wooden and solid and I liked the white paint, the deep red trim, and the fancy transom with a whale's tail design. The water heaved against the quay. It was a murky green patterned with restless sepia and olive dapples. A fish and chips box floated on the surface and the water smelled of wild ocean doing battle with sewage, oil, and greasy food.

The skipper agreed it was rank. We stood there regarding each other, and then he said, 'You the kid for Verloren Island?' And he leaned forward and added, 'The name's Bert.'

I stood on one leg with the other hooked behind it and asked whether she was a good boat.

'My word. Found her abandoned and falling to pieces. Built her up myself with the help of some mates.'

'Can I get on?'

'Be my guest.'

We stood on the aft deck in silence. There was a break in the clouds and a huge swathe of light lit up the mountain. Snow was gleaming down its flanks.

Bert wore big boots and a woollen jumper with holes at the elbows. Everyone else was rugged up against the blasts off Antarctica so I could tell he was sizing me up in the clothes department. 'This isn't the tropics,' he said, but I told him that I like the cold.

He squatted down out of the wind, whistling tunelessly while the water tested the sides of the boat and the rigging clattered. He had huge hands stained with oil.

'I suppose, being such a salty seadog, you've got a tattoo?' I said.

He looked at me, surprised, and so I hastily confided that Dad's got one, and I slapped my bum to indicate where. He went on whistling. The boat rocked. A gull stood on the wharf, one leg tucked up into its white feathers.

'Know much about the island?' he asked, and I told him that I knew it had seals. Then he said, 'Verloren. They say it means "to be lost" or "drowned" and the fellow who named it came close to getting himself wrecked on a rogue rock called The Dagger. Full of reefs, Verloren is, particularly down the southern end. Plenty of boats have smashed up …'

I said 'wow' in a faint voice. He also said the French explorer, Baudin, named the mountain Mount Naturaliste and that 'she's a shallow sea, full of shiftin' shoals.'

I twisted a strand of hair around my finger and gazed at the river. It wasn't even the open sea, and it was already full of toothy waves. Then Dad came over to talk business. Bert was taking our gear all the way to the island. We'd join the *Rosy Wrasse* on Flinders Island.

~

When our house was empty and everyone was partying at Sally's place, a shadowy feeling seeped into me, and I slipped back home. I walked around the outside, stopping at the windows, laying my face on the cold glass, stroking the walls, and staring in at the empty spaces where we'd once lived.

The house had become a stranger and I felt a stranger inside myself too. I sat on a branch of the pepper tree feeling sad. We'd loved our view from Mount Stuart down the built-up foothills and valleys to the river, even though it hid a multiplicity of human sins, like heavy metals and the *Anson* sailing daily down river to tip jarosite waste over the edge of the continental shelf. Then Sally came looking for me.

She said losing a house is nothing compared to gaining an island, but she doesn't understand how lonely always moving on actually is. We sat swinging our legs. She was wearing a baggy black jumper over her jeans and a beanie on her head, but she was still cold, so we climbed down. We walked down the damp pavement to her place, where people were crushed up against each other and food, music and voices spun colour through the air. Mum was outside by the bonfire talking to Marti and Janet. Dad was inside, teasing Suzie, the lead singer of The Crazed Desert Gophers, as usual.

It was a good thing Mum couldn't see.

12

Gadigal Country (Paddington, Sydney) 2000

Peramangk and Kaurna Country (Adelaide Hills) 2000

———————

Time's Illusions

BACK HOME, I CHECKED my emails, tensing when I noticed one from Arno suggesting that I pick up my belongings, 'assuming we're over'.

I flicked it into trash.

At precisely eight o'clock the phone rang. I hesitated, wondering if he was following up. He wasn't. It was my first ever phone call from Steve, and pleasantries over, he said, 'I'm getting Freya for you. I want you to treat her with kindness and respect. She's got something important to tell you.'

I heard his footsteps retreat and a door close. Somewhere near my flat a car backfired.

Freya, when she eventually came to the phone, sounded artificially upbeat. Her small talk was strained. She seemed to be at a loss as to know how to begin.

'Why did you *really* call?'

'Steve thought – we both thought – you should know that I'm

having a mastectomy on Tuesday. They're being non-committal, but they've warned me it looks – advanced.' Her voice caught on the last word.

But she's only in her fifties! Reality had whisked away its mask and I had glimpsed the abyss.

'*No!*' I whispered, my throat unbearably tight.

We cradled the silence between us, and eyes squeezed closed, I rocked gently.

'It's not the end of the world, Nicky.'

I swallowed. 'It's a lot to absorb.' Unanticipated tears welled. 'How are you feeling?'

'I'm fine, sweetheart. No need to worry about me. Steve's being magnificent.' And her voice shook a little as she talked about the support she'd had from friends.

Eventually, 'I'll phone you tomorrow,' I said. 'Once I've absorbed this news.'

I put down the phone and sat quite still for a moment, experiencing the physical sensation of reality's poles shifting, my world assuming a different dimension. A surge of emotion uprooted me and frightened by a spiralling panic, I phoned Arno – an automatic reaction.

'My stuff. Can I come around now?'

'Is this about your stuff or something else?'

'My mother … Arno, my mother …'

'I'll come to you?'

'Thanks, but I need to do something, I'll see you at your place.'

With panic coming in rapid waves, I drove across Sydney Harbour

Bridge to Manly. He was waiting outside and without a word opened his arms then held me until I'd regained my composure.

On his couch, with the wine he'd poured me clutched in both hands, I told him about Freya, detailing our relationship more comprehensively than ever before. He listened, his arm around my shoulder, and then clarified what a good daughter would do. Course of action confirmed, he said he respected my decision the other day, but thought I needed to work out why I had over-reacted and jumped to conclusions.

'This is the first time, Nicky, you've dropped that cool enigma with me,' he joked and said he was giving me space to sort myself out.

'I can't talk about all that now, Arno.'

'Sure,' he said, and gave me a gentle hug.

We didn't make a move to pack my stuff. It was past midnight. That night, being in his arms gave me courage for the following day.

I booked a flight and informed work. I arrived in Adelaide as Freya came around from the anaesthetic. The hospital was silent and oppressive. A crucifix dominated the wall of her room.

~

'Hello,' I whisper.

We hold each other's gaze.

'Thank you,' she smiles. '*Thank you.*'

~

Curled up in the chair in Freya's bedroom several days later, I have time to regard her as she sleeps. That pale skin. That look of sheer exhaustion.

The mauve half-moons beneath her eyes. She has aged so much since I last saw her, more years ago than I care to recall.

The sound of a goat bleating is just perceptible.

'Giles,' says Freya. 'Given to us by a friend. Love him. Wish he'd stop wrecking the garden though.'

There is birdsong, such serenity, but I'm unsettled that Freya lived with those lumps for so long. Later, after she's slept, I ask her why, and she sighs.

'I couldn't help hoping they'd go away if I didn't believe it was happening to me.' She raises her chin. 'Denial, Nicky. I admit it. Complete denial.'

I look down at my feet and my blood-red toenails look brightly back at me. We couldn't be more different. I'd have acted, pronto.

I feel for the lighter in my pocket; my new friend, bought on impulse at the airport.

'Big city living – it's not you, really,' says Freya, when we are talking about Sydney. 'And Nicky, I'm so sorry about my part in all that's gone wrong for you.'

What would you know about anything to do with me? I want to say, but I tap the lighter and remain silent. She puts a hand to her lost breast.

'Don't smoke. I worry about you already; not that too.'

I ignore this comment. In her company, I'm struggling to discard past attitudes, to pivot our relationship in a new direction. Unresolved issues, dark and volatile, still lie smouldering between us.

But yesterday she was told the cancer has spread.

'I'll be back in a minute,' I tell her.

Outside I light up and inhale. It's like I'm sixteen again, when the boyfriend Nan called 'Bad News' embodied the abandonment and rebelliousness I was feeling.

~

One evening, in the kitchen, Steve talks about Freya's cancer, his story expanding on hers. He says she'd gone for a routine mammogram. They suggested an ultrasound as well, 'just to be sure.' She considered it over-servicing when they advised her to have a biopsy and so she sought a second opinion, even a third. By the time she submitted to the procedure she was in shock. They both were.

'The unrelenting torture of waiting. And when we finally heard … You know, Nicky, it only takes a single moment to obliterate the future.' And he smashes his fist into the palm of his hand. 'She doesn't deserve this. Your mother, Nicky, is a wonderful, loving, open-hearted—' and he stops to gather himself, examining his hands, and for the first time ever, I feel a real warmth for this man I have spent most of my life loathing.

'We came home, and we sat in the study. Our grief was an almost tangible thing.'

'She seems so calm.'

'That's called courage. In front of you, she'll be trying not to let it slip.'

We watch a honeyeater feeding from the grevillea beside the window. 'It's made her reassess her life. Time has a finite quality now.

She says it's changed her perspective on living, like she's veered down an unmapped tributary while everyone else floats on by.' He slowly rubs his hands together as though he wants to comfort them. 'Those days before the operation – she said she'd rather do the ironing than go to the theatre.'

'She would?'

His voice raw, he says, 'For me, it's as though she's out there struggling in white water and all I can do is watch helplessly from the banks.'

We stand side by side staring out at the garden. *Fast, dark river,* I'm thinking. The bird, startled, takes flight. My abandoned journal, my discarded past … when was it that I decided words were too worn to encompass the great tragedies of ordinary lives?

Steve begins to tell me the story of Freya's cancer again. The words he uses are almost the same, as though through repetition he can weather the situation into a manageable shape. Occasionally I nod, but there's a small splash of purple in a far corner of the garden and my arm feels gripped by Freya's hand and my body is tense with the memory of my father being washed downstream away from us. Tears well. My face reddens.

He clears his throat. 'This whole experience – this is life, isn't it? Birth and aging, sickness and dying.'

I slip a cautious arm around his waist, but I'm not really there; not really doing that. Instead, I'm remembering the map spread across my desk so long ago, with Wheeler's handwriting all over it. Maps, words, symbols. But Steve is right. We've embarked on a journey with Freya across formidable emotional terrain, without waypoints and our bearings in turmoil.

'It's hard coming to terms with suffering and transience. But thank you, Nicky. That hug means an awful lot to me. It will mean even more if you'd go and give one to your mother.'

13

Peramangk and Kaurna Country (Adelaide Hills) 2000

Bass Strait (Verloren Island) 1984

Crossing Water

THE NEXT DAY FREYA gets up and joins me in the garden. We have a tray of tea and biscuits that Steve organised before he left to work on his boat.

'Remember that day we spent on Flinders Island before going to Verloren?'

I tense, instantly that girl again. Between the two of us, the past has always been a taboo topic.

'Green paddocks, black swans, and rain. That's about all I remember,' I reply, unwilling to mention the fight we'd had, my final act of resistance against being banished to the island. They'd left me to sulk and I'd watched through the window as they walked down to the wharf and greeted Bert, on the *Rosy Wrasse*. A rust-bucket scallop boat was docking.

'The most exciting event of that whole dreary day was a ute that came down to the wharf while you were with Bert. A man climbed slowly out and stared at the water. He stood there about ten minutes. Then he got slowly back in and slowly drove away.'

'That's entertainment on Flinders Island,' says Freya. 'Slow time. We could all do with more of that. I remember going to the pub. That's where we first met that pilot.'

Dorothy, small and slight with chestnut hair and a little triangular gap between her front teeth was the local pilot we'd relied on.

'She told you stories about Yolla that you came back and told me.'

'She did? You'll need to remind me.'

I'd gone to bed while they'd enjoyed meeting the locals, and dreamed the three of us were in a white boat on a green creek snaking across the hot, humid Kimberley. There were finches in the pandani and the bauhinia trees. The creek banks were muddy and held together by mangrove root systems. Up on the plain there was a eucalypt savannah, but the river slid beneath a canopy of trees that obscured our vision. Freya, rowing, stared downriver while Wheeler trailed a line for barramundi. I watched great flocks of clattering cockatoos cross the sky beneath cumulonimbus, tall as skyscrapers, building up about us. The heat was excruciating.

We came to an island. Wheeler and I got out and stood on a spit of pebbles, smooth as sealskin. He cast out lots of fishing lines, then climbed up a slope to where boab trees were gathered, majestic fat ladies whispering secrets. He sat on a bough, describing in poetry everything he was seeing, but his voice became faint, then disappeared, although his mouth kept on moving.

Freya sat on the transom, her feet in the water, eating cake and peering at the river through a magnifying glass. I watched her, perplexed, from where I sat on my haunches in the water. The more I looked at the pebbles the more detailed and alive they became, vibrating with huge, restrained energy. I lifted one up and a tiny silver fish darted out from beneath it while the pebble lying cupped in my hand transformed into a mango.

Freya, still staring downstream, said, 'Here comes the change' and a stupendous crash rolled over us. Thunder shook the planet, and the tension in the sky expired into a wind that swept downriver. Raindrops, large as tadpoles, dived into the creek, leaving small hollows that pockmarked the surface and set tiny waves in motion. The crocodile watching us caught my eye then sidled into the water.

I lay back on the pebbles feeling the water rise, relishing the wind, until I was split by lightning.

~

Freya had forgotten to take her seasickness tablets. She lay in the saloon clutching a bucket, Kes whimpering beside her, ears flattened, eyes terrified, not knowing when the horror would end.

I stayed in the cockpit with Wheeler and Bert. He said she was a big sea and that the cold front had caught him unawares; she was blowing thirty knots. He had turned off that deep-throated engine and the smell of diesel had faded away.

'She's a boat at her best in a bit of a blow,' he said, so it didn't bother me when she heeled, or when a wave broke over the bow. We were close hauled, making our way beneath a wisp of sail and I could tell by his grin that Bert was a sailor at heart because that's all they talked about – sailing – and Bert let Wheeler take the wheel whenever he adjusted the sails.

I was loving being out on the ocean, trying to decipher its personality, keeping my eye on the long, slithery waves and the white crests breaking, frothy spume flying away in the air, but I wasn't allowed to touch anything.

Bert said this stretch of sea was as well-known to him as Mount Stuart was to me, that the stars were his map in the darkness. I watched him pick a line through the maze of waves, the sea more like a wild animal, with its own briny smell and personality. When I mentioned this, Bert glinted a friendly eye at me and said, 'Hold on girl, there's a big one coming.'

I decided that the sea is a creature with a penchant for hollows and that the sea and the sky are distorted images of each other, the currents and the breeze, the foam and the clouds, the plankton and the pollen, the fish and the fowl, and they both nibble and push at the earth along their edges. One likes the heights, the other the depths, but they both disperse and carry.

'Shallow,' said Bert, as a gust hit us. 'My oath, she's shallow. Full of shifting shoals, never know where they're gunna pitch next, shipwrecks scattered all over the seabed.'

She was full of islands too. Wheeler wanted to know their names and Bert would look like he was thinking, then say 'Badger', 'Goose', 'Vansittart' or whatever it happened to be. Wheeler would check them on the chart, then observe the compass and arrange the world for me around its needle.

A lone gull wheeled on the wind, its *ow* a long thin line of sound like kite string. Most of the birds we'd seen were cormorants and gulls on rocks and islands sitting out the wind, like we should have been doing.

Bert's eye was on every swell, his concentration on the wheel and the tell-tales.

'You gunna get the heave-hos too?' he asked me when Wheeler finally spewed over the side. But I didn't. I sat in my uncomfortable life jacket on the leeward side and watched cormorants flying fast and low on the wind and he told me how we'd be on the island when the short-tailed shearwaters (which he called *yolla*) returned. Spray was flying over the cabin top. We were getting soaked, but it was exhilarating.

'The last week of September – that's when they'll come home,' he shouted.

In the afternoon the wind died down and Bert pointed to Verloren Island emerging on the horizon. It was looming over us when Freya finally staggered up the companionway. I saw that it was bigger than the islands we'd long left behind, excluding Cape Barren and Flinders Islands. It looked like a misshapen, mutilated chook splayed out massively upon the sea. South Verloren (by far the bigger part) was dominated by Mount Naturaliste, its summit hidden behind a dismal cloudbank, with Lone Egg Island lying to the southeast as though it had rolled out from beneath the remains of the battered wing that was Digit Point. North Verloren was little more than a squat, scrubby hillside. A neck of sandy isthmus tethered the head and the body together and beaches, cliffs and coves stretched along its length, Bert said, giving way to rocky reefs and cliffs further south. He muttered names like 'Wright Rocks', 'Phoques Point', 'Tinman's Reef' and cursed 'The Dagger' – a lone sea stack off the southern tip.

'Lighthouse once had two keepers' houses,' Bert said as we rounded North Verloren. 'Bugger all trace of the second these days. Real ferocious house fire. Killed two kiddies.' A feeling of foreboding overwhelmed me when he told me that the jetty we were heading for was in the Dead Lady's Gulch, a small natural harbour.

'Boat overturned,' he said. 'Her little booted foot stuck up above the waves for a couple of days.'

It was a lonely and imposing island. Seabirds cried. The lighthouse was a pale finger against the darkening sky. Waves slapped against the boat. The sails were down. The diesel thudded once again, and with the fenders in place, Bert eased the boat in through the entrance of the gulch as we surveyed the jetty with trepidation.

'Don't know how you manage this boat alone,' Wheeler said to Bert as we helped secure the mooring lines then liberated Kes from below.

When I stood on the island a drained, dislocated feeling settled in me. I wanted to keep its presence at a little distance. Instead, it seemed to be breathing beneath my feet. I felt a sense of belonging towards the boat and the island felt alien. There was a sense of waiting, and a lost, lonely sort of feeling, and a starved feeling and a wanting to go to the toilet feeling. We had to get to know a strange house in the quickening darkness at the end of a long day, and I was glad Bert was with us. If he hadn't been, I would have sat down and wept.

The hill rose in front of us. It had a pelt of yellow grass, and the bushes were like bruises in the failing light. Our surroundings seemed full and empty at the same time, as though the island itself was watching us. Bert had fetched a rickety wooden cart and he and Wheeler were heaving our stuff into it. I was about to start helping when Wheeler said, 'Look!' and I saw a pale arc of light flick out across the sky.

Our lighthouse!

Just for a moment my spirits lifted.

The automated beam was a silent, purposeful presence as we stumbled up the hill. The ground heaved beneath our feet, and I was silent, deep inside the cavern of my own being. Freya was ready to collapse. She said, 'Wheeler's grand idea – Wheeler's responsibility.'

He and Bert, pulling the cart, passed the occasional comment. I heard the word 'graveyard' and a little later 'convict built'. Kes was somewhere in the darkness, sniffing through the tussocks, a wet nose felt against my ankle and then gone again.

The hill flattened out. The old lighthouse keeper's house was behind the light and we had to make our way around large granite boulders. We reached the veranda as the lighthouse gathered its light and pitched it out again. Wheeler turned the key and opened the door. Cold, musty air flowed out around us.

'Can't see a damned thing,' he said. 'But that certainly felt like my old aunty Mabel.'

My skull prickled. Freya put her hand on my shoulder. 'Good one, Wheeler,' she mumbled. 'Just get on with it, won't you?'

Wheeler called out for a torch and Bert said he'd left his on the boat. Freya's fingers were digging into me. Then I remembered my backpack. I'd packed a whistle, some chocolate and some wet weather gear, because you never know when you might be in peril on the sea. And my torch, right at the top, to use for signalling should I be floating about in the ocean after dark.

Just for a moment it was like being inside a play and I forgot my tiredness. I created a small light that flickered around the room, picking out a fireplace, some chairs and a table. In the middle of it stood a tilly lantern and some candles stuck in beer bottles.

'Good on you,' said Bert, who had remembered his cigarette lighter at least.

He got the tilly lamp going. There was wax and dust around the bottles, chipped paint on the mantelpiece and dirt marks on the wall above it. The furniture emanated hostility. The house seemed full of secrets and through the sash windows I could see the light pulse like an erratic heartbeat, dying and renewing itself.

I noticed the couch and the armchairs had broken springs, and the covers had faded into patches of bleached crimson and apricot with splashes of an antique blue. Freya collapsed onto the couch. Wheeler followed Bert down the passage. Kes had curled up in an armchair, his shoulders hunched up against the world. I didn't want to go down the dark passage and so I went out to the cart and started rummaging for food. When I came back in with a few damp bags I could see a candle twinkling at the far end of the passage, and I could hear them talking about the generator.

I gave Freya an apple and then because I was busting, I went back outside and crouched down in the dark. I felt the scratching of grass against my feet, heard my father's voice out to the left, and thought what a curious feeling it was to be out in the dark on salted legs, not knowing my own patch of the planet.

The sky and the sea breathed against each other. The light threw itself out across the night sky and loud bird conversation drifted up from the beaches. I looked up at the universe. The Seven Sisters were travelling below the horizon, it being winter, and the Southern Cross was somewhere above the clouds. There was a waxing quarter moon in the sky and the stars seemed close and numerous. I was tired and humbled, and I didn't want to move, then quite close to me, something honked. I walked back and sat on the doorstep and lost myself in space again, watching a meteor move across the night sky. Then the generator began to thud against the darkness, light blazed from the windows and I found I was satisfied to be where I was and that I was even looking forward to the next day.

~

Wheeler was talking to someone in the distance. Not to Freya, I knew, swimming up from sleep, because I could hear her downstairs, along with the sound of waves, and a breeze billowing up and fading away. I looked around the bedroom. It had a high ceiling and peeling paint. There was a pile of ash in the fireplace and the wooden floor was dusty. The walls were built of foot-thick slabs of granite. I climbed into yester-day's wash-ready clothes and went downstairs.

The front door was open. There were white clouds in a blue sky and a breeze was in the passage. Its freedom infected me. Outside, at the edge of the hill I stood in silence. This place didn't know the meaning of restraint. The island was magnificent! And the lighthouse was a great stone beacon with a line of small windows all the way to the top and a flight of steps that arched up to reach the door a few metres above the ground.

'Work of art,' said Wheeler, but Bert, who'd overnighted on his boat, just grunted in a strangled sort of way and jiggled the key in the lock. He pointed out that it was granite like the house, and that it shouldn't take us long to find the quarry. They went inside, but I walked around the hilltop calling Kes. Where the grass bordered a mosaic of native pigface and helichrysum stood monumental boulders freed from the sand by the Roaring Forties, each with its individual wind-sculpted shape, each with large quartz crystals visible in the stone, each dappled with lichens – acrylic oranges, yellows and greens, and, in the cracks that the wind and rain had made in them, sometimes a wisp of yellow poa grew.

I went into the scrub behind the house, sandy underfoot, and sloping in gradual declines down to two beaches that I later found out were called Sunlit Cove and Restless Bay. They lay to the east and west, south of the hill. Misfortune, a bald lump of rock, splashed with guano and vibrating with birds, broke the surface of the sea a little north of Sunlit Cove. Far below me on Restless raced Kes, gleefully barking, sweeping along the damp sand after seagulls, whirling in circles, cooling himself in the breakers before repeating the performance all over again. We had lots of training to do, and in a hurry.

A path led down through a blowout to Restless Bay and beyond the two beaches North Verloren trailed away into the isthmus of sand. It had a scratching of moorland down its centre and the brown glint of a dune-captured lake at its southern end.

Beyond the isthmus, South Verloren rose by slow degrees up into the wooded slopes of Mount Naturaliste. Its spurs and valleys were suggestions of black, denting its olive-green forests, and there was a hint of cliff along its eastern edge. I could see islands to the north, east and west, fingers of hazy land that blurred into each other so that it was hard to tell where some began and others ended. Although I strained to see the Tasmanian mainland, I could not make it out.

~

Freya was sitting on the steps of the front veranda drinking tea. I told her that everywhere I looked there were bones and feathers, and scats that looked like big fat cigars.

'Cape Barren geese. Did you see any?'

'No, but I heard honking last night,' I said, sitting down beside her.

'We really should have left Kes behind. He absolutely does not belong on an island with so much birdlife.'

Fortunately, Wheeler and Bert emerged from the lighthouse just then. Bert stood on the edge of the cliff considering the swell. He was waiting for high tide before leaving. It made me heavy-hearted to think of him sailing away from us.

'Mum, why are there cow horns on either side of the front door?' I'd noticed them last night and thought they looked suspicious.

'I was wondering that myself. Some symbolic meaning?'

'Homer?'

'Hesiod? True dreams coming through gates of horn?'

'Possibly.'

'Okay, let's leave them up and keep the gods happy,' she said. 'Although these were never their skies to rule.'

14

Peramangk and Kaurna Country (Adelaide Hills) 2000

The Cellar

As we sit reading on the garden bench, Freya says, 'I hope you don't mind, but I peeked at your journal before sending it off to you. I loved the references to archaeology.'

So disrespectful! Another betrayal. It adds to the hurt I'm already feeling that she gave something so intimate to Sally to give to me.

'Any of your letters I can peek at?'

She deflects me. 'You know, I've been thinking about Anneke so much lately. How close we were, before our father left. We'd adored him, you know. He was funny and warm and charismatic.' She sighs. 'I lost him, then Anneke. She stopped hanging out with me after meeting Marti. He was a great refuge from our unhappy home.'

'It really was that bad?'

'She wouldn't have run away if it wasn't.'

'Are you back in touch with her?'

She shakes her head. 'But I'd love to see her again.'

'Have you tried to find her?'

'She could be anywhere. I wouldn't know where to begin.' She looks at the ground. 'Really, I've left it too late.'

I straighten my back and watch a peaceful dove preening itself close by.

'It hurts,' she says, lowering her voice. 'So you see, I do understand the way you feel.'

I doubt it!

'We've all of us been betrayed, and we've all betrayed each other.'

I don't react, only because she has cancer, but a kookaburra laughs from a river red gum in Giles's paddock.

'Nicky?' She looks uncertain. 'There may be letters somewhere, ones I wrote to Anneke. Risky for me, but I think your understanding is more important.'

'Thanks. That means a lot.'

It's almost imperceptible, but her face relaxes.

'How I wish, Nicky, you'd call me Mum again.'

That's a step too far. I know I've reddened. 'It's getting too hot out here. I'm going inside.' As I close my book and stand up, Freya sighs and then she follows me slowly back into the house.

She retreats to her bedroom and I to mine. Behind my closed door I lie on my bed where I can safely untangle my petulance. Her request was confronting and for all I know, meant to be loving, but my cruel response has unleashed a self-hatred that swiftly sweeps me away, down into darkness.

~

My visit is unexpectedly extended by Max asking me to meet with an Adelaide client. It gives me a chance to get away from the house – a relief, because the more time I spend with Freya the less comfortable I feel about where our conversations are heading.

When I return from my morning in the city, I let her sample the perfume I've bought – *Grand Amour* – because there's no harm in hoping. Perfume is safe territory. We sample some of hers too, and then by some circuitous route, she begins to talk about her cellar, and how it would help if I could sort through it for her. She thinks there is stuff of mine down there and certainly some of Nan's belongings.

'You'll need to ask Steve for the torch,' and she gently hefts Amber, her much-loved cat, off her lap.

'I'm not likely to get through much,' I warn, setting off to find him.

The torch is a heavy old one made of metal. Steve likes old things: the gramophone, the radio, the old and beautiful M.G. Their exquisite house is full of delicate antiques and paintings, but the cellar itself is hot and I worry about redbacks, repetitively checking that the door is firmly open, even after leaning a rock against it. If it wasn't for a strengthening curiosity about where the other volumes of my journal might be, I'd be inclined to leave the boxes for another time.

The torch catches the ruby glow of wines in racks beside the door. Then, in the beam of light I notice sculptures that cause a shock of recognition. They're Nan's! Impulsively, I move towards them, touch and commune with them, then leave them for another time.

Nearby I locate decaying boxes stacked up against each other where the cellar is enclosed by boards and the footings of the foundations. I drag one up the steps and on opening it discover random mementos of Nan's Parisian childhood, including a mouldy album containing photographs of her young life, and find a photograph of a beautiful young woman leaning against a tall, immaculately dressed man. He looks past the camera while she smiles into it. Nan and the grandfather I never knew.

Sitting on the boulder beside the cellar entrance, album in my hand, I'm startled out of my reverie by Steve calling me in for tea. I show Freya the album but there's little she can tell me.

'You *must* know! You're her daughter!'

'How much do you know about Freya?' Steve passes me a plate.

He's right. We are strangers and he's the usurper. All the long years apart. All that blame and hurt and anger. We turn the pages. There are pictures of my philandering grandfather with the girls when they were younger. There's one of Nan, her arm around a teenage Freya; Anneke, a little removed, defiant.

'Look what I found,' Freya says. 'Celeste's perfume.' And she hands me the Lalique flaçon.

'*Je Reviens*!' I whisper.

'Anneke probably knows more about these photos,' she says.

'She should know that you're sick.'

'I'm in remission,' she says firmly. 'No matter what the doctors say.'

Denial again.

Steve looks at her thoughtfully. 'But she should,' he says.

I gather the dishes and head for the kitchen.

15

Peramangk and Kaurna Country (Adelaide Hills) 2000

Bass Strait (Verloren Island) 1984

Tentative Connections

BEFORE SWITCHING OUT MY light, I reach for the flaçon and release that antique fragrance. As Nan's comforting presence envelops me, I pick over my attitude to the past like a bird searching through leaf litter. Somewhere an owl hoots and I can hear Giles bleating and the soughing of the wind through the trees. Adrift on the edge of sleep, images loom, transform, and fade away – a violin trapped in a forest of kelp becomes the dampness of clay, and hands become roots then the tree. A creature that is half-bird half-girl hurtles towards me and I jump, startling the images away, and am left remembering a cliff and the small sounds of pebbles falling.

I have a midday flight so I get up early, and I'm fumbling around in the cellar when my fingers touch the surface of a bookish object, and stumbling up into the sharp light of another hot day, I discover it's one of Wheeler's ledgers. I dust it down, squeeze it into my suitcase and join Steve and Freya for breakfast.

~

'Something for you,' says Freya as we say our goodbyes. 'Far too precious to relegate to the cellar.' And just like that she passes me the rest of my journals.

'I'll book a ticket for another visit as soon as I get home.' We hold each other long and tight when we say our farewells. A cautious affection has re-entered our relationship, but I'm still distrustful. I bet she's read all my journals.

In the car with Steve, I stare out the window. There's a lump in my throat and I close my eyes, digging my nails into the palm of my hand. He reaches over and pats my leg. He chats to me about his yacht, talks about his favourite places in Adelaide, and then at the airport buys us coffees and waits until the boarding call. His hug is warm. 'You take care of yourself, Nicky,' he says. 'We'll see you again soon. And don't worry about Freya. I'll look after her.' And he kisses me emphatically on my cheek.

~

I look down at the ocean from my window seat above the clouds and think about the chunks we've removed from our mother-daughter Iron Curtain. Last night, instead of deflecting her, I'd let Freya talk about our first day on the island when she'd sat on the jetty, long after the *Rosy Wrasse* had gone, wishing she'd taken the opportunity to escape.

She'd walked back up to the cold house. It had an ocean mustiness. She wanted it fresh, awash with light and colour to help establish a mental toehold and lift her out of despondency and so she began transforming the house into a home.

She'd placed the bird-girl on my bedroom mantelpiece and a vase of correa sprigs beside my bed and to thank her, she reminded me, I'd given her a paper nautilus. She'd thrown open the windows and set Satie's music free to float across our hilltop. A dusting, a scrub, some judicious splashes of colour, and even that sour old lounge had turned cosy. Our big bright posters were water-stained from the crossing, but once up they made a big difference to the ambience.

She'd scrubbed the kitchen table and filled a deep blue bowl with oranges. The water tank was half full, the stack of firewood was small. Cold fronts were queued up between Tasmania and Antarctica.

'I couldn't stop longing for Hobart,' she'd said.

And I'd remembered the teal leaf falling.

~

Somewhere above the Coorong, I reach for my journal and find the place where her memories and my words collide. Accepting a cup of tea from the cabin crew, I begin reading from when we stood on Whale Rock and watched the *Rosy Wrasse* diminish with distance, how the sky grew cloudy, the wind cooler, and the sea threw down its waves like a hand of cards it had lost faith in. The gap between the *Rosy Wrasse* and the island widened and loneliness flooded in.

We were alone. Three tiny figures with a brooding island at our backs, the sky staring down at the sea, the sea staring up at the sky, and we were of no significance. None whatsoever. And yet the island seemed alert to us, like a shaggy monster focused on the tiny progress of a trio of fleas through the forest of its hair.

'Come on, let's go exploring,' Dad's words jarred against the silence. He shadowboxed around me, and his movements carved a small territory for us to move and be in. Kes, loping behind us, his nose seeking scent trails in the sand, began swinging his tail and sniffing about in search of a stick. I hopped along the granite boulders, picking a path ahead of them, leaving Mum alone on the jetty watching the rain approach.

'I hate the name "Dead Lady's Gulch,"' I said. 'And there's not much in these tidal pools.'

'You'd need strength to hold on tight.' And later we did find washed-up kelp with granite clinging to their footholds.

We passed half-worked boulders strewn about in the old quarry used for the lighthouse, and, on the southern side of the headland, the footings of an old jetty. Dad grabbed my hand as we jumped off the boulders onto Sunlit Cove's beach, a gentle curve with a boat shed halfway along it, backed into the little dunes. There was a dense wrack line of pale shells and brown seaweeds and I stooped to pick up a large, white shell entangled in a knot of golden kelp.

'A paper nautilus,' Dad said, and then, while he looked at a rough map Bert had drawn for him, I dug my hands into the kelp bubbles gathered like drifts of raisins in the sheltered hollows of orange-lichened boulders. But a thought whirled in my head: *I won't see anyone my age until Sally comes to stay.* Loneliness nailed itself into my bones and I could not dislodge it.

We found short-tailed shearwater and little penguin rookeries slung in a band behind the dunes. 'Great avian real estate,' said Dad as he began collecting driftwood to stake, delineating a respectful walking track behind the rookery. 'It's your responsibility to teach that dog to observe this boundary.'

'He'll learn quickly, you know that.'

The timber boards of the boat shed were in a bad state of repair and through the gaps and rotted-out places we could see a dinghy in the dark.

'Maybe we'll use it to fish, or to row over to Misfortune,' said Dad.

'Uncle Arthur might not like that.'

'It'll be fine.'

'Mum won't approve.' I was wishing she'd come with us.

Clouds were walking the horizon on thin legs of rain by the time we reached the grey casuarina trees on the low headland at the end of the beach.

'Wherever I've gone in the world, I'm always lured by the big blue magnet. And here we are again, a new adventure on the edge of the octopus ocean,' said Dad, high-fiving me.

The day had developed the stillness that comes with a drizzling sky. When a spot of blue began expanding, the sea brightened, luminously transparent beside us, with washes of turquoise and silver further out. We followed the shoreline to the start of the isthmus, sticking to the sand, because to walk through the yellow tussocks was to high-step and stumble.

Skinny Loccota Strip on the eastern side was steep, the sand soft, so we tramped west across the isthmus to Emita Beach, with its vast shallows. Lots of waders were there, because it was pockmarked with the tiny burrows of a vast army of soldier crabs that had formed a pink crustacean ribbon at the water's edge. We could hear them clicking as they marched across the swash.

'Let's go home. Mum will be worrying.'

Each time I asked, he'd direct my attention towards something new.

Led by Kes, we climbed the dunes, because, Dad said, 'Now that we're here, we might as well explore that dune captured lake.'

Wallabies bounded out of the scraggy scrub, stopping to stare back at us from a safe distance. Cape Barren geese rose heavily into the sky, honking warnings, and flew down to South Verloren to escape us.

The lake was a world apart from the beach, cupped by dunes that muffled the cadence of the ocean.

'Got to bring your mother here.'

'She'll probably jog down here tomorrow. Dad, let's go back.'

'Feel that water!'

It was warm after the chilly sea, and brackish. I looked through liquid topaz, down to pale sand, sculpted into tiny ripples, a drowned dune field of miniature proportions, with coarser, dark particles settled in the little scalloped hollows.

'And so the sedimentary layers build,' Dad said. 'And look, another up-market suburb of burrows over here.'

'Dad, come on!'

He pointed up at the sky. 'See that magnificent bird way up high? You're looking at your first Verloren sea eagle.'

~

No phone, no television, no nothing … I was reading on the veranda when Mum came along and said she'd love to make the lighthouse her study. We couldn't go up it because Dad had the key. Instead, we climbed the poky stairs to the attic, its walls covered with old newspapers dating back decades. It had a mouse-mustiness overlying a smell of linseed oil and something else with pungent edges that I'd never experienced before.

'Whiffs of seafaring,' Mum said.

Later, we made a makeshift bookshelf for the living area, spread the kilim on the floor and put a red vase on a trunk, and Mum was making a coffee when the generator died. The call of seabirds immediately filled the silence.

She took a bunch of journal articles and settled herself on the couch.

I considered the room, alarmed that we'd brought so much gear for what they'd said would be a brief stay. 'Are you glad we came here?' I asked her.

She sighed. 'I don't know yet, Nicky. For all this space, I think we might start to feel claustrophobic.'

I was digging in boxes and in one I found a better map of the island. It named more bays and noted a farm and there were crosses indicating wrecks.

'This is a headland bypass dune we're on, so let's call it Mount Aeolian,' she said, adding it to the map, and outside she showed me how some long ago person had stitched the sand together with kikuyu grass from Africa. It surrounds the house then gives way to the boulders and tussocks.

That's where we were standing when the generator kicked in again.

'Good thing Wheeler's got a sweet touch with that beast,' Mum said. 'At last I can have that cup of coffee.'

16

Bass Strait (Verloren Island) 1984

———————

Lighthouse

I WAS LOOKING AT my father stuffing his face over one of our first lunches. His hair had been licked into angular clumps by the salty air, and he was in the clothes I knew he'd wear every day – wrecked shorts, Blunnies without socks and one of the tattered blue singlets from his building site days, though I thought it possible he might start roaming the island in his kilt. We were teasing each other while Freya kept glancing at her unnecessary watch.

Well, we did need a watch for one thing. Dad discovered a pile of meteorological gear in the lighthouse and wanted us to record the weather. Parents are such schemers, that's all I can say. It'd no doubt mean lessons.

Once the dishes were done Dad said, 'Where's that lazy hound dog? He can nap outside while we go up the lighthouse.'

It wasn't just breathlessness that silenced us on reaching the top. It was the ocean and the way it shimmered where the sun, pouring through the clouds, laid pools of silver light upon its surface. Cloud streets cast shadows, enormous dapples on the sea, and distant islands basked in sudden sunlight. A gull flew by so close I saw the breeze lift the tips of its pinions.

'Is this not paradise?' said Dad, breaking the spell. 'What a great school!' And he swept his arm around to indicate the island, but nearly decapitated me instead.

'Look at the lamp, Nicky,' and he started spouting boring details, although the fact that it is the equivalent of seventeen thousand candles burning together is awesome, and 'candlepower' is a word worth remembering.

'Three flashes every thirty seconds,' he said.

It wasn't facts I wanted – it was images, and words like *nuance* and *resonate*, my current favourites.

Far below us the island stretched south, and right beneath us Kes was asleep on the grass. We saw Misfortune and the small, dense shadows of the graves amongst the tussocks in a hollow between the gulch and Restless Bay.

'Most of the graves aren't marked,' said Mum. 'They buried the people from the *Mansfield* shipwreck there, but that headstone standing at a tilt is Alison Blair's. She drowned in 1854 and her two little boys died from fever less than a year later. I read that she hated living here, tough Scot though she was, but she couldn't persuade her husband to leave.' She gave Dad a gentle nudge. 'That better not be you, Wheeler.'

'It's like all these people are still part of this place,' I said, and a shiver went up my spine. A granite coal shed squats near those graves.

It used to house the convicts who built the lighthouse there. I had no desire to meet a convict ghost.

In the small room beneath the light, I dutifully listened to Dad yakking on, sliding my hand over brass and wood, checking out a dusty nautical chart. I had an uneasy feeling that every conversation with my parents was going to have the ulterior purpose of educating me and I could see our relationship disintegrating fast.

Dad said this room was the perfect 'shed' for the salty seadog he was fast becoming and surely Mum didn't want to be encapsulated in such a phallic structure, and he winked at me when I giggled.

'Check,' he said. 'Look how neatly I've stacked my books!'

I saw the hurt on Mum's face as he slipped his arm around her waist. He laughed when I said, 'We'll call you Priapus if you're going to sit up here!'

'Maybe it will unleash your dad's creative powers,' said Mum. 'We'll see just how fertile his imagination really is. And it better be, Wheeler, because I'd have liked this as a study too.'

I gave them a push towards the door.

'Grave island, harsh history,' Mum continued as we clomped back down the narrow stairs. 'And in a different way, surviving the Ice Age here would have been tough too.'

I'm not sure I want my life braided into Verloren's story, I was thinking, as Mum talked about the ancient Bassian Plain. She reckoned that beneath the sea there were clues about that era when this was quite another sort of place.

'Nicky,' she said, reading my thoughts. 'There isn't an inch of this island that hasn't experienced a death, albeit a microscopic one. The past is going to be my livelihood, but we all need to live the present skilfully – though I have to say, when you're being difficult, I don't feel too capable at all!' And she laughed, as we walked over to the drystone wall, behind which Dad is planning to grow vegetables. Mum said the soil was shallow and impoverished so she doubted we'd raise a single spud, but if salty scats made good manure, we'd grow monsters. It was impossible to take a step around there without standing on excrement – my parents had brought me to an absolute hellhole.

~

Dad set up the meteorological equipment near the lighthouse.

'I'm pretty damned sure the people who once lived here would've had amazing knowledge about the weather. Colonialism. Like an enormous eraser. Come on, Nicky, what's happened to your enthusiasm?'

I stomped off, because the truth was, I felt so lonely those first few days, stuck on an island with Priapus and Mum, both far too keen on sharing their passions. We needed visitors and we needed them now.

The island was definitely getting under my skin because that night I dreamed we got wrecked on Misfortune, the wind screaming in an octave close to the edge of sound. The waves were heavy blows in the dark 'with the kick of seventeen thousand horses', Wheeler shouted, his wet face against my ear as I choked on spindrift flying off tall black waves. I was up to my knees in water and the boat was sinking. I was screaming for help, but no sound came. I clutched at the starboard gunwale, but the wood crumbled beneath my hands, and I was left holding fragments.

I couldn't hear the words Mum was yelling, her hair whipped by the wind, and even as we sank, she pulled and cursed the tiller, now beneath the surface. Wheeler was laughing while the wind slashed the sail to ribbons that snaked and cracked above us. He clutched the mast, but it toppled in his hands. 'Look to the stars!' he shouted and hurled his compass into the waves.

Then I was rolling in the sea. Misfortune loomed above me. Time passed, and I became conscious of rock beneath me and the cutting wind against my skin.

A man lifted me up. I wanted to say, *don't put me in another boat*, but I was mute, in that thin flat space beyond terror, looking at a man with bristles on his chin, who pulled at the oars and talked to two small boys wearing old-fashioned clothing.

They took me up to our house. A lady settled me on the couch.

'It's braw,' she said with a Scottish accent, stroking its fabric while two little boys stared down at me.

'We must cut off your hair,' she said. 'We need a fire to beckon a ship.'

I wanted to ask her where my parents were, but no sound came. My hair was a fire on the hill and the smoke in the sky read 'save our souls'.

But that couldn't be, because at the same time the rain was falling.

17

Gadigal Country (The Rocks, Sydney) 2000

Bass Strait (Verloren Island) 1984

The Island Orchestra of Light and Sound

WHEN I PHONE FREYA to let her know I'm safely home, I permit a conversation about the island. We talk about safe things, like the night soundscape – the wailing and cries of the seabirds, the smash of surf and howling gales.

'Oh!' she says. 'And the light! Cloud formations and moonlight, the falls of sunlight on the ocean, the rainbows.'

And an aurora. But that's not for sharing.

'Some real adventurers came ashore,' she says.

The yachts that brought them were mostly Tasmanian or Victorian, and, especially when it came to Steve, I'd have preferred if they'd sailed on by.

'We were mostly happy then, weren't we?' she says.

I don't respond. It was never that simple. But as she's read my journals, I suspect she's trying to reframe my childhood.

Later, Arno phones to find out how my visit went.

'You sound more relaxed,' he says.

'It was the right thing to do.' I'm trying to be more open, to prove his assessment of me was flawed. 'And I'll go again as soon as she's finished chemo.'

'*Bravo*, Nicky!'

'Do you feel like a South Australian break?' *You fool*, I think, *don't go there.*

'Don't sacrifice time with your mother. It's far too precious.'

He's keeping his distance, I can tell. He talks about cycling to Barrenjoey Head and a baby nephew in Italy.

'And the woman you met when you were there?' I finally ask.

'I didn't say "woman" – all I said was that I had a conversation. You overreact, Nicky. It's *crazy*.'

One, I'm sure he met someone. Two, he's probably already booked his ticket home. Three, I'd never move to Italy. And four, he can't be trusted.

I cut short the call. Who needs a man anyway?

~

A friend who knows I've jettisoned Arno suggests we catch up with our usual bunch for drinks in The Rocks. At a terrace table with harbour views, they get stuck into him on my behalf. '*So* superficial,' they tell me, and 'way too conscious of his appearance,' and, 'the way he swaggers,' says another.

They're trying to be supportive, I get that, but that's not Arno and these reactions are why I went to ground. As they make sly digs, I recall his clever wit, his lovely accent, and the reassurance of his optimism. I did love his energetic sense of direction and his kindness, but not the way he synced it with criticism at L'Heure Exquise.

I leave early, seeking the solace of my couch, returning to that bundle of Freya's letters, to one she was writing in front of the fire at the end of August, the house quiet, Wheeler and Kes out somewhere along the isthmus, me apparently in my bedroom reading.

… Nicky complains about history lessons, but she reads about Verloren avidly. We swap facts, steal each other's books, drop them accidentally in the bath and the sea and abandon them to the sun to dry out. Open any of the books piled next to a chair and there will be tell-tale trails of sand in the creases of their spines. We've really aged and dishevelled them!

According to Nicky, the island has ghosts 'because this book says so!' Wheeler's response – put a sock in it and do something useful. Instead she stalked down to the beach, her hair flaming behind her.

He's making me a cup of tea and I must say it's cosy in front of the fire, eating our freshly baked bread and chatting, Miles Davis on in the background …

~

The North Verloren Cape Barren goose couple set the sky rattling with their honking at first light. We live inside their territory. As soon as they spot us, they depart, complaining loudly. We've called them Philip and Elizabeth. They both have metal bands on their sturdy pink legs.

'They might get visitors,' said Dad as we watched them graze. 'Given their jewellery.'

Just then, the radio crackled into life. 'All ships, all ships,' we heard, and swapped channels to hear that there would be snow down to two hundred metres on mainland Tasmania with a gale force warning of fifty knots for all Tasmanian coastal waters. We listened to fishing boats reporting in, and later Dad said that the weather would delay the new firewood supply. Then Bert's voice came over the radio, and so Dad showed me how to change channels.

'*Rosy Wrasse, Rosy Wrasse*, this is the Verloren light, the Verloren light, do you copy?' he said.

Over the static Bert's faint voice responded. '… Sitting fast in the Tamar River until the weather improves …'

My parents were in their Aran jumpers, but I was in a t-shirt. We were wondering how those Straitsmen who were trying to make good, but also the convicts, plunderers, pirates, sealers and vagabonds coped with this tough environment. Mum said, 'You've got to imagine the lives of good men who valued their Aboriginal wives' local knowledge was vastly improved.' And on she went about marriage through the ages.

Dad stroked his chin. 'I think my novel will be about a Straitsman called Gunther who gets dropped here, forgotten by the mother craft and builds a life for himself.'

'Right, Mum said. 'Remember the women,' and kissed him, before going upstairs to work on her thesis.

~

That night, as the storm raged, we sat close to the fire and played Scrabble, Dad playing 'Sail On, Sailor' too many times between turns. But he put his guitar down as messages started flowing from the yacht *Birngana* en route from Eden to Hobart. We messed with the squelch on the radio and, over the sound of the static and the howling wind, learned that she was being storm-tossed in Bass Strait, that she had engine problems and a ripped mainsail.

'Rather a lighthouse than a yacht,' said Mum.

'Quite an adventure,' said Dad, a strange gleam in his eye.

'Forget it, Wheeler,' she said. 'Nicky, time for bed.'

~

Birngana sought refuge in the Bay of Fires, but a fishing boat anchored in Sunlit Cove said they'd lost gear overboard, it was hell out there, and one of the crew had busted his thumb.

'Want to come down to Restless?' Mum asked me after breakfast.

Tonnes of freshly deposited sand had created a new beach landscape. Boulders that had stood proud had completely disappeared. As we gazed around in amazement, I found I was staring at a dark, solid thing, half buried amongst kelp and driftwood. A sodden violin case. A violin still inside, wet and swollen, although the strings were intact, and the bow was half in place on the inside of the lid. Where the rosin should have been, there was a sea-cold ring, its delicate clasp supporting a single pearl. I slid it onto my finger. It had a simple elegance, and Mum and I were still marvelling at our find when Dad and Kes arrived. He held up a flathead he'd caught at Emita, then tried to strum the violin.

'None of us will get this to sing,' he said. 'We need Anneke for that. She could play a mean violin.'

Mum laughed and slipped the ring on her finger. 'Your nan once had one exactly like this.'

'What happened to it?'

'She reckons she lost it gardening.'

'You can keep the ring and I'll have the violin.'

She gave me her most radiant smile and we walked home arm in arm, trailing Dad.

He pan-fried the fish for lunch and we shared it, laughing at his hilarious stories about working in a pub in Dumfries. Dad is such a good mimic.

~

It was a few days before the sea settled down enough for us to row the clinker around to the gulch. Her paint is peeling, she leaks and dribbles, one of the oars is split and she's generally shabby and unreliable but does her best to lurch along in the approximate direction we want her to go. She's called the *Sophia.*

It was fun and when we got there, we hauled her up on the beach that makes itself available at low tide and ate sandwiches on the boulders.

Then Mum went home and Dad and I took the boat back to Sunlit Cove, and we thought how much more fun she'd be with a sail.

At Sunlit Cove, I jumped out into the water.

'Home you go, Nicky.'

And before I knew what was happening he was rowing over to Misfortune. He ignored my shouts and waves, so I stormed up to the house.

Mum and I stood on top of the hill and watched through binoculars as he disappeared around to the eastern side of the rock.

'That stupid man!' she said.

We were standing on the veranda, our arms crossed, when he returned.

'It was fine! Promise! There's a narrow spot where the boat was safe, but I nearly tripped over a fur seal – looked like a rock until it didn't.'

'You cheated me out of an adventure!'

'I plead guilty. Next time, Nicky.'

'The cormorants' nests aren't just made of seaweed anymore,' he told us as we walked inside. 'Some have plastic bait box straps strung through them too. The poor buggers don't know the meaning of their circumstances. But man, the smell was overwhelming and it's a discordant orchestra of light and sound over there, all that guano gleaming white, all that racket as they fled into the sky! And the colony has fleas,' he said, scratching himself. 'Not sure you would have liked it,' and he gave my hair a gentle yank.

'I feel itchy now,' Mum said. 'Go and have a shower. Immediately! You've probably transferred some into Nicky's hair.'

While he'd been on Misfortune, we'd decided to go on an expedition by ourselves to Stumpy's Bay, but later that evening we relented and said he could come too.

It was on this walk that we discovered that we were not alone on the island.

18

Bass Strait (Verloren Island) 1984

Not Alone

THE DAY WE WENT to Stumpy's Bay the mountain was the palest of purples. A light breeze chopped up the surface of the sea. Mum chanted the names of Verloren's plants, bedraggled feathers were entangled in the tussocks, and carcasses and bones were everywhere.

'Somewhere on this island,' Dad said, 'there's a naked goose – and I'm the one who's going to find it.'

On Loccota, the soft sand made my leg muscles ache and I plopped down against the dune and opened my messy notebook. I breathed in the briny air, so crisp and heady. It struck me with great force that simple moments like this are *ineffable* but every day I'm here there are still moments that thud with loneliness.

Mum wanted to know what I'd written, so I peered into my notebook. 'My mother has a nose so long that upon seeing it, a young elephant died of envy.'

She tapped her nose. 'I couldn't compete with a proboscis monkey. Whatever you're writing is perfectly safe,' and she flicked sand onto my legs.

We had smoko at Sam's Soak, the lake in the middle of the isthmus dunes. Pipits gave small, forlorn cries. Chats flitted above the tussocks and alarmed geese flew down to the sea.

'Massage my tympanic membrane,' Dad ordered. He made me tell him the tiniest details I was seeing, but I started with a large one that was puzzling me. 'We're sitting at the lake. It's shallow and it's salty, yet it's higher than the sea.'

Mum was lying with her head against her pack. 'It's in a deflation hollow gathering runoff from the mountain. It's only saline because it's so close to the ocean.' She got up. 'Might get a head start on the two of you lazy lumps,' she said.

~

The mountain's presence dominates the entirety of South Verloren. The first beaches on the east coast are a series of coves with smoky cliffs streaked from the runoff filtering through the vegetation above them. Squally Cove is the biggest. We walked along the edge of the poa, following narrow paths worn by cattle, although all we saw was one sheep carrying three years' worth of wool, tottering along on its thin grey legs, off to the west of us.

'That old coot will die this summer,' said Dad.

'Can't Sally's uncle come and shear it?'

'More to the point are hooves trampling chicks in their burrows,' he said. 'Uncle Arthur needs to get his animals off here. These islands rightly belong to the birds.'

We caught up with Mum. I was the first to notice the huge moonbird rookery on the cliffs at Beagle Bay. We clambered up the headland to get a better look and discovered a birding hut way down the slope, half hidden in the poa. It was a ramshackle place made of corrugated iron, all alone on this rugged side of the island. The wind blew through the bent heads of the tussocks. A bit of roof flapped in the breeze, and we could smell bird as we approached it. I was clutching Dad's arm. Kes was sniffing scents along the ground, tail wagging slow and relaxed, then slow and thoughtful, then tucked under. His hackles were raised as we walked around the hut.

Dad wanted to open the rickety door but Mum said no, that would be trespassing. 'I can guarantee there'll be feathers on the floor, the smell of the birds and racks for cooling them,' she said to me, as we carried on walking.

'Somebody's staying there,' I said. Kes's tucked-under tail was loud as a shout.

Someone was watching us, and it made my head prickle.

'When does the birding season start?' I asked.

'March. And we won't be here.' She told me that I must see it in context, that birding is cultural. It provided much-needed sustenance too.

'I'd like to prove shearwaters were part of the diet of the people who lived here long ago.'

'Why don't you ask their descendants?'

'That's a reasonable question.'

'Those birds have so many names it's confusing,' I said. 'Short-tailed shearwater, sooty petrel—'

'Yolla, mutton-birds, *Puffinus tenuirostris,*' she added.

'Where do you suppose they are at the moment?'

'In the Arctic? Maybe on their way?'

'I think they leave Alaska at the beginning of September.'

We caught up with Dad, who'd stopped where the burrows begin. He reminded me that tiger snakes also live down them. We'd already seen a few lying around, too dormant to care about us, so we stood around for a while admiring their water views.

'Still,' said Dad, 'not much privacy from the neighbours.' Cattle had materialised out of nowhere, hugely out of proportion among the poa. We felt surrounded and hurried over the dunes and onto the beach.

'These footsteps are fresh,' Mum said, pointing at the sand.

Beagle is a long, wide beach with limestone headlands at either end. The footsteps emerged from the dunes, stretched along the beach then circled back into the interior.

'Probably a birder,' said Dad.

I knew it! One pair. Barefoot. Long, I wrote in my notebook.

'I'm ravenous,' Dad said, so we stopped to eat in the shade beneath the headland, treating Kes to peanuts, which he cracked open as deftly as a parrot.

Dad stretched out on a rock with his hat over his head and his feet in the sun. 'This is the life! Sunscreen my feet, one of you.'

Mum passed me the lotion. 'You do it. My proboscis is much too sensitive.'

'It's a rare nose that appreciates the subtle bouquet of Metatarsal Chardonnay '46,' said Dad, from beneath his canvas hat.

'I'm sure it was intoxicating in 1946, at least to your mum, but the quality deteriorated rapidly,' and Mum gave the deep, hooting laugh I like so much.

'Your feet would make a rat retch,' I said, happy because they were happy.

'I'd better watch out then, with you two around.' And his hand whipped out and grabbed my ankle.

~

Stumpy's Bay had a wild grandeur, but it was the sea-arch backed by Stumpy's Stack at the southern headland that awed us. It was a massive outcrop that looked like a gigantic head with a beaten-up nose and a small secluded cove had formed there, protected by cliffs on three sides, into which the sea had hacked a cave. It's got a dark, wet breath that smells of underwater life forms. At high tide the ocean would wash you in there and swallow you whole.

The sea made sucking noises that echoed around the cave's interior. There were barnacles, soft, slimy sea squirts and red waratah anemones, and it was tranquil until Dad knelt on a boulder, his hand on his chest, and facing Mum recited a love poem by Neruda from the book he'd been carrying in his pocket.

Parents! *So* mortifying! I implored him to stop, but he laughed, then chucked the book at me and told me to read the rest. I hastily followed Mum, her hands in her pockets and a strange smile on her face. Dad walked behind us whistling 'Love Letters in the Sand', just to irritate me even more.

She gave my hair a gentle tug as we waited for him to catch up, then they waltzed together on the sand, Dad singing and Mum laughing at me. In that dorky moment I felt happy because everything was going to be all right.

I let them go ahead of me with Kes, wanting to look at the sea arch again. From that tiny cove, when I looked back along the beach, I discovered it was no longer empty. A boy was walking along the swash about two hundred metres away. When he saw me, he stopped. We stared at each other, and then he turned, and walked back towards Beagle Bay.

I ran after my parents. 'I just saw a boy!'

'What did he look like?' asked Mum.

'Tall, but not all that much older than me. Tanned. Dark hair. He wasn't friendly.'

'Not such a lonely island after all, eh Nicky?' said Dad.

'But we're the only people allowed to be here!'

Mum laughed. 'We're hardly the owners!'

We walked home through afternoon sunlight that came and went behind a cavalcade of cumulus clouds. Kes had ripped his paws on barnacles and they were tired and sore. Mum spotted the remains of past feasts in a dune, layers of white shells, and by the time we reached Restless the sun was low and the lighthouse was suffused with a pale pink glow. Mum decided to jog ahead.

As Dad and I reached the top of Mount Aeolian, we stopped. He laughed, deep and low. Light was streaming through a sudden break in the clouds, illuminating small areas of ocean as well as the hill. I felt disembodied, my mind unbound, because everything seemed part of this luminous light, sharing an awareness, settling and yet not settling, still and yet not still, touching the ground and us like no touch at all, dissolving everything into itself.

The gulls flying through the light disintegrated, their colour and movement washed out by the radiance. It felt as if the island had decided to accept us, but I realised that words wring the magic out of things too profound to be described.

Later, a southerly came through and it rained glassy streamers that shattered on the window. I lay in bed, thinking about that boy. I hoped I'd get to meet him. My parents were downstairs, and I could hear my dad singing. Behind the rain and his voice, the sea was crashing on boulders. Across the island birds were huddling and marsupials were making night tracks. And in Alaska, the moonbirds were preparing for their journey.

I put out my bedroom light. I thought about the extraordinary light we walked through. Weirdly, it was like love. And maybe I found a word for it. It's *numinous*.

19

Peramangk and Kaurna Country (Adelaide Hills) 2000

Bass Strait (Verloren Island) 1984

Sails, Wings and Dreams

FREYA'S CHEMOTHERAPY HAS BEEN leaving her tired and nauseated, but when I visit, she's keen for me to get to know Steve in more relaxed circumstances, and so, with the breeze around ten knots and a kindly sun in the sky, we head out to sea on their classic Swan 36, after a tour of the yacht that isn't just about safety, but an opportunity for me to admire its nautical magnificence. We put on some music and idly chat, and while I occasionally trim the sails, Steve tells me about the yacht's history.

When Freya and I are organising lunch in the galley, I mention that I'm shapeshifting my journals into a memoir.

'I love that idea.' She looks down, bites her lip. 'Our relationship. Please don't be too harsh.'

Best to move away from that. 'I wonder what you remember about Dorothy Brisa and the island?' I ask her.

She laughs. 'You could say she was our Hermes, delivering visitors and mail.'

'I have a few pages here about that. I'll read them to you later.'

'I would love that.'

We heave to for lunch. There are jellyfish below the surface, light waves dancing up the hull, and occasionally seabirds fly by. A pod of dolphins heads south. The land is low-lying, Norfolk Pines prominent, and the sun is high in the sky, as we make idle conversation beneath the bimini. It couldn't be more peaceful.

We're making way at about four knots when Freya and I retreat below deck to wash up. She's desperate for me to remember the happy times. While she puts away the plates, I start reading my narrative, from where we heard the drone of a small plane growing louder and saw the glint of metal in the sky as it descended towards us, circling Mount Aeolian, heading south before banking into the light northerly.

'It's going to land on Emita,' said Mum excitedly as Dad ran down the lighthouse steps. By the time we reached the beach the plane was taxiing along the sand. Dorothy was delivering vegies, mail, and some other stuff Dad had ordered.

While he dragged the cart back, the three of us put together a picnic to take to the gulch, where we spread it out on Whale Rock.

Dorothy told us that she's been flying for seven years, that she likes to be alone with the drama of the sky, that it's the ultimate freedom. She likes looping and twisting, dropping the plane's nose and plummeting, feeling for the perfect moment to strike the joystick so that it rears and shudders on its tail. She likes flying at mountains and rolling aside at the last minute. I can't imagine having no fear.

What she especially loves about Verloren is Mount Naturaliste, only she calls it the Sleeping Buddha because she says that's what it looks like from the southeast and that her friend, Yolla, loves Greek mythology and calls it Mount Morpheus because she thinks it's a dream spinner. She stuck those cow horns up at our front door. She'd found them on the mountain, near a cave, which explains why I've never had so many dreams in my life as I've had here.

'I have to scrape them off my eyelids in the morning.'

'There you go,' said Dorothy.

'We're all being plagued by dreams,' said Mum, and she excused herself to go and help Dad.

Dorothy told me she has a PhD. It's in psychology. Jung is her hero and she loves collecting dreams.

'What's the best one you've got?'

She thought a moment. 'Well, Yolla had a dream that changed her life.'

And she told me how, before her friend had changed her name, they'd rowed the little distance from Flinders Island to tiny Fisher Island, to catch up with the moonbird researchers staying there. Yolla felt queasy. She went into the hut to nap while everyone chatted outside and she dreamed she was in the Mount Naturaliste cave. On an altar, candlelit, was a luminous egg and a camera. As she reached for the camera, a snake reared up behind it.

The large egg cracked.

She took the camera, put it to her eye and clicked. Lightening flashed in the snake's eyes. The last vestiges of shell fell away and the moonbird shook out its damp wings.

'Takes much longer than that to hatch,' said Dorothy, assessing the tide. 'But the minute she woke she knew what she was meant to be.'

'A photographer called Yolla?'

Dorothy looked at me thoughtfully. 'We stood beside the hut door discussing the dream. Yolla tapped the sign above the lintel. She said, "from now on, call me Yolla."'

'Why?'

'It's a sign. A hand-painted one. That's what it says: Yolla.'

'And when was this?'

'About seven years ago.'

'We heard she was crazy.'

'My dream is to fly all the way to the Arctic with the yolla.'

'That's amazing.'

Dorothy shrugged. 'They probably call me crazy too.'

I told her about the dreams I'd been having, and about the weight that pushes down on me.

'That's anxiety. Nicky, would you like to talk about it?'

I shrugged, and quickly told her about Sally, who says she wants to be a singer, like Patti Smith, and how she can throw back her head and let loose an undulating trail of semi-quavers and how sometimes she sings with The Crazed Desert Gophers, but only when they're practising.

Then Dorothy told me about her friend Len, and how he dreams he can stop the damage we, the barbarian hordes, are doing to Tasmania. 'You might meet him here too,' she said.

The boy, I thought to myself.

Dorothy said she's interested in the impact of nature on the mind, and I should make notes about my dreams for her, and then she observed that the tide had turned and it was time to head off.

'Dreams,' I said, as we neared the top of the path below the lighthouse. 'Sometimes I wonder whether we dream them or they dream us?'

'We are the dream,' said Dorothy.

'But if we are the dream then who is dreaming us?' I wondered. I looked across at Mount Naturaliste, snoozing innocently in the sun. *Are you the culprit?* I wondered to myself.

'One day,' said Dorothy. 'You'll meet Yolla. Of that I am sure.'

I didn't much care. I'd rather meet that boy. But I did like Dorothy and out here even a conversation about a stranger's dreams is a change from talking to parents.

20

Gadigal Country (Sydney) 2000

Peramangk and Kaurna Country (Adelaide Hills) 2000

Bass Strait (Verloren Island) 1984

Uncomfortable Recognition

SUMMER SLIDES NORTH. AUTUMN foliage glows on the deciduous trees, but all I notice are the spent leaves falling. Temperatures drop. I long for night and the descent into sleep, but when night comes insomnia strikes. My mind is tight and heavy, yet thought is too ephemeral to support the weight of a decision. I've lost my enthusiasm for cafes, movies, and shopping, and although I still walk and swim, it's not pleasurable. Keeping in touch with friends isn't worth the effort. There's no single misery I can isolate – it isn't just Freya, nor Arno either.

When I least expect it, he visits, bringing the gear I've never bothered collecting.

'This place is so untidy! That's not like you!' He makes me walk with him along the Maroubra to Bondi coastline and wants to know why I'm still feeling so stuck. He teases me by calling me a 'cautious investor' and jokes that for our relationship to have worked I needed to be more bullish. He's moved on, it's clear. I still love his warmth, less so the banality of his language. He talks about a job opportunity in Rome.

'What do you think about that?'

I give a small shrug. I'm feeling nihilistic.

'I'm worried about you,' he says. 'I'll stay in touch.'

Shunning company, I find my calls and visits to Freya are growing more frequent. The peacefulness of their Adelaide lifestyle begins to work a certain magic on me. She's stopped mentioning the cellar. She's more interested in my future and occasionally suggests that I contact Sally. There never seems to be sufficient time.

She has secondaries cropping up everywhere. They're subtle. Their stealth dismays us. She says she feels ambushed, as though she needs to keep renegotiating her contract with reality. And for all her reassurances to the contrary, I must be right in believing chemo and radiation have not been successful; that time is running out.

On one of her better days, on a wine-tasting drive through the Barossa Valley, just the two of us, we reminisce about Verloren.

'Remember when Rob arrived?' I ask as we sit amongst others on the patio of a small winery. There's dappled shade, birdcalls, and the sound of a sprinkler.

'Awkward,' she says.

Rob's visit had begun innocuously enough. I was reading, and I'd lifted my head to have the sea surprise me. There, suddenly, was the *Rosy Wrasse*, giving a lift to the day.

Bert wasn't alone. A tall, energetic man stood at the bow, ready with a line as they entered the gulch. Kes was whipping up and down the jetty and the stranger wasn't impressed.

Bert indicated with his chin and said, 'You've got yourself a scientist here. Name's Rob,' and when I got in the way as he passed boxes down, he said, 'What are you skylarking about for?'

I looked at Rob's fieldwork-dirty army surplus shorts and his slim legs and later, when I told Mum that he reminded me of an emu she said, 'You're shocking; I think he's good looking,' but laughed anyway.

As soon as Rob was on the jetty, Kes's nose gravitated to his groin. '*Get off*!' he snapped, flapping his arms.

Dad reached out to shake his hand. 'What brings you here?'

He said he'd just finished monitoring geese on Flinders Island. 'I've got other islands to cover before heading back to Hobart. I'll be here a few days, depending on the boat,' and he gave an almost indiscernible nod in Bert's direction.

'Up to the weather, cobber.' Bert reached for a craypot. 'This do, Wheeler?'

'Aye, Bert. She's a beauty.'

Bert surveyed the southern sky and said he might be here longer than he'd planned because 'that front looks like she's comin' through pretty darn smart.'

'I'll second that,' said Dad.

I hopped onto the cart and started opening boxes. I liked the look of those vegies, but when I told Bert that I was sick of dehydrated potato, Rob suggested we try to establish a vegie patch.

Bert cleared his throat. 'Got a cold one in the esky for me, cobber?'

'There's always a beer for you, Bert.' Dad pointed his chin at Rob. 'You coming up to the house?'

'Best be on my way, guys.' He wiped his salty glasses on a handkerchief and said he might call in on his way back, then pulled out a map, as thin on detail as ours before we started scrawling names all over it, and told us he was heading for the farm.

'You'll only see one pair with their chicks on North Verloren,' I said as he hoiked his rucksack onto his back.

'Good to know. Well, catch you all later,' and he started up the track, flapping shorts and heavy boots, an old canvas hat pulled down over his ears. His hair was tied back in a ponytail.

'You might learn some useful stuff from him, Nicky,' said Dad.

Bert made a sound in the back of his throat. 'Bloody academics and those National Parks types. Bunch of shiny arses, the lot of them. With a bit of bad luck you might have a few more arriving later in the season too.' He looked cautiously at Mum as though he thought she was a shiny arse too, but she was staring at an oystercatcher on a nearby boulder as though she hadn't heard a word.

Dad said, 'Well, mate. It's good for business,' and Bert said, 'Yeah, mate. But not for the ticker, mate. The crap a bloke has gotta listen to. Tells me the climate is changing, ever heard such nonsense? All they know is bookwork. That fella's lucky he didn't find himself paddling in the great blue yonder without his mum to hold his hand.'

Almost imperceptibly, Mum's jaw clenched.

'Use those muscles, women!' yelled Dad, as we all began pushing the cart. Above us, Philip and Elizabeth circled Mount Aeolian, honking.

~

Bert was sitting in an indecisive patch of sunlight on the lighthouse steps when I flopped down beside him with my notebook. I had questions, and because I like the way he speaks, I wanted to get his words down properly.

He shifted uneasily and took a cigarette from the pocket of his shirt, squinting at me through one eye because of the sudden glare.

'Fire away then, sweetheart.' And he lit up. I told him my questions were for a goose essay. 'Will you tell me everything you know about Cape Barren geese, please?'

He grinned. 'They make good cray bait, love.'

My face dropped.

He patted my knee. 'Stick a bit of gannet in the pot and the crays are fighting each other to be first in.'

It couldn't be true.

He inhaled slowly, rolling his cigarette between his fingers. 'Geese, though. Like flies on Flinders.'

'Do the locals eat them?'

'My word, darling. The young ones make a good plate. They breed on the smaller islands like Verloren, see? Then the juveniles come over to Flinders and have themselves a party in the paddocks. I don't care what any of those scientists says. A cow hardly has a place to plant her dainty hooves when those fat fellas arrive.'

'Do they shoot them?'

'Got to keep the numbers down, love. Two hundred, sometimes more of them sitting on a paddock.' He tapped his cigarette against the steps. 'Shoo them off and they just hop into the next one. That professor – that Rob fella – full of fancy notions. Never been over here in his life before. Fed tall stories in the university then thinks he knows everything. I've been around a while now, love. I know the place.' He shook his head. 'Let's go and have a cuppa before my ticker chucks it in.'

'He could have been more friendly.'

Bert gave me an approving smile. And even though he talks so slowly, I didn't get down everything he said.

~

The weather turned gusty. Bert rode it out in the gulch and the next morning, when the weather had moderated, he came up the hill for breakfast. Later, we sat on the veranda, and he told me how he makes craypots.

Mum reckoned Bert has the biggest hands she'd ever seen because of all the physical work he's done over his lifetime. His fingers looked like burnt snags because of the oil on them. Nan used to say that beauty isn't the front cover of *Vogue*. Beauty was *wabi sabi*, it lay in interesting lines, and colour, and texture. I thought Bert had *mesmerising* hands. I wanted to hold them down and stare at them – at the colour of them and the veins, the oil embedded in them, the blood blisters and cuts and scars, and the wrinkles, dry patches and age spots, and the fierce, wiry hairs on them.

Beauty wasn't the Queen's English either. If I could've, I'd have spoken like Bert, that country way.

'Now you need your wire for the frame and your cane for the neck of the pot,' he went on. 'You need to make a come-on-in entrance and space for the little ones to wander on out.'

He explained how you weave the wood around the wire and then he paused. 'And don't you go thinking it's easy, girl. It's a skill. Some of my mates use plastic and steel mesh pots, but I tell you what – them cray can pick the difference. There's nothing like the real McCoy to catch a lobster. Only these days they make you put them spawny shes back. It's your newfangled regulations concocted up by city smarty-pants that know nothing about the ocean.'

He threw down his cigarette butt and I watched it roll away. 'Wind's eased, tide's right. Time to move.' He got up and wandered off.

I watched him go. I picked up the butt. If you had to slice off a gannet's head to become a local, then I was happy to stay a smarty-pants from the city.

~

Bert had shown us how to bait and set the pot down in shallow waters. He said you often pull up other critters. He's found pear helmets, road-night's volute and beerbarrel tuns in his pots. Later, we found a big, angry cray in there. A whelk was sharing the pot with it.

But Dad still prefers diving for cray. 'I despair,' said Mum when he left next morning without even telling us. I said I'd go and keep an eye on him.

'What about your work?' she called, but I pretended I couldn't hear.

I meandered along the beach, keeping him in my sights. At the end of Restless he started boulder-hopping to get to Superstition Reef. I gave him time to drop into the sea before settling myself on a rock, and it wasn't long before he surfaced with a cray in his gloved hand.

'It's berried,' I said.

The closed season was in force for females. Even so, he came home with a berried cray a week back. Mum made him take it back to exactly where it came from. She stood on Mount Aeolian, watching through her binoculars. He'd thought we'd be impressed by the size of her, and we were, only not in the way he intended. A cray takes about five years before it breeds. What's more, Dad was the person who told me this. He said that in midwinter, when we were arriving, crays were down on the ocean floor 'copulating their little cray hearts out' and that big ones can have about five hundred thousand eggs attached to their bellies.

'Go home, Nicky!' he shouted.

But I leaned against Kes, who had followed me, both of us focused on Wheeler's diving. The sea was turquoise, and azure further out. That morning there was seaweed floating on the tide and probably cray larvae in the water and crays tucked on small shelves beneath the limestone reef, or walking in a line along the ocean floor, a red streamer against the white sand.

~

The easterly brought drizzle, and the humidity made the furniture sweaty. I had classes with Dad and later with Mum. I read *The Heart Is a Lonely Hunter* and stared out at the rain. Dad was in the lighthouse and Bert had just reported a one-metre swell on the sked from his position near Goose Island. Paganini's 'Love of Three Oranges' was playing on the tape recorder. Bread was baking in the kitchen.

Meanwhile the mist was pressing up against the windows, sneaking in under the doors. I took my notebook out from under the chair where it was lying in a small drift of stardust, and this was our conversation:

'Mum?'

'Hmm?'

'Did the first people on this island eat Cape Barren geese?'

'I reckon. And they lined their huts with feathers and shaped bones into tools.'

'Better check the bread,' I reminded her.

She opened the oven and tapped the crust. 'Perfect! Can you call your dad? He deserves a reward. He's been working hard all afternoon.'

She slid the loaf from the oven. Steam rose. I breathed in deeply.

~

The sea was snitchy. Water smacked the rocks. The wind drifted, snapping at bushes. It had got inside us. It made us cantankerous too.

Mum came down from her study. 'Let's go and find out how Rob is getting along.'

I couldn't close my maths books fast enough. Dad said to Kes, 'Don't look at me like that, Dog. You have to stay at home.'

We followed sheep tracks through the tussocks to Honeymoon Cove. Casuarina trees with dark tessellated bark and stringy grey needles were growing above and between the granite boulders. There were more boulders just off the beach. From a certain point, Lone Egg Island was visible to the south.

On the island, the whole life cycle of birds was impossible to ignore. We'd found heaps of nests and eggs, seen chicks, and stepped over bones and carcasses. As we approached the farm, I watched geese rising heavily into the sky, flying low, their necks outstretched, their large wings beating the air, their honking too loud for the wind to absorb. We had disturbed them.

Mum called us over to look at a particularly elegant goose nest. Little white feathers flew like flags from the tips of the tussock above the nest, which was clean and snug, a haven of tranquillity and secret goose life. The down was so deep that we only got the tiniest glimpse of the eggs.

'Good parents,' said Mum. 'The last nest was so scrappy in comparison.'

'Rob would have to know we're here by the number of geese that have flown down to the beach,' said Dad. We looked across the remains of the paddocks to the derelict farm buildings spaced out about us. The dilapidated sheds looked too large in the landscape. The broken windows were sinister. Long ago the Martin family cleared the bush, and built the drystone walls that run haphazardly across South Verloren. They burned to improve the pasture and then they grazed sheep and cattle. Their 'improvements' were disasters for the wildlife.

We couldn't see Rob's tent but two abandoned chicks peeped forlornly in the tussocks while the adults made a racket down towards Little Boot Point. A lone mother goose returned, anxiously circled the farm, crying out, then disappeared back to the coast.

Mum and I sat on the veranda. Some floorboards had rotted, and we could see the grass below. She took a bite of an apple and passed it to me. 'Look at all the arum lilies growing around the house. They've been here since the farm began.'

To avoid an archaeological conversation, I went to find Dad. He'd found Rob's empty tent on the far side of the drystone wall.

'Let's walk on to Little Boot Point,' he suggested. We hadn't gone far before Rob appeared, alerted to our presence by the geese.

He jammed his canvas hat down on his head. 'If the wind stopped blowing this place would be magic,' he said. 'And really, the university ought to get an archaeologist out here. Look at all the cultural relics lying around!'

I looked at Dad, but he hadn't seemed to have heard.

Rob suggested a cup of tea as Mum caught up to us, so we went to his tent and huddled beside the drystone wall because the wind was strengthening. While we waited for the billy to boil, Rob gathered flask tops and bowls that would do for extra mugs.

'It's going to blow all night,' said Mum.

Rob pointed at the sky as a goose flew over. 'Hear that trumpeting? Male bird. The females grunt.'

I told him I'd heard that the CBGs (which was what he called Cape Barren geese) nearly went extinct.

He poured the smoky tea and handed us our makeshift mugs. He said, 'Now's a time of plenty, because if there wasn't so much suitable habitat, they'd have to disperse more widely.'

Mum told him about the research I was doing on the geese. She thinks I'm Einstein in a skirt. So embarrassing! Dad obviously thought so too. He pulled down his hat and pretended to doze.

Rob smiled. 'The farmers on Flinders have been generous. Not that they see it that way, but when the vegetation on the smaller islands starts to yellow up at the beginning of summer all the juveniles and non-breeding geese head for Flinders. They can only eat green plants, and there are the paddocks laid out for them. It's a gilt-edged invitation.' He turned his mug upside down and the remains of his tea pooled on the ground.

Mum began muttering that we had to get back. 'Rouse yourself,' she said to Dad, giving him a little shake.

'This teacher's enjoying being off duty.' But he got up slowly.

'Come again.' Rob said. 'Come tomorrow. It's my last day.'

Dad stood up. 'Mate, I've got a message for you. Bert's sitting out the weather off Cape Barren Island. You're going to have to hang in here a while.'

'No worries. I can't think of many other places I'd rather be.'

Then, as we were leaving, he said, 'Somebody else is camping down here. No sign of a boat.'

'Spoken to him?' asked Dad.

'Or her?' said Mum.

'No, mate. Got the feeling they didn't want company.'

It's that boy. I'm sure of it.

~

The next day's forecast was for highland snow across Tasmania. Grey-bellied cumulus congestus clouds moved across the sky. We didn't see much of the mountain, but that evening, when Dad and I were singing along to a Men at Work album, he pointed at the window.

'Here's the goose boy!' And he went to the back door to let him in.

'I'm after that beer,' Rob said, and helped himself to *my* chair.

They started drinking. The stew made slow, plopping sounds on the stove. Garlic and tomato aromas filled the air.

Mum and I continued with our puzzle. Kes slept, and Dad got into banter mode. Rob settled in for the long haul. He only opened his mouth to talk natural history, and then he wouldn't shut up.

Dad got up to stir the stew. I reached for the pack of cards lying on the table and began to shuffle. Rob knew all about the Bass Strait islands. He knew their history. He knew how the *Farsund* got wrecked on Vansittart Island, where sea eagles nest in the Furneaux, the behaviour of terns and the migratory habits of species I'd never heard of. I thought, *He's quite interesting really*, which was just as well as I couldn't see how we'd ever be able to stop him talking.

And then the subject changed.

'Look, the weather's turning wild. My tent's got a leak. Guess I could kip in the farmhouse, but I was hankering for a bit of company. Do you reckon I could have a bed for the night?'

'No problem,' said Dad. 'There's a spare room if you don't mind the odd bedbug.'

'There's a ghost at the farm,' Rob said grimly. 'She sobs. I'll take the mattress. Ta muchly.'

'So,' said Mum when my dad went to get another beer. 'What's led you to be doing this sort of work?'

Rob nervously tapped his knee. 'You know, I just kind of *fell* into it?'

Freya leaned forward. 'Yeah? Like how?'

I held up the cards. 'Anyone want a game?' I could see Rob wasn't the kind of person who wanted to cough up a potted history. He looked at my cards and hesitated.

Then Mum, who was a big bulky shape in the corner with her shadow looming against the wall, said *no* on his behalf.

I began to deal myself a lonely hand.

'I'm from Queensland, grew up on the Atherton Tableland,' Rob began as Dad returned.

'Aye, the Tableland.' Dad was putting on some reggae. 'Those mysterious lakes in those hot, damp forests. Quite the erotic landscape.'

I giggled, and he gave me a wink.

'Volcanic.' Rob tapped his glass on his knee. 'Then I came here to do my degree and I stayed.'

There was a silence. I started to draw a picture of his emu-shaped head, his eyes large and alert, and the more I drew, the more I realised he wasn't bad looking.

He was talking about islands and the endless number he'd visited and all the ones he still wanted to tick off his list. Under the table his leg swung up and down.

'That's quite an inventory,' said Dad.

'I guess.'

'We all have dreams, whether we act on them or not,' Mum said.

Dad leaned over and patted her arm. 'Freya keeps a swag of them on my behalf too, don't you Frey?'

I took a careful peep at her. She was rolling her tongue against the inside of her cheek and staring into her glass of beer.

'One day I'm going to work on the islands along the Alaskan Panhandle.' Rob closed his eyes and smiled rapturously.

'Give me a hoy when you're leaving and I'll tag along,' said Dad.

'We'll pay you to take him.' Mum started getting the plates out, rather noisily.

I took careful note of the angle of his right eyebrow. I was on sketch number three of *An Emu's Head*.

Dad opened another beer.

'And I'm thinking of giving this island an international profile.'

'The hell you are. It hasn't even got a local one.'

'I'm writing an article about the geese, and I'm coming back later with a friend, to help with her fieldwork. Might write an article on this island's history.'

'I may be able to help you.' Mum had her back to us, dishing up.

'Right,' Rob nodded slowly.

I thought, *He doesn't think she can help him really.*

'Freya's an archaeologist.' Dad smiled at her as she returned with our meals.

Then a truly terrible thing happened. Rob hit his forehead with his fist. 'I've got it – I *thought* I recognised you. I've seen you on campus. You hang around with …' He glanced quickly at Dad, his face confused.

Mum thumped his plate down loudly and Dad jumped up and asked if any of us would like water.

The air was static with alarm. My heart pounded.

She sat down slowly and smiled at us. 'My archaeologist friends – we're a tight bunch. Rob, I'm in the process of writing up my PhD.'

We all breathed again.

'Your thesis is based on these islands?'

'Actually, no – South West Tasmania.'

'Well, I guess it makes sense on some level.' Rob laughed, and some stew fell off his fork.

Hers was poised halfway to her mouth. 'But I do have a small grant to do some work on this island.'

'Hah! I'll await your report with interest.'

'Knowing my wife, it will be thorough,' said Dad.

'You know,' Rob said. 'The CBGs. The male makes the nest but the female plucks her breast to make a lining and she'll lay an egg a day until she's got about four. Then for the next thirty-five days there she sits. She won't leave them for more than a few minutes, unless she's disturbed.'

I winced, thinking about how often we'd disturbed them.

'They usually pair up for life. Same as the shearwaters. Good, good stew.' He wiped his mouth and nodded at Mum.

'Wheeler made it.'

'And they stay together to survive.'

'For love,' I insisted.

'Animals don't feel love.'

Beside the stove Kes gave a dreamy little grunt. I shook my head. 'Why would we be the only species to feel love? It doesn't make sense.'

Rob was amused. 'Scientifically, you always need proof.'

'Science has its limitations,' said Mum.

I couldn't mention my numinous moment or say Nan would back me up too.

We've had long talks about how intangible concepts, emotions, and ideas fill the universe and act through us. 'I expect Einstein would agree with me,' I said.

'You seem bright, Nicky, but I doubt you know much about Einstein.'

Under the table Mum put a hand on my leg.

'Me and Einstein, you and Descartes,' I said.

'Nicky,' Mum said, a warning in her voice, but Rob laughed.

'I do admire Descartes,' he said. 'Nice meal, people. Thank you.' And he leaned back in his chair. 'As I was saying earlier, I'm not denying these old-timers know these islands. Problem is, there's a bit of pain involved in understanding the causes and consequences of the changes taking place. It's hard to convince them of the facts.'

'Sounds like you guys have got something to learn from each other.' Dad stretched out his legs.

'Guys like Bert? It's like pissing into the wind.'

'He's a good bloke. More depth there than you'd imagine. He's been around. Pays to listen first – you going to come and help me with the weather, Nicky? It's a howler out there.'

Mum pushed me towards the door. It was our ritual, even in what Dad calls *dreich* weather. And I like being outside at night because he usually makes stargazing fun. We're getting used to living by the phases of the moon, and saying goodnight to the mountain is what I do to keep nightmares away.

But, after Dad had turned off the generator and the house was in darkness, a lone eucalypt leaf fell against the vastness of my closed eyes and old uncertainties pressed in on me again.

21

Peramangk and Kaurna Country (Adelaide Hills) 2000

Bass Strait (Verloren Island) 1984

Learning How to Drown

In October 2000, with the Sydney Olympic Games over, tension building in the Middle East and the dollar tumbling, Steve phones to tell me that the cancer is deepening its hold on Freya's bones and lungs.

I arrive to find her wracked by a cough, needing to rest after a few dozen steps, each breath demanding energy she increasingly does not have. I'm profoundly shaken by her deterioration.

We spend as much time as possible in the garden beneath a cockatoo sky, birds clattering in the treetops. The spring breeze, the light through the trees, the fragrance of flowers, become the backdrop of the days.

The intricate arrangement of veins in a leaf, the care with which a fly cleans its legs, the incremental unfurling of a particular blossom – these moments anchor us, and I now understand why ironing once took precedence over the theatre when first she learned that she had cancer. In the face of her mortality, the tiny comforts of life are poignant.

Shaping this memoir has been helping me gain a more mature perspective on events, to find beauty, not horror, to bring more understanding to my complicated relationship with Freya. There is real nostalgia in recalling summer days on Verloren when windborne butterflies danced above the tussocks.

I take the opportunity, when I'm alone, to return to this work, beginning with Freya's letter written on 10 September 1984, when she told Anneke about the effort she was making to rebuild family cohesiveness, and about a walk we'd all done down the east coast to the Tinman's Teeth and Pot Boil Point, ruthless places with unforgiving but biologically mesmerising limestone reefs. At Gullet Cove, the water icy but calm, we'd swum with seals, and the kelp was tall and dense as a forest, quite different from the seagrass meadows off the beaches. I loved that she praised Wheeler for the effort he'd been putting into teaching me. He was inventive. Maths became a treasure hunt across the island. Clues to the next location had to be unlocked by completing formulas and equations.

… Occasionally we see a fishing boat or yacht moored at Sunlit or Honeymoon Coves. Sometimes yachties come up to the house for conversation or water. We met Alaskans the other day. These conversations ease a particular sort of claustrophobia that comes with not seeing others for long stretches of time.

I have government permission for my work here. There's no legal obligation to ask the traditional owners for theirs but I've thought about asking Bert to put me in touch as I don't know where to begin.

I think he might put obstacles in my way, though, because I'm just a 'sheila'.

Sometime in the next few days, we're all going in search of the old sealing site down south. It's eluded us so far but sealing has become our main topic of conversation and if we can make this fun perhaps Nicky will get interested in archaeology. Overall, we're relishing the island and often I find myself drunk on the ocean or a bird's line of flight. The rest of the world has fallen away …

~

Dad had left a note on the kitchen table: *Gone snorkelling.* From the top of Mount Aeolian, I could see Mum jogging along Emita Beach. The geese were grazing outside the kitchen door and a sea eagle flew by, struggling to gain height, a large fish glinting in its talons.

I took a wizened apple and tracked Dad's footprints along Loccota Strip as far as Sam's Soak. The black swan couple who live in its reeds flew away but the dunes enfolded me. A water rat had left tracks and there was an orange that I thought Wheeler must have left behind. When I closed my eyes, the noises were the little peaceful ones of insects and tiny birds. Sam's Soak seemed a self-contained world.

I got out my notebook and wrote: *The mountain's thoughts take a thousand years to form, but each one is profound.*

Then I heard someone sneeze. I froze. I could see no one. The clattering reeds and muffled surf transformed, became sinister, and the mountain wasn't interested in my terror. Unable to endure the thumping of my heart, I leapt up, intent on racing home, when the boy appeared.

T-shirt and shorts as worn as Dad's. Dishevelled hair. Tall and slender.

'You,' he said.

I drew myself up to my full height. 'What are you doing on our island?'

'*Your* island?' He spoke like he was testing the words for taste and finding them not to his liking. He shook his head and whistled between his teeth. 'It's not *your* island,' he said.

'Marti's Uncle Arthur said it's his island and we're the only ones allowed to live here—'

'Marti's Uncle Arthur, huh? That's a fuckin' good one. Just because he's got a little piece of paper. Doesn't mean a thing to the island. Doesn't mean a thing except suffering.'

He pointed north. 'Lighthouse – the government,' swung his arm south. 'Farm – settlers. That old bloke who runs his cattle here, damaging Country – it's not his either. They all just took it.'

I nodded, and a blush of shame bloomed across my face.

'How long are you staying?'

'Too long for my liking.'

Then he said, 'All you people who come to look at the view and enjoy yourself for a little while. No connection to this place. No relationship to it. No understanding. Just plunder and destroy.'

'I get it. I hate the destruction too.'

'You don't actually get it.' But he'd softened.

'What don't I get?'

He sighed and muttered something I couldn't hear.

'I'm Nicky, by the way.'

There was a long silence before he said, 'Len.'

'Are you living here?'

He shook his head. 'Needed time away from school to sort stuff out. This is where I come. Your mother – I've seen her at the dunes studying ... what do archaeologists call them – *middens*? She should ask the Elders for permission. She's not showing respect.'

'You should tell her that.'

'You people.'

'What?' I stared at him, uncertain.

'It's not up to me. It's up to her. Fucking educate yourselves! Think about what you're doing.' He gave a small, despairing shrug and started walking away.

'I just meant that she'd be really interested. She's been talking about that sort of thing. But I'll pass that on.' I trailed along after him. 'And I do love this island, it's only that ...' And I told him about our continental drift.

'You love this island,' he said, not looking at me. 'You love it like a – like a new skirt, as if it's impressive to dig in the dunes and rob us of culture, of our identity. For us, the island is our relative. It's family. Country is everything. You people are killing it.'

Were we? Were these things true? Freya said archaeology had already provided support for Aboriginal identity and land rights. Was that not a good thing? I liked this boy and I thought he had a right to be angry but I was disappointed that he didn't like me, is what I thought, as we stood beside Sam's Soak and stared into the water. A pelican arrived and we crouched down and watched it, and slowly a friendliness developed between us as I listened to this boy talk gently about the island, until the pelican heaved itself into the air and flew away.

I forgot about Dad. Instead, I walked home differently, softer and slower, trying on the feeling of the island being an honoured relative, like Nan, maybe, and thinking about the landforms holding stories and lore, of lost songlines beneath the sea. And I started to get it and to wonder how much I was missing because I didn't yet have the eyes to see, and how much Len and his family had lost because of our blind ignorance.

He was a fierce boy. He had dazzling stories. And he had the most amazing sea-grey eyes.

~

Mum was drinking coffee on the lighthouse steps. 'I met that boy again. He doesn't like you meddling about on the island,' I told her.

'He said that?'

'He doesn't even like us being here.'

She put down her coffee mug. 'You know that conference I went to last year? Well, some of us agreed it was important to acknowledge that Aboriginal Australians own their ancestors' remains, their cultural artefacts – their heritage, you know, Nicky. And so obviously what followed was that we need to consult and involve them, ask for permission, but I don't know who to talk to.' She ran her hands through her hair, looking anguished. 'There's intention but no process yet. Plus I'm stuck on this island.'

'Maybe start with him? Anyway, I'm going to read at the gulch.'

'I'll join you.' She got up. 'I love this work but I keep thinking about the good old boys like Dr Crowther, plundering Aboriginal graves and stealing their bones. It's confronting. What if I'm continuing the legacy of cultural appropriation?'

We climbed Whale Rock. The sun was highlighting Misfortune and the guano shone like freshly fallen snow.

'And it's a human rights issue too,' she said.

'Maybe that's what your PhD should've been about.'

'Anyway, enough about archaeology. Why don't we take the boat and go over to Misfortune? We'll be old ladies before Wheeler agrees to take us there.'

Dad had told me she was hopeless when it comes to boats – concerning, because as we left the lee of Mount Aeolian, the wind freshened, and it wasn't long before the waves grew and we realised that this was serious ocean, and we were contending with a bolshy breeze. Mum didn't feel game to turn back in case the boat broached. We didn't comment on our gross stupidity, mourn our lack of lifejackets or remark that the tide was going out, but we did note that Dad had removed the anchor. The only safety device we had was a rusty jam tin. We debated heading for Sunlit, but the break looked intimidating. We rowed with silent urgency, except that occasionally Mum said words I get into trouble for using.

I stopped noticing the birds, too aware of how far away both Verloren and Misfortune had become. There were glints of black and purple in the turquoise waves.

A cloud blocked the sun and the water darkened. Mum was panting with the effort. Misfortune looked inaccessible as we drew close, but a wave rose beneath us and slammed us onto the rock side-on.

Incredibly, the boat didn't crack, but I slipped getting out and cut my leg, although I only noticed that much later.

A cloud of cormorants rose into the sky. Eager to see the seals, I ran up Misfortune on shaky legs while Mum held the boat and bailed. The air reeked. I wanted to gag. I barely looked at the nests and I forgot about seals because I was shocked; I was standing on a ledge like the one I'd lain on in my dream. I wanted to get off the island as quickly as possible, but now I was paranoid about the sea.

Mum was still bailing when I returned, *Sophia* bashing against Misfortune's leeward side, but I noticed a gap in the waves and Mum slithered into the boat and I pushed off. She rowed slowly. Her arm was grazed from a fall onto barnacles.

Soon the waves reared up again and the jam tin I was bailing with might as well have been a thimble. I felt better when, close to the point of collapse, Mum started synchronising the boat with the sea and pursuing the path of least resistance, but a particularly large wave swept over the transom and the boat broached. We were swamped. With horrible slowness *Sophia* turned over, tipping us into water just too deep for us to stand. It was momentous, watching her sink, as we were carried away from each other.

I was taking in mouthfuls of water between screaming for Mum. She made a heroic effort, managed to reach me, grabbed me from behind, and with her arm around my neck and under my arm, tried to swim with me. As each wave approached, 'Bodysurf it,' she'd shout, letting me go, and then we'd struggle back to grab hold of each other again, but we were tired, and at last could no longer reach each other at all. There was a rip. I could tell I would end up being swept past Misfortune. I started swimming parallel to the beach, letting the current take me.

Then there was Dad, up to his waist, throwing us lines, hauling us in, and we were hugging each other and crying, and he was kissing and cursing us at the same time, and Kes was leaping around, barking madly.

Everything glittered with life.

We didn't feel ourselves again for days. He said if he hadn't seen our idiocy from the top of the lighthouse we would have surely drowned and in my dreams my hair blazed on Mount Aeolian.

22

Peramangk and Kaurna Country (Adelaide Hills) 2000

Bass Strait (Verloren Island) 1984

———————

Sapphire City

I CAN HEAR THE sombre strains of Elgar's 'Cello Concerto' through the floorboards as I sort through stuff in the cellar. Earlier, I asked Freya if listening to wistful music didn't get to her. She said 'no' rather sharply, thinking I was being critical of Steve. Now I see that he chooses the music specifically for her, as though it were a gift, seeking to suit it to the tenor of her mood.

Carla, her palliative care nurse, is present, and while they need privacy, I'm reluctant to spend a precious day in the cellar. The first box I manhandle to the door contains archaeological texts, and I put aside a copy of Plomley's *Friendly Mission*. Among these books is an antique hatbox containing much of her correspondence with Anneke. I hastily replace the lid as Steve arrives with an ice-cold glass of water, sprigged with mint.

'You could get a reasonable price for your grandmother's work,' he says, looking at a couple of smaller pieces I've put to one side.

'Yes, but I'd rather keep them.'

'Freya always said, if not for you, she'd have sold Celeste's work ages ago. The house is already too full of art.' He's distressed, I can tell, but I'm dismayed by the comment.

And having dragged a box to the door, he returns to his study.

I walk over to my habitual spot in the garden to edit a little, the cold glass in my hand, somewhat thankful I'm not reading this bit to Freya, because it begins with the morning I woke to find a grotesque pimple on my face, my first ever and, I read in my journal, before I could do anything about it, Dad said, 'With that yellow pus bucket glowing on your forehead we don't need a lighthouse. Cheers, Nicky, I'm off to climb the mountain.'

So unkind!

While Mum laboured in the struggling vegie patch, I did school-work. It's September. It's cold. The moonbirds have left Alaska and are winging their way south. They connect the Arctic circle to the Antarctic, summer to summer, and that's an amazing thing. It's also amazing to have little penguins, aka *Eudyptula minor*, as neighbours and I'm surrounded by them. They dig into the rim of the land and often we encounter groups returning to their burrows while the rest of their companions continue to spend their weeks at sea. They spruce up their homes and flirt a little.

A few nights ago, we headed down to Sunlit, leaving Kes moping at home. Penguins were surfing in on the waves. Wings held out to dry, they preened, dithering a little, discussing us, before waddling towards the dunes, white breasts gleaming. Mum said, 'We're alarming them,' but Dad said, 'Rubbish!' and flicked torchlight over them. They bunched together, sizing us up, then formed a tight group and waddled away to their burrows, leaving a trail of their watery lives on the air behind them. Outrageous noises were coming from the colony. Dad said, 'Now that's uninhibited lovemaking!' and as Mum's breath implied laughter I knew it was safe to laugh too.

~

Mum was singing 'Summertime' in the bathroom when I asked if I could put my tent up on the edge of Sapphire City. She settled her hairband in place and said, 'It's a rookery,' and I said, 'Yes, a rookery called Sapphire City,' and she said, 'It's a bad time to ask. I'm about to do the provisioning and this time I've got to get it right.'

It doesn't pay to forget a staple item, although Dad wouldn't notice if she forgot to order soap or shampoo. Just then the radio crackled, and I heard Bert's voice fading in and out as I trailed Freya through to the lounge. I cajoled her by brushing her hair while she drew up the order, but then she started wondering where Dad was, and why he wasn't teaching me, which meant I had to quickly fabricate a story about penguin lessons planned for the afternoon.

'If my tent was there, I could monitor their behaviour, very educational.' (She's becoming suspicious about Dad's flexible teaching hours so I haven't told her that over in his eyrie he's reading sailing magazines he'd smuggled over and that there are boat plans hidden among them.)

She sat with her pen poised above her notepad. 'I know you. You'll be feeding and cuddling them. You'll be bringing them home.' She gave her neck a little scratch and it made the skin just there go briefly pale. I watched the colour flood back in again.

'I won't!'

She was silent while I brushed.

'Well, as long as you watch and don't interfere! And be careful of snakes.'

I pranced upstairs to get the tent. She decided to get enthusiastic and came down the hill with me to help choose a site, a snug hollow surrounded by tussocks, before setting off on a jog in search of Dad.

As soon as it was up, I lay down and watched the pipits flit above me. A furry green caterpillar clung to a blade of poa above my face. Burrows honeycombed the ground. Nan says happiness is the feeling of a peaceful mind. Nan is right about almost everything.

Late in the afternoon Mum called by to ask if I'd like company for tea. She hadn't found Dad and the house was lonely without me. Most of the birds had packed up their fishing for the day and the beaches were quiet, the tide slack. We made a driftwood fire and boiled a billy and after finishing our pasta we toasted marshmallows on sticks. She told me stories about her childhood. I've listened to many variations, and I've found that if I'm patient another little detail will emerge about her father.

'What was the best thing about him?'

'He was funny, I suppose, and he was pretty good about spending time with us – until he wasn't. I was the youngest, but I was the one mothering Nan and Anneke for a time, and always having to be the peacemaker,' and she slowly turned her marshmallow above the flames. We popped them in our mouths and prepared the next ones.

'We thought he was kind when he helped Mrs Cunningham next door whenever something needed fixing. Later, we wondered.'

Just like I wonder, when I'm in bed at night, about Freya and that uni guy, especially since Rob had dinner with us.

She folded her arms around her knees and rocked slowly from side to side. We fell silent. The sky deepened and the stars took up their positions. Mount Naturaliste and the distant islands were mere suggestions in the darkness. I studied the sky, hoping for an aurora, or a star to fall.

'And then he vanished completely.'

'Maybe Anneke knows where he is?'

'No idea.'

'Don't you wonder whether he's still alive?'

'He's buried down deep in my memory. I'd prefer he stayed there.'

A silence welled around us as we contemplated this statement from our different perspectives.

We leaned against each other, and I took a deep breath of the warm fragrance she was wearing.

'Do you miss Anneke?'

'I do. I worry about her. And you know, I once made her a promise. It wasn't a sensible thing to do in retrospect, but I made it and I'm bound by it and I'd like her to come and release me from it.'

'Was that the promise to keep writing to her?'

She hugged me. Kissed the top of my head. 'If only.'

'You're not going to tell me, are you?'

She squeezed me again. 'You're the first person I'd tell if I could.'

Which was nice of her to say, and evidence that she's the best mother, and also my most trusted friend.

'Are you going to wait with me for the penguins to arrive?'

'Thanks, Nicky, but I want to check if your dad is home. I wish he'd said where he was going.'

I could tell from her voice that she was worried. 'I think he went up the mountain.'

'No. He said he'd do that with us.'

She hugged me again, and kissed me goodnight.

I wriggled into my sleeping bag. I hoped Dad was all right wherever he was. I opened my field guide to calm my anxiety and began reading about penguin lifestyles.

I've observed different architectural designs around here, from shallow scallops of sand beneath outcropped rock for the relaxed, self-assured, or just plain lazy, to the metre-deep tunnels preferred by those with troglodyte tendencies. The only new thing the book told me was that fishermen once slaughtered penguins and used them as cray bait. What is the matter with people? Maybe Bert once fished for cray this terrible way! He'd admitted to using gannet.

I'd dozed off when twitterings began to rise from the burrows, followed shortly afterwards by calls coming over the dunes. I wriggled outside and surveyed the beach. The torchlight merged with the glow of the waxing gibbous moon and caught and held in its path small bodies bobbing on the water. Some headed straight for their burrows and called at the entrance before entering. Others did a careful inspection, gave the entrance a quick spruce-up or stood outside their homes, whistling and calling, necks back, beaks directed at the moon.

There were flirting penguins in my tent. It was damp, fishy, and scuffed with sand. I longed for my bed, but if I'd returned, Dad would have called me a wimp. I encouraged them out and zipped up the flap. Outside the wailing grew. Yet over the noise, close by my tent I heard footsteps stop. And then continue. Maybe Dad on his way home, or a curious wallaby. Or, just maybe, Len.

23

Bass Strait (Verloren Island) 1984

Not Mr Popular

I WOKE AT SUNRISE and lay in the tent reading and watching cormorants fishing before going up to the house. Kes was sleeping on the kitchen steps, and Dad said Mum had already gone down to South Verloren. Over the radio we heard a crew member on the *Freak*, a scallop boat out of Whitemark, say that their engine had failed; they might need assistance.

'Good thing they've got calm weather,' said Dad.

He made me brekkie and said he and Kes had reached the mountain summit yesterday, but it had taken considerable bush bashing. From the top the ocean looked like liquid opal reeling below, and the mountain tapered down like scales along a dragon's back until the island narrowed away to nothing. Sea eagles were circling, and the islands were spread out in every direction.

Instead of doing the maths he'd given me, I wrote down my latest dream for Dorothy, because in it I know I'm on the island even though there are icebergs and many more islands. Verloren is an outcrop on a grassy plain and there's a tree growing through our wrecked *Sophia*. A group of us watch a curl of smoke hanging in the distant sky, straining to work out the meaning. A stance stiffens, a mouth tightens, someone frowns, voices are lowered. A small boy sits on the ground. We are all family. We wear animal skins and move across Country, always watching – the horizon, the sea, the sky, but one by one people disappear and finally there is only the little boy and me, walking hand in hand.

We stop eating. When smoke hangs in the sky we watch it with dread, sitting on a beach, filmy-eyed, until, past hunger, we follow a splashing stream up the snowy mountain to a cave.

It's icy in there. The little boy's sobs fade away. A white silence permeates everything, eating up sound and even, eventually, the shallow rhythm of my breathing.

~

I tracked Dad to where he was diving and sat on the rocks with my schoolwork, and when he bobbed up we talked about how we might be able to save the *Sophia* if we get a good spring tide. I really love these moments with my dad.

'Come on, girl. Orate your discoveries.' And he got out and cracked open a beer and listened to me talk about the things I'd found and the clues he'd left on his way down here.

That's school on Verloren Island.

The other day Dorothy delivered letters from my friends, along with one from Mrs Porter. I didn't tell Dad – she sounded concerned I was falling behind the class – but as we sat there I mentioned Sally's.

Hello Nicky!

Guess what??? I've got a boyfriend!!! You don't know him, but I met him at Cheryl's party. And here comes the sad bit – she hooked up with Sam Doody! Don't worry! He is such a waste of space! He acts like he's got a crush on her but then he wants to know all your news, so who knows!!! You have missed out on two parties but until I met Danny I'd have swapped them for the island.

Mr and Mrs Jones will let me visit in January, so now my task is to make sure they don't come too …

I'm in exile, Sam Doody is a jerk, but, I said to Dad, at least Sally still wants to visit, even though she's got a boyfriend.

'I feel so left out,' I confided.

Once I'd believed my parents that we'd be home by December. But just when I felt like they were the best parents in the world again, and that we were happy, I discovered that Dad was not Mr Popular because Mum wanted us to fly back to Hobart so I could touch base with school. She told me living on the island was more expensive than Dad had calculated. We couldn't afford a trip back and she was so upset about this that I began to wonder if school was the only reason why.

24

Peramangk and Kaurna Country (Adelaide Hills) 2000

Bass Strait (Verloren Island) 1984

Coastline, Moon, and Stars

STEVE'S VOICE DRIFTS TOWARDS me from the garden gate. Warm, understanding Carla, raven-haired and large-eyed, is leaving, and keen for an update on Freya, I join them.

Her expression is calm, her voice low as she discusses the decline she's noticing, and she shares some suggestions for making Freya more comfortable. Steve, visibly anguished, disappears inside. I linger and when Carla finally leaves, I feel deeply the lack of someone to talk to. Sally is in Adelaide, and I know would drop everything, but I feel overwhelmed by listlessness.

I lean against the gate twirling the moonbird feather I'd found in a box, then I make cups of tea for us all, and return to my editing. So great is my need for distraction that I immediately dive into a letter written on 17 September, before turning to my journal.

… A curious thing, Anneke – I've noticed the dunes are being undercut by spring tides and storm events, particularly where there is marram grass. That might be bad news for dune-dwelling animals. It may mean the sea level is rising, a sign that the climate is changing. I spoke about this to a visiting yachtie who happened to be a geologist. Across the sciences, our impact on climate and habitats is a growing concern.

Anyway, my eye for detecting artefacts is improving. I found a scatter of worked quartz flakes and tiny thumbnail scrapers, probably used for cleaning skins. I record them and leave them in place but the pleasure I get from this work has been falling away. When I encounter issues, there's no one to discuss them with. I miss my colleagues.

Today, as we stood near the lighthouse watching gannets dive, I asked Wheeler to show me the mountain cave, but yet again he decided the sea was calling, so Nicky and Kes came along. Nicky led me there so easily it was as though she'd visited it before. When we came level to a cliff face, we had to sidle along while a raven watched us from a nearby tree.

There was the cool smell of earth and rock, and the exhilaration of tiny ferns growing in damp corners. There were moss banks, and a risky bend to negotiate before reaching the entrance. The cave felt sacred. Smoke stains the ceiling and a fire had been made there recently. Nicky didn't like the raven's undulating caw in the silent forest and she wanted me to hurry – she soon disappeared along the cliff face and when I left, the raven flew away, its wings whipping the air, so close it fanned my face, kind of eerie! Will continue this letter later.

The cave really had creeped me out so I chose to stay in the house that night and we played Canasta, while outside the wind wailed and the surf roared. Later, in bed, I watched the beam flick through the darkness and thought about the sea floor littered with corralled bones, and pearly eyes – yes, I'm reading *The Tempest* and sometimes I feel like I'm living it.

After the storm the morning sea and sky were pearlescent, the waves subdued. Mum and I went beachcombing. On Restless the beach had eroded, all the way down to the rocky reef. The sea had swept thousands of tonnes of sand away, and poking out of the dunes was what looked like part of a decrepit wooden wreck, re-exposed.

Mum hopes it's the *Britomart*, a trading ketch that wrecked somewhere in the islands in 1839. She's found shards of pottery that the moonbirds kicked up to the surface in the process of burrow-making last year and says maybe the crew salvaged some of the cargo and camped behind the beach. She looked at the wreck and its old rusty nails then went up to the house for a camera and notepad. It was spooky on the beach alone, like the crew were still there, staring down at me.

After she'd made notes and taken a sample, we meandered along the dense wrack line. In amongst the tangles of seaweed, we found cuttlefish carrying goose barnacles and sponges that Freya called dead man's fingers.

'Strange story,' said Freya, picking up a barnacled twig. 'During the Middle Ages, in some parts of Europe, people thought these barnacles were the fruit of the trees that washed up on beaches and that the barnacle goose hatched from them.'

'I don't believe that.'

'Linnaeus thought swallows buried themselves in lake floors over winter and popped up with the arrival of spring.'

'That's crazy!'

But I wasn't really listening. I was wondering where Len was. He might as well have been buried in a lake floor for all I'd seen of him.

25

Bass Strait (Verloren Island) 1984

Encounter at Honeymoon Cove

'THERE'S A YACHT AT Honeymoon,' Mum told us, as Dad and I studied a map. Verloren Island's moonbird community is homeward bound across the vast Pacific Ocean and we've been applying our dodgy formula for tracking their 21,000-kilometre journey.

'There was a woman on deck,' she said. 'We looked across at each other and waved, and she was going to untie her tender and come on over. I could really have done with a chat, but …'

'But what?' I asked, not looking up.

She went and put on the kettle. 'Well, there was something about her that brought Anneke to mind, and I felt depressed and carried on walking, having a long conversation with her in my head.'

'Yacht might still be there tomorrow,' I said.

'We don't know what the wind will be doing,' Dad said, returning to our map. 'All we know is that these birds travel at about forty knots, three to fifteen metres above the sea.'

Still, we've been noting dates and marking tentative positions.

Mr Napper, once the lighthouse-keeper here, didn't know his migratory route roughly duplicated that of the moonbirds when he brought his family from Alaska to this island. He lost two children to sickness, one to snake bite and his wife to the ocean. Mr Napper left Verloren alone one April. The winds are quieter then. It's when the adult moonbirds fly north to Alaska.

When we still had them positioned off the New South Wales coastline, Bert radioed to say they'd been sighted east of Wilsons Promontory.

In a week they'd be home, these remnants of the great flocks that once blotted out the sun.

~

It was my turn to leave a note on the kitchen table. I packed a bag, wrote 'Gone to Honeymoon Cove', called Kes and set off.

It was a low neap tide, the weather perfect. I marched with the soldier crabs across Emita and gave the oystercatchers a wide berth, not wanting to interrupt their foraging. Kes was ahead of me, his tail carving circles of happiness. There were pelicans on the water and a trail of moon snail egg masses along the wrack line.

Together we clambered over the orange-lichened boulders on the point and walked along the narrow path beneath the casuarinas to where the path ceases above the beach. The yacht Mum had mentioned was still there. I looked down into the cove and saw a dinghy, a towel and an umbrella. A woman with long, black hair lay beneath it reading a book and eating an apple.

She had no clothes on.

I backtracked as quietly as I could, but it was no good. Kes was down on the sand, eager to make a new friend.

'Where did you come from?' She sat up to give him a scratch and then looked up and laughed. 'Oops!' she said and wrapped a sarong around herself in far too leisurely a fashion.

I stayed exactly where I was. 'Are you alone?' I asked.

'Just me, and only briefly. A pity. I love this place. Come on down.' She walked towards me, smiling, an arm outstretched.

I quite liked the idea of somebody new to talk to, and so I jumped down onto the beach and placed my things at a little distance from hers, near the southern rocks. Kes wanted her to throw him a stick and while she obliged, I slipped off my sandals and went down to feel the water. It was incredibly cold, but the cove was sheltered.

'We haven't introduced ourselves,' she said, as we stood on the swash. 'My name's Yolla.'

'Yolla,' I said wonderingly. 'I'm Nicky from the lighthouse.'

'That's my favourite name.'

She waded in deeper, her back towards me. She was tanned, a little bit of flab hung below her shoulders, and she was wearing big loop earrings. She stood there in silence, holding up the bottom of her red sarong, then over her shoulder she said, 'And where is your family right now?'

'At the lighthouse.'

She walked back up the beach and settled herself beneath her umbrella. 'Bring your towel over here so we can talk.'

Soon we were into a deep conversation. She told me how from time to time she'd spent months here, but it was unfortunate that the last time her path crossed with 'the grumpy little farmer'.

She described herself as a freelance photographer and artist, and of all the adults I've ever met, she was easily the best listener. She was interested in me, and I was interested in her because of the stories I'd heard.

She wanted to know about my childhood, about school, about everything.

'What's the worst thing that's happened to you?' she asked.

'When Dad fell over a cliff, and I thought I'd killed him.'

'And the best?'

'Hobart, my Nan and Sally.' I looked at the sea. 'I love this island and my parents are the best, but I hope we go home soon.'

She nodded. 'There are costs attached to moving a lot. I know because I'm something of a nomad myself.'

Kes was lying beside me panting. I'd forgotten to bring him water. Sometimes he gets dizzy when he's thirsty, walking like he's drunk, then falling over.

'I'm glad you've got caring parents. When I was young my parents' divorce was catastrophic. But the worst thing that's happened to me was giving away my baby. One moment this tiny being you feel drenched in love for is snuggled in your arms, the next ...'

'I can't even begin to imagine. I'm so sorry.'

'You *never* get over it. But a boat, a dream and this island helped me find a new sense of direction.' She pointed at the mountain. 'Dreams pour out of the cave up there.'

'I know! Every night!" And I told her that the previous night I'd dreamed I was sitting near the lighthouse, a hot wind blowing, and a fisherman walked up from Sunlit Cove to get water. Mr Napper, the lighthouse keeper, told him that he'd have to go to the farm to fill his pail because they only had a teaspoon left, and when the fisherman got angry, Mr Napper showed him the boulder closest to the veranda, and tapped it. A bead of water appeared on the surface, and he said, 'It used to flow sweet as a stream. Now it sweats if we're lucky and it's powerfully salty. We're getting awfully thirsty.'

She seemed interested so I carried on, telling her how the fisherman stormed down the hill and moments later smoke rose near the dunes.

'Fool's dropped a match,' said Mr Napper. I was standing beside the boulder with the boy who was in my cave dream, only he was taller than me now. He stood on one leg, dark as a shadow, skinny as a tree, tossing a pebble from hand to hand.

We ran to the penguin colony. The fire was crackling, the moulting penguins were terrified, many aflame, as we plunged our hands into burrows, burning our fingers. Meanwhile, the fisherman stood nearby and laughed, and with the going down of the sun, the returning penguins discovered a holocaust.

She was fully listening. 'It felt so real my heart ached when I woke up. I could almost feel blisters on my fingers.'

'That has happened,' said Yolla. 'Whole communities of penguins and moonbirds have been burned out this way, often. Smoke has swirled, and this is what the penguins have seen, over and over, as they've returned from the sea. They've suffered shock. They've died of despair. Often.'

'Nan once told me that small wars go unremarked.'

'Did she?' said Yolla thoughtfully. 'But this isn't a small war. People damaging the earth, hurting the sentient beings that inhabit it. We stepped out of nature and started running amuck. We even trash our own children.'

'Sometimes it makes me wish I'd never been born.'

'*Please*,' said Yolla, briefly hugging me. 'Never say that. You are remarkable. Your life has purpose, and you are loved beyond your parents' love, just as you are. Nicky, we put too much emphasis on our individuality, we Westerners. We're the sum of all that is, the energy of the universe momentarily working through us.' She slowly gestured at the sea, the island. 'Nothing is as it seems. Time's illusions play us all. And you know, the cave – most of the dreams aren't meant for us.'

I looked at her quizzically.

'They're for the animals and the plants, and the people who were once here. They're in the language our ancestors smashed.'

I nodded. 'I wish you could meet Nan. You'd love her.'

'Tell me about her.'

After that she wanted to know about my parents. We sat there for a long time, sharing our food. Then she took out a hefty camera and asked if she could take some photographs of Kes and me, and she showed me her Verloren sketchbook, mostly shells and seabirds, but also some abstract-looking landscapes.

'We have a breeze, Nicky.'

It was making patterns on the water.

'It's a good time to head off,' she said. And then she added that she was going on safari, a month in the Okavango Delta. 'Some staggering good luck. But I always love getting back to these islands. Dorothy has a house at Killiecrankie, did you know? On Flinders Island? I often visit. If you ever need a friend, contact Dorothy. She has a lot of time for you.'

'She said she wants to follow the moonbirds to the Chukchi Sea.'

'We're planning that project together.'

Every time she stood up to go, we'd start another conversation, but finally I helped her push the tender into the water and I gathered my gear. She gave me the longest hug. 'It was so meaningful to meet you here, Nicky. An honour, really. This island never ceases to surprise me. I'm sure we'll meet again someday.'

I was excited to tell my parents about Yolla, but as I came bursting through the door I could tell there'd been an argument. My heart dropped. It wasn't the right time, so I escaped to the gulch.

When I'm unhappy, my misery seems to sweep out of me and settle in the landscape. Mostly I love the island so much I want to wrap myself in its tussocky pelt, but even though we've all been so happy, at night I'm nagged by anxious sadness. I know what will happen now. Mum and Dad will *say* they love me, but they'll ignore me. Her head will be stuck in archaeology and he'll do more fishing. When they argue, it's about me. We should be setting a date to return to Hobart, but when I bring it up, she says she's tied here by her project and he always changes the subject.

26

Peramangk and Kaurna Country (Adelaide Hills) 2000

Bass Strait (Verloren Island) 1984

Shostakovich and Shearwaters

MY MOTHER IS LYING on the couch with a book when I ask if I can read her one of her old letters.

She looks up at me with uncertainty. 'Should I be worried?'

'Not at all.' And I sit near her feet and smooth the paper.

21 September 1984

Dear Anneke,

Bert radioed the other day – a cryptic message for Wheeler. 'Tell him she's still coming over and she won't need no pumping.'

I took my coffee and walked down to the vegie patch, trying to work it out. The waves were rumbling along the rocks below …

'Stop right there, Nicky,' she says. 'How angry I was!'

'Yes, you most certainly were. But it clearly took you a while to work it out.'

We laugh, but her laughter turns into coughs. I get her water, and she returns to her book and I to a journal extract.

~

My parents are weird! The other evening they didn't hear me come inside and when I said, 'What's going on?' they jumped away from each other, laughing, and I took advantage of their confusion and swapped Brahms for a little JJ Cale. But then they sidestepped into an argument. Mum gave the exasperated sigh she long ago perfected. 'I know where you're coming from. We've discussed this before, and I said *great idea* to incorporate the island into the curriculum but the longest school day Nicky's had can't be more than a measly four hours.'

'Over-exaggeration, Frey. You give me no credit. Come on Nicky, we're leaving your snaky mum inside. You come with me.'

We went to the lighthouse and spotted an anchor light in Sunlit Cove, then he poured a whisky and said he was going to teach me about quarks, which isn't in the curriculum, and I was half asleep, drooped over the table, my head resting on my arms, wishing like anything that Nan was back and I could fly home to Hobart.

Then he poured a bigger drink and opened his drawer of bones, ones we've found scattered among the tussocks and I immediately said it was too late for a lesson and so he took out his secret stash of yachting magazines instead, and said if it wasn't for Mum, he'd have built a boat by now and we'd be sailing the world.

I'm glad we're not.

Mum doesn't know he has whisky up there and sometimes there's that old familiar smell I associate with The Crazed Desert Gophers, but when I ask him what it is, he changes the subject. I can't tell Mum. She'd go ballistic.

Wednesday, 26 September

… We are shoved up against one another on this island, and sometimes it seems there's nothing to talk about. So lonely! My colleagues are sailing up in early December. I'm hoping I can participate in their survey but it could cause tension … I'm so looking forward to seeing them, but anxious about it as well …

The wind had picked up again. I took Mum a cup of tea. She was sitting at her desk in a sleeping bag, typing with gloved fingers. Just one look and I knew she was in pain.

I gave her a hug. 'You know the other day when I was at Honeymoon?'

'Yes, but Nicky, please be a darling and heat up this hot water bottle for me?'

Afterwards, I stood at the edge of the hill. A fishing boat had sought refuge in Sunlit Cove, its bow facing southwest. Dad came over and told me their anchor had dragged when the big gusts hit, and they got scary close to the rocks before they managed to reset it.

I said, 'Dad, you know when I was at Honeymoon the other day? You won't believe this, but—'

'Whoa, Nicky – I've just remembered something I need to get from the lighthouse …'

I looked down the island and wished I knew where I could find Len. Just maybe I'd get a five-minute conversation.

~

A week later Bert arrived with heaps of fresh vegies. He brought me a Killiecrankie diamond from Flinders Island and I put it on the mantelpiece with Nan's bird-girl sculpture. I showed him the pile of flotsam and jetsam I'd dragged up from the beach and he bent over and picked up some fishing net.

'Looks like mine.'

'How would you know?'

He said he recognised his handiwork in a fixed bit. 'Might still come in use. Easy to lose a net overboard. It's a wild ocean out there.'

My silent accusation hung in the air.

'This is just a little bit of net, darling.' His mouth tightened. He tapped his cigarette.

I turned and walked over to the house, and up the stairs to my room. I lay on my bed and pressed my fingers into the corners of my eyes because for some dumb reason I was crying. Not because of that stupid net but because Sam Doody has a crush on Cheryl, my friends are at parties and I'm stuck on this far-flung island and the only boy here keeps avoiding me. Worse, later Mum played the *moderato con moto* from Shostakovich's 'Sonata No. 2 in B Minor' over and over until she drove me down to my tent and Dad up the lighthouse.

The *Essie Black* out of Cape Barren saw a raft of moonbirds north of Flinders Island so we put aside the formula that didn't work and that night, as I climbed Mount Aeolian, a bird whipped by so low I had to duck to avoid a collision.

But was it a moonbird? I thought they arrived in a crowd. Wheeler says the flocks are smaller now – perhaps because they get snagged in the nets of smarty-pants fishermen.

On 26 September, I found fresh guano and fans of scratched sand spread outside some burrows and on the 27th, I waited on the dunes alone. A light northerly was blowing and there were creamy cloud streets out to sea. The sky deepened and the lighthouse rolled out its first beam. Then the sky was swimming with stars and the penguins grew restless, their chatter drifting up from the sand. As I was about to go home, a bird flew swiftly overhead and during the next few minutes the number circling the dunes increased rapidly. Their wings sliced the air. They whirled, they wheeled, they zipped past me fast as bullets, so close that I ducked to protect my head. Some crash-landed with thumps in the tussocks.

The Verloren moonbirds were home! And loudly so!

Across the isthmus that magic evening the mountain was black and still, its skin full of the movements of animals. Out across the sea, the islands, too, were dark against the immense, star-sequinned sky. The sea glittered quietly where the moonlight lay upon its surface and around me birds whirled and babbled. In that moment of awe, alone in that watery world, it was numinous.

27

Bass Strait (Verloren Island) 1984

A Boy and His Fishing Rod

'SHE'S A PEARLER,' SAID Wheeler about the day. 'Those slinky little waves, that jitterbugging light.' And so we went skin diving, then sat on the boulders at Squally Cove and counted the abalone we'd collected.

'Did you see the flounder change colour as it settled into the sand? And the banded sea perch?' I said. I'd also seen a stingray shift from beneath the sand and flap slowly away over seagrass, the sun dappling its pale back as it rippled through the water, and we were caught together in time, before our lives took different courses. 'Weren't those red sea fans magic?'

We dived again. Seals came to look at us. They gambolled like puppies and the light made waves along the contours of their bodies.

We walked back across the farm, avoiding the sunbaking snakes. Goslings were fledging and adult geese moulting. The older chicks, savvier than the newborns, prowled through the tussocks, alert to every anomaly. And then, as we did from time to time, we saw a humpback whale breach.

180

Dad was chatting about his novel, how Gunther Berg built a community here with other Straitsmen, originally employed as sealers. Their Aboriginal wives contributed traditional skills, diving along the reefs, catching moonbirds and harvesting bushtucker. They incorporated *Britomart* wreckage into their huts and where the stream drains from swampy ground and meanders into Beagle Bay, is where they made the three rock-lined soak holes we discovered with Mum the other day. All I can do is describe my real life as story and hope Mrs Porter likes it.

That's when I saw Len watching us from under some casuarina trees. I gave him a tiny wave, and he gave me a little nod.

'This is my dad,' I called, and Wheeler walked over and immediately engaged him in a fishing conversation and invited him up to the house for lunch.

But he showed us the fish he'd caught, and said he'd best be on his way. I felt as though I'd never get to know him.

We ate pan-fried abalone in sunshine on the kitchen steps, but in the late afternoon the mountain retreated behind a blanket of cloud and the boulders around the house were veiled in mist, so it was a few days before Mum and I were inspired to pack a lunch and set off for Gullet Cove via Hannah's Hope Bay. When we reached Sam's Soak, I ran up the dunes that Dad now calls Alveolar Ridge. The swan couple and a few hooded dotterels scattered when they saw me.

I looked around, hoping to see Len again.

'I saw someone in the distance at Beagle Bay the other day and there was smoke at the hut,' said Mum.

'Probably Len.'

'I'm surprised I haven't met him yet.'

'Well, he'll know everything you're doing.'

We cut across the farm to Honeymoon Cove, scattering geese. Then we had to go a little inland because of the cliffs and a small stretch of casuarina forest and on out into lightly wooded heath, this being the edge of the dry sclerophyll slopes of Mount Naturaliste. We heard a kookaburra laugh and there were wattlebirds calling out to each other in the eucalypt trees. Freya was walking in front of me, chanting species names, so, because she was being annoying and her big bottom was in easy reach, I leaned forward and pinched her through her baggy red cotton pants and when she tried to get me back, I ran laughing down to Possum Boat Harbour with Kes.

And there was Len, fishing off the rocks, startled to see me, just as I was startled to see him.

'Len! Hi! Come and meet my mother,' I called.

A shadow passed across his face. He wound in his line slowly as I picked a path towards him. Behind me, Mum came striding out of the bush.

'Come on,' I said when I got closer. 'She won't bite.'

He winced.

'We'll leave you alone, just come and meet her.' And I turned, hoping he'd follow.

She waved at him, her face breaking into a rather too eager smile as he slowly walked towards the beach.

I thought he would tackle her about what she was doing, or that she would launch into an explanation, but she kept the conversation light, before telling us that she was going to walk down Little Boot Point and did we want to come?

We both shook our heads. We sat on the sand and watched her go. The silence rang. Lone Egg Island drowsed in the sun. Waders were poking about looking for a meal.

Kes came and lay beside us and Len and I talked about the moonbirds. He'd watched them arrive at Beagle Bay. 'See you've got a tent in the dunes,' he said.

'I wondered if that was you walking past. You could have said hello.'

'Didn't know I'd be welcome.'

'Anyway, I can't use it anymore. I thought the nights were full of bird conversation before but the moonbirds are like an all-night orchestra – correction; a discordant one – and they really rev up just before sunrise. It's crazy.'

He laughed. 'They never shut up. But they'll disappear out to sea for a couple of weeks in November, after they've fixed up their burrows.'

'To feast.'

He nodded. 'Yep, before the egg laying and chick rearing.'

Then I told him how I was missing school, and he said he liked learning new things but the school he'd been at had been tough. It did his head in listening to teachers talking as though his people didn't exist. It was hard making friends when people casually made racist comments.

'It kills you,' he said. 'You feel unseen, like you don't even have a right to exist.'

'My dad could teach you, just don't expect to learn the curriculum,' I said. 'He'd like to hear your story though.'

Little Boot Point is mainly poa tussocks and olearia bushes, so we could see my mother walking back up. When she reached us, she was red-faced and excited. At the far end of the point she'd found an old circular cairn in a state of semi-collapse.

I looked at Len and rolled my eyes. 'This is what I have to put up with,' I said, and he laughed. We were getting to be quite friendly.

'She's harsh,' my mother said, sitting down and unpacking her lunch. 'Len, I hear you have concerns about my work?'

He seemed very adult when he took her on. 'Archaeologists, they act like they have a right to do whatever they like to our culture, things that belong to us. What do human rights even mean if we have no say over the little that's left for us?'

Mum was nodding. 'I agree,' and she told him about the conference. 'Look, Len, there's a cave further along the coast – you know the one? Come and see what I do. Then you can talk about it with anyone who shares the same concerns, anyone you think I should be speaking to. I'm happy to give you whatever information you need.'

He didn't look convinced and the conversation turned to other things. After eating we explored the edge of the reef. 'Time to move along,' Mum said. She headed off along the beach, and Len and I walked into the water talking, standing knee-deep, so close to each other that sometimes the waves caused us to touch, and the more we talked the more I realised we had quite a bit in common.

'I think the moonbirds are breeding now.' I mentioned.

'Yolla,' he said. 'That's their true name. Not moonbirds.'

'That's what I should call them?'

He stared out to sea as though he hadn't heard. 'They lay their eggs over three days in late November,' he added eventually. I knew that, but all I said was 'oh,' and eventually we followed my mother along the beach, and he told me how he'd been reading about colonialism around the world and the way it had destroyed so much knowledge and if more of that knowledge still existed and was respected, he thought our broken world wouldn't be so messed up.

We reached the cliff where the cave is. Mum was sitting outside.

'Thought I'd wait for you,' she said. 'Len, would you like to show me the cave? And if you want to share anything you know about it, that would be great.'

He really didn't look like he wanted to, but he went with her.

This cave, I knew, would keep her occupied for a long time. I just hoped she wouldn't offend him.

He was inscrutable when he came back out. 'I'm turning back,' he said. 'See you around.'

I had hoped he'd suggest catching up tomorrow.

As he walked away I shouted after him, 'Come up to the lighthouse if you like,' and he raised his arm but didn't turn around.

'What did you say to him?' I asked my mother suspiciously.

'Nothing offensive, at least I don't think so. But I might have put him in an awkward position. He said I need to talk to an Elder, and he gave me a name.'

Mum and I stumbled through the tussocks behind Preservation

Beach and stood on the tip of Digit Point looking down into Hannah's Hope Bay. It's a wide beach with shady trees and from where we stood we could also see the rugged stretch of coast that extends down to Wright Rocks and the Dagger, where the sea is wild and untrustworthy.

'I like that boy,' said Mum. 'And he's got amazing eyes and what your Nan would call a Renaissance bone structure.'

'You mean good-looking?'

'Just a pity he's lost his way,' and she turned to walk on.

'Maybe he's actually finding his way,' I said. And then, 'I met Yolla at Honeymoon Bay.'

Mum stopped. She opened her water bottle. 'You did? Why was she here?'

I watched her drinking. 'She was the woman you saw on the yacht.'

'Now I wish I'd waited that day. Did you like her?

I paused. 'I did. She was really interested in us, actually.'

'That's nice. We better move along, Nicky. I hope your dad is making tea.'

And so we did, getting home after dark, only to find he hadn't. He'd sliced open his leg on an underwater reef and was lying on the couch looking pale and helpless, waiting for us to pamper him.

'One day your luck is going to desert you,' said Mum.

She shouldn't have said that. She should have known how dangerous it is to tempt fate.

28

Bass Strait (Verloren Island) 1984

A Tender Business

I DREAM OF ORANGES, but the only ones available are those we occasionally find on the wrack line, which we pretend float over from the 'tropical' islands surrounding us.

'This disgusting food!' I said last night, and Mum snapped. Later, sitting with Dad beneath a vast peacefulness of stars, surrounded by the unbelievable clamour of bird conversations, he said she's snappy because of mistakes she made provisioning. He put his arm around me and told me to give her some breathing space.

But what if her mood is because that uni guy is actually her boyfriend and she's missing him? I kept this worry to myself. 'They're crazy loud,' I agreed.

Then Dad belched, long and low, and laughed.

'You dag. You starry toadfish!'

And we raced each other inside.

~

When Dad had spoken to Bert on the radio a couple of days previously, Bert said he'd take him out fishing on the *Rosy Wrasse* next time he came over.

'A boys' day out!' Dad chortled, 'Finally I get to see more of the island from the sea.'

Behind me Mum was quietly singing 'Danny Boy' as she stood in the doorway watching Phil and Liz crop pigface around the boulders. I noticed the hairline crack in her voice when Dad said that. He put on The Grateful Dead and Mum sang, 'As dead I well might be' as she slipped out the door.

'Can't we all go?' I asked as he strummed along to the music. 'We also want to see the coast, you know.'

He put down his guitar, said, 'Yeah? Fishing? But you don't like that,' and with a whistle to Kes, swaggered down the passage.

~

The *Rosy Wrasse* made towards us over the stippled ocean and once it had arrived, been secured and Bert greeted, Mum and I opened boxes, looking for letters. I asked Bert why he had another dinghy on board when he already had a tender and a strange thing happened. He and Dad exchanged a look and Mum spun around and went marching up the hill.

Dad watched her go, whistling between his teeth. These days, I never seem to know what's going on.

Later, I sat on the lighthouse steps and in between eating fresh fruit, I tore open the letters from Sally and Mrs Porter. I read Sally's first.

Dear Nicky

I no longer have a boyfriend. He was such a waste of space! But a guy has moved into that brick house across the road, some kind of genius at physics and music, Amanda Healey says. She is all over him. He has a baby sister, and his mum has purple bags under her eyes. His father has gone to live in Melbourne, that's why he's always pushing the pram past our front door.

My folks, being their usual loving selves, are thrilled at the prospect of getting rid of me in January, so they can go sailing. My gran is riding to Brisbane with her boyfriend. All that way in the sidecar of a Harley! Mr Jones has a lot to say about that!

Love from your friend Sal, who misses you with all her heart.

PS There is snow on the mountain. Chloe's parents took us walking up there and I came home with a leech. Just where I'll leave to your imagination. I am never going up there again. Ever!

PPS Sam Doody sends his love!!!!

Sam Doody can stick his love. Hobart seems so far away and when I look across at Mount Naturaliste, I do still miss my other mountain, but Mum and Dad keep finding reasons to keep me here. I read the postcard Nan had sent, then opened Mrs Porter's letter. It was enthusiastic, even though I haven't sent her much, and what I've sent is censored because she is a teacher, and Mrs Jones's best friend.

~

'You sheilas coming fishing?' asked Bert. Dad rubbed his cheek as though he hadn't heard. Immediately, I went to call Mum. She was lying on their bed with her arms across her face, the old battered copy of Lao Tzu's *Tao Te Ching* Nan gave her when she went off to uni beside her. She moved one hand to protectively cover a letter. My stomach tightened.

'What's the matter, Mum?' I tried to get a closer look at it.

'Dollars.'

'Us sheilas are actually allowed to go too.'

'I could not be less interested.'

'Please? It won't be as much fun without you. You know them – fish, fish, fish – that's all they'll talk about.'

'You can tell me about it later.' With her other hand she put a wisp of my hair carefully behind my ear, kissed my hand and waved me out the room.

I heard Shostakovich before I even passed the boulders.

~

Salt clung to Dad's rods. Mum said sloppiness and abuse were responsible for wrecking his tackle. He'd chosen quality equipment before we left Hobart, but when she'd found the price tags she'd done her usual little panic.

I loved being back on board the *Rosy Wrasse* with the sea running beneath my feet. I leaned against the rail, looking out for whales and gazing at Restless going by, and watched a sea eagle wheeling lazily on a thermal, high above a scattering of gannets and gulls off Honeymoon Cove. There was only one small cloud in all that blue electric vastness.

It changed its shape, moment by moment, dividing up then realigning, until it finally faded away altogether.

'Good omen, that eagle.' Dad gave me a thumbs-up. The sea was liquid diamond and mesmerising as fire. The breeze freshened further down the west coast. I heard Bert tell him that fish like a bit of a chop, it reassures them, and then he cut the engine south of the Tinman's Teeth. It was the closest I'd ever been to Lone Egg Island, a seal haul-out. The swell was slapping against the boat. Out on the water sounds are events magnified against the vastness of the sea. The leap of a fish. The dive of a gannet. The slap of a whale's tail on water. Bert's cough. Dad fiddling for a hook amongst his sinkers. Scraps of laconic conversation, a bird's cry. The thin singing of their reels as they cast their lines towards the reef.

The smell of diesel hung in the air. I dangled my legs over the water and watched the wave's reflections dancing up the hull. I opened a book, but daydreamed instead, gazing at Verloren, getting to know it all over again from a sailor's perspective.

Northwards, the lighthouse on the hill was a slender exclamation against that great round of blue. Somewhere beneath it was Mum and Shostakovich. She was probably rereading the letter from the uni guy; not something I could tell Dad.

A fly landed on my arm.

'That's my little mate come up from the galley – how about another of those tinnies?' he shouted to Wheeler, and proceeded to talk about burleys and how reading water takes practice.

Then Wheeler caught a stripey trumpeter and a while later Bert hooked another, rather on the small side. Things were quiet for a good while after that until Bert reeled in a passing salmon.

'How did the Dead Lady's Gulch get its name?' I asked as he gutted it. He grunted, fixed bait on his hook, then said, 'Don't think you'll like the story,' and turned to Wheeler. 'What d'ya reckon mate? Is she tough enough to cop a horror story?'

He cast his line and made himself comfortable beside me. 'A brigantine called the *Frances Gertrude* used to ply the stretch between Melbourne and New Zealand in the 1870s or thereabouts. Well, she hit a gale in Bass Strait and ripped her sails and so the captain made for that island there, see?' He pointed a finger at an island bleached with light. 'Needed shelter to make repairs.' He paused to watch a shag sweep by. 'That done, they sailed past Verloren, but noticed the ensign was Union down.'

The tip of his rod quivered. He paused a moment. 'Distress signal, see. Turned out a lighthouse keeper had carked it. The family was keepin' the corpse cool in the bath. They collected the lot of them – the corpse, the missus, and the kiddies. But at the entrance to the gulch, the boat breached. Just like that – swamped.'

He let out a little more line. 'Shouldn't be talking when a fish is biting.' He was taking a long time to strike, but Bert does everything slowly.

'Bugger,' he said, as the line went slack. Then, 'Everyone except the lighthouse keeper's missus made it. Her long dress snagged in them rocks. They couldn't reach her. Just her skirt in the waves and sometimes a foot appearing, in a little black boot.'

He gave a dramatic strike, and the fight was on.

'Looks like a beauty,' said Wheeler, ready with the net. The fish, seeing us through one upward-looking eye, was shocked into fighting with last-minute desperation – another trumpeter.

'She'll be good tucker,' said Bert. 'Can't do better than a stripey.'

I handed him his pliers and turned away so I couldn't see it flapping on the deck, all iridescent silver and thick charcoal stripes.

'You do the scaling, sweetheart,' he invited.

I feigned nonchalance. The smell rose like sharp flames, smothering my hands. Scales fell like petals of shell. Those still eyes accused me.

'You've still got them soft city attitudes. Gotta kill to eat, girl, and that's the truth of it.'

He threw the entrails into the sea. Against the wide blue, they were as shocking as a slap across the face. They dropped, and the water closed over them. A smudge of red spread briefly, then faded away.

Ten minutes of silence went by.

'Likely to be many sharks around Verloren?' I pushed down the 'record' button on my little battery tape recorder.

'My word, on account of the seals. You'll be risking your neck, mate, if you dive around that colony,' he said to Dad, pointing towards Phoques Point. 'Though the most common shark here—'

'—is the gummy,' said my father, reeling in.

'No mate. The swell shark, mate. Also called the draughtboard. Likes a rocky reef. Eats small fish and crustaceans.' He turned to me, 'It's just your old man's toes they'll go for. Caught a swell shark in a craypot a few months back. Little 'un.' He thought for a while. 'You seen them egg cases on the beach?'

'The mermaids' purses?'

'Be swell shark egg-cases, most likely.'

He wound in and checked his bait. On the water's skin dapples of deeper colour danced and transformed themselves with a speed my eyes couldn't follow.

'Who is Rosy Wrasse?' I asked.

'She's a fish, darlin'. I wanted to call her after a humble little fish. My mates said to call her the Real Bastard Trumpeter. They said call her the Cowfish or the Prickly Toadfish or the Common Stinkfish, which just goes to show that ya shouldn't go lookin' for names in a pub.'

Bert said he lives near Trouser Point in a fibro shack he shares with his wife. He grows vegies, and with his big hands makes little wooden sculptures for sale at the Whitemark tearoom. I'd hoped that *Rosy Wrasse* might have been more mysterious, the love of his life. 'You could have called her the *Stargazer*,' I said.

'Next time I get a boat I'll come straight to you, love. Ugly fish but a pretty name.'

'Don't get another one, Bert; the *Rosy* is a lovely boat.'

'I'm going to call mine the *Cosmopolitan Leatherjacket*,' said Dad.

I squinted up at him. 'You'll never get a boat, which is just as well with your lousy navigational skills.'

'What a thing to say to your old man. Anyway, you know I always keep my compass on me.' And he pulled it out of his pocket to prove his point.

'He even takes it to bed at night,' I told Bert.

Bert looked down at the water. 'I bet your missus has a lot to say about that,' he said.

'You get back to that book of yours, young lady,' said Dad, giving my leg a little kick. 'And you can turn that machine off now and give us men some peace.'

'I'll pour you a tea to make amends.'

'That won't win you any brownie points. Chuck us a beer.'

I enjoyed the roll of the boat while they wove a slow, meandering piscatorial conversation around their fishing and their drinking, until Dad, looking over to me, said, 'I have got a boat though.'

'*Sophia* drowned,' I told Bert.

'Another Verloren dead lady,' he said.

'Not that wretched clinker, Nicky. The ducky, there, in front of us. Meet the *Cosmopolitan Leatherjack*. Decided we needed a boat to get maximum enjoyment out of the island,' and Dad gave me a cheerful wink.

What had he done? Mum would freak! We were going to be drowned beneath a Shostakovichian tsunami unless I could contrive to smash the records.

~

Two stripey trumpeters later, we got underway again, rounded the reef and headed north.

'Sea's as bad as stonechoppers here.' Bert pointed to the surf breaking on the Tinman's Teeth. It was vicious water, but not to the seals who lolled, one flipper up like so many Mr Beauforts sampling the breeze. Others draped themselves into the contours of the boulders. Gannets were plummeting into the sea. The cliffs laid shadows down upon the water. The sun lit up the fringe of casuarinas above them. The world was all leaping particles, solitons and waves and there was no more difference between the tapered tips of my fingers and the air around them other than a mere slackening of particles, a loosening of the pattern.

We passed Stumpy's Bay and tiny coves I hadn't properly seen before, just big enough for a towel, a beach umbrella, and a picnic basket. The island loomed as a surfacing of ocean crust. The bays, the beaches and rocky reaches belonged to themselves in a way that they hadn't when we'd walked across them.

'It's like the island has a different personality when you see it from the water,' I said. But the words failed to encompass the shivery aliveness of the place. I remembered the power of my numinous moment and turned to Wheeler. 'Remember the day we walked to Stumpy's? The light on Mount Aeolian? *Remember?*'

'Aye,' he said, but he was looking towards the coast and waving, and there on a rock was Len, waving back at us, but getting smaller with distance.

~

Mum's fury ruined everything. It wasn't a conducive atmosphere for appreciating the flavour of the sacrificial trumpeter. She said the ducky should have been a joint decision and muttered darkly about dollars.

Later, she kissed me on the top of my head. 'Just one of those days when I wish I'd never said "yes" to this island,' she said. 'I'm so sorry, Nicky, for all the ways we've let you down. You and I, we're both feeling so lonely out here.'

I swallowed, keeping my eyes on the tranquil pearl on her long, slim finger.

Later, up in the lighthouse, Dad said that boat with its little outboard motor was mainly for Mum's fieldwork. A gift. And maybe 'the beginning of something grand'. First the rubber ducky, then a traditional Bass Strait trader for a complete tourist venture. He said the islands need the money tourism provides and that it offers the perfect lifestyle.

I told him Mum would hate this plan. And then he asked me what I knew about those archaeologists planning to sail to this island.

'Nothing,' I said.

But I knew the sort of dream I'd be having that night.

29

Bass Strait (Verloren Island) 1984

____

Lost and Broken, Rich and Strange

STORM CLOUDS WERE LINED up on the horizon as Kes and I went walking down to Beagle Bay on the off chance that we'd meet Len. I thought about him every day, and I was hungry for company – anyone's company, but most of all his.

Five dolphins were travelling south and I was watching them when Kes started sniffing footsteps. Fresh and recent, long and thin. But the rain was coming and reluctantly I turned for home.

Dad was sitting on the lighthouse steps reading, his guitar beside him, as I came puffing up the hill, bringing the drizzle with me.

'I saw Len's footprints.'

'Saw an abalone boat earlier. Think they're poaching,' he said, getting up to move inside. Later that day, once the rain had passed, a thin trail of smoke stained the sky down the southern end of the island. Len, I supposed. I went to my bedroom to write poetry, but my attention kept gravitating to that ribbon of smoke. I hoped that tomorrow I'd see him.

~

We bumped into each other near Squally Cove. He mentioned that a mate with a fishing boat had dropped him back here after a bit of time away.

'Why do you come here so often?' I asked.

'Main reason – my mum died last year.' He looked at the ground. 'We were tight. I come here to be close to her and to care for Country, and to try and understand the lost and broken things.'

'I'm *so* sorry, Len.' I panic just thinking about losing my mum. I couldn't imagine life without her hooting laugh, her off-key singing and her warmth. Even when pain or her thesis put up a barrier, she is still someone I can lean into. 'That must really hurt.'

'Still waiting for it to ease,' he said, and turned to look at the sea.

We stood together for a while in silence. I didn't know what to say but I could feel that pain spread across the landscape and wash through me too. So, 'Len, do you know Yolla?' I asked, as we sat down on the sand.

'Yep.'

'What can you tell me?'

He shrugged.

'Well, I met her a while back. She was at Honeymoon, skinnydipping.'

'Sounds like Yolla. Nothing much to tell. She's solid though.'

'How do you mean?'

'She's good on a boat. I trust her.'

'What else?'

'You ask a lot of questions. There are other ways to learn things.'

'What do you mean?'

He scooped the sand on either side of him. 'Like about this island … you could start by listening to the island.'

I giggled. 'I hardly think the island is going to tell me about Yolla!'

'Have you noticed the yolla have gone?'

It was the first week of November and they'd left to feed at sea, leaving their burrows empty. Dad had said it was their last fling before they have ankle-biters hampering their lifestyle. I could have pointed out that parents have hampered *my* lifestyle, but I didn't.

'It's like someone turned down the volume. It's a full-throated island, this.'

'They'll soon be back,' said Len.

'Maybe we could watch them arrive together?'

'Maybe.'

I'm counting down the days.

~

I felt so happy on my walk back home. The world seemed magical and I realised that it doesn't matter how awful life gets, you can be at your happiest merely sitting on a boulder contemplating the planet's every tiny wrinkle and little freckled spot.

The waves rolled in as I enjoyed the idea that there's spirit, mind and energy flowing through and around everything. I looked at the barnacles and they seemed different, quite magnificent really, and I looked at the sea and saw that it really was alive, and that even the boulders had a powerful energy, were silence intensified. I waited for the ocean to reward me for this insight by tossing a dolphin into the air, but along came a beetle. I looked at its jewelled body and watched it cleaning itself daintily on the back of my arm. That beetle could teach Dad a thing or two about hygiene.

Mum came down from the dunes. We walked home, and everything was flowing – the air, the sea, the sand – and my ideas were flowing too. We found a candle and one old thong on Emita and sure enough it had a few goose barnacles on it. I picked up a large maroon seed with thin black lines on it like the branches of a tree, and Mum decided it was from a palm tree endemic to a remote Samoan island and I said maybe it came from those 'tropical islands' we can see around us, full of palm trees and orange blossom where the sun always shines, even when the mist covers us over.

She laughed and the breeze shook her hair and I felt a great tug at my heart, because when she is all lit up, she is like a goddess, and I know that I'll never be half as wonderful as she is. In those moments, she's the best mother ever.

30

Peramangk and Kaurna Country (Adelaide Hills) 2000

Bass Strait (Verloren Island) 1984

Parents Should Never Be Trusted

MY TOUCHSTONE! STUCK FOR so long in this stuffy Adelaide cellar! I enclose it in my hands, enjoying its coolness, admiring the patterning on its surface, remembering Len giving it to me down at the gulch.

Steve left a short while ago for the marina, so I wander inside to check on Freya, just as she surfaces from sleep. I kiss her forehead, then offer water to ease a bout of coughing. As I settle into the chair beside her, Amber stretches, then departs, her tail poised in an expression of contempt.

'You're such a jealous cat,' I tell her, and Freya smiles.

'What are you doing?' She indicates my lap.

'You know, my memoir.'

She nods, turns away and drowses. I wait until she drifts off, then pick up my pen and slash away at teenage angst. Encountering myself through my writing has a strange physicality; I feel that the girl I once was is keeping me company, is standing in this room like a heron, watching from the shadows.

I'm steadying myself before reading on. I know exactly what's coming. It's my 10 November entry. I once drafted it so obsessively it became branded on my brain and it's not one I'd ever share with Freya.

It's about the day I stopped calling them Mum and Dad.

~

I don't want to write, but I'm going to make myself start at the beginning, with the lesson that exposed the hypocrisy of the people I live with. I'm going to record every tiny detail to help me finally understand.

They're not fair but I *will* be. Wheeler is a good teacher – more interesting than most – but as Nan says, he's a man who likes to have many fronts open at the same time. Teaching is one small front. Fishing and diving and music and thinking about writing (but maybe not actually writing), and planning new lifestyles are huge fronts, as are what he calls his 'ideas of the moment'.

Honesty is *not* a priority.

Today, while we were doing maths, I saw 'the look' move over his face. The next moment he said, 'Finish your sums, do some history, I'll be back soon.'

I watched him disappear down the slope with Kes, rod in one hand, tackle in the other and his snorkelling gear in a backpack. Freya was jogging on Emita. The sky was cobalt blue but precipitory megafauna were beginning to wander over the horizon and the breeze was flouncing about like a prima donna. Far away, to the west of the closest island, I could see a yacht.

Forget lessons. I'd read a novel!

I put on the kettle and took a short stroll outside to commune with the mountain. Another little dip into my novel … Half an hour more and then I'd begin. (This is how things are when you think you understand the life you are living.)

Footsteps outside. 'You're working hard,' Freya said dryly. 'Where's Wheeler?' And she looked around the room as though she expected him to pop up from behind the couch.

'I'm researching.'

She went to check what gear of his was missing. I picked up my books and escaped to my bedroom.

I didn't know that our relationship was about to be shattered. The music should have been a warning. She could have put on 'Isle joyeuse', but no – she freed Shostakovich to rant like a wild thing.

I'd fallen asleep, so they must have been talking beneath my window for a while before I realised that something was up. There was no music, only my parents arguing away, getting louder by the moment.

Kes crept into my room, his tail between his legs, looking at me with alarm.

'You're supposed to be teaching. You're *so* irresponsible, *so* deceitful and *so* self-indulgent.'

Wheeler said something about waiting to see how much I'd done by tea, but his voice was angry and defensive, and she mumbled something snitchy, then yelled, '… I'd never have taken on Nicky if I'd realised what a *no-hoper* you'd turn out to be. And I wish I'd never agreed to come here. You're not teaching Nicky. You're running down our savings. You're destroying everything.'

'Has it ever occurred to you that you might be some of the problem, Freya? That your promises are problems? And let's just add to all that the fact that I can't trust you; all that time on campus. Suspicious fieldwork. You break my heart, you truly do.'

'Trust! That's a bit rich, coming from you.'

I'd moved to the window so I saw him whip around and storm off to the gulch, Freya following, but shortly afterwards the rubber ducky (which we've all been pretending doesn't exist) zoomed by, heading south against a blustery breeze.

My head was reeling. She had to know I was in my room. She must have meant me to overhear. She wanted me to know that I'm a burden.

I threw myself on my bed. Impossible to please one without offending the other and I lay on my stomach chanting, *my fault, my fault* into the pillow. I felt trapped. Wheeler would want me to finish the work he'd set, to prove his system worked. She would want me not to, confirming her point. Either way, there'd be another argument.

I sat up slowly. The room was unusually cold. I searched for a jumper and as I was putting it on the answer struck me. If I could make them both hate me at the same time they'd be more united. Maybe I should run away. A little flame of rebellion expanded and quickly consumed me. I was in tears as I rushed down to my tent, Kes at my heels. I did not know how to save the situation.

And I had to do something because if I didn't, my parents were going to get divorced.

It was only when I was safely inside the tent, picking over their argument, that I paused, startled, over Freya's words – *'I'd never have taken her on.'*

What did she mean? Did she mean on to the island? Was she referring to an argument with me? Or challenging me about schoolwork?

It didn't make sense!

I lay there, not understanding. Then a slow, cold realisation flooded me. I couldn't believe I'd overlooked those hard words. (How many times might I have done this before – heard them talking about me but not understood?)

I'm *adopted!*

Impossible at first to believe, then obvious.

So obvious!

My friends say I'm clever. Well, I'm the most dim-witted person on the planet. A hundred questions assailed me. They'd have told me – surely?

Surely?

Perhaps I was wrong?

But those words repeated and reverberated and there could be no other meaning.

So who was I really?

And where were my real parents?

What was this all about and how many people knew about it? Did Nan?

Everything I knew about myself and my parents began peeling painfully away until I felt a bland anonymity, even an annihilation. The only certainty was that they were stuck with a kid they didn't want.

Reality had a slow, *Sophia*-broaching moment and I began to experience a peculiar sensation as though my spirit was draining out of the soles of my feet.

I could hear Wheeler calling me from far away, but I didn't move from my position. Kes licked my face and whimpered.

'I'm divorcing my parents,' I wept into his salty black coat, and he patiently kept licking my damp face, my only true friend ever.

I waited until I was certain they weren't around before heading up to the house for supplies. But Wheeler was in the kitchen. 'Grief!' he said. 'You're wearing a jumper. Hang on a tick while I get the camera.'

I marched past him. Went upstairs. Got my gear.

Freya came out of her study. 'You were gone a while,' she said with a guilty and uncertain look on her face.

I slammed the bedroom door.

Silence.

Then, 'Tea's ready when you are,' and she tapped my door with her fingers, the way she sometimes pats my head.

'*Fuck* tea!'

A shocked silence.

About a minute later I heard her tiptoeing slowly down the stairs.

Fuck, I muttered, over and over. It made me feel powerful enough to stomp down the stairs. It made me satisfied to see their alarmed faces. It gave me the courage to slam the door, really, really hard.

'*I hate you both*,' I yelled, and stormed down to my tent, birds wailing around me.

31

Bass Strait (Verloren Island) 1984

Guilt, Promises, and Betrayals

WHEN THE PENGUINS CAME in from the sea and ramped up their cacophony, the odd chick, cumbersome in a bulky coat of brown and grey down, came and peeped in at the flap. It wasn't magical anymore. I couldn't stop crying. Later, Freya came and flopped down beside me at the closed entrance to the tent. I felt an enormous loathing and a terrible sadness, both at the same time.

'What a hullaballoo! I don't know how you'll manage to sleep,' she said as if everything was normal. The penguins drowned out my muffled sobs. 'I can see an anchor light in the bay.' Silence. 'Fishing boat, I suppose,' she added.

The waves tipped themselves on to the sand with small splashes. In the tent, I was a nautilus floating away.

'And I can see the Seven Sisters.'

Like I cared.

'Please let me in, Nicky?'

'*Fuck. Off!*' It was strange to hear my disembodied voice.

208

'Nicky, at least tell me what I've done to make you so angry?'

The birds wailed. She sighed. 'I think I know. I'm just not sure I know.'

The minutes rolled by. All by itself my body wriggled lower into the sleeping bag. She stood up. Her fingers drummed lightly on the tent. 'Night sweetheart. I love you so, so much. Take all the time you need, then come up to the house and let's talk.'

I wasn't fooled for a moment by her sad little voice.

Her footsteps receded and then returned. 'Um, Nicky … If this is about something you might have overheard … if it is, then I'm concerned you might have got the wrong impression?'

Silence. Her sigh. Another retreat.

I listened to her progress up the dunes and out of my heart. A tear slid from my eye into my ear, but for some weird reason all I could think about was how much I wanted to see Len and how little he seemed to want to see me. I'd never felt so alone or fragile and the din around me fragmented my thoughts.

I woke to the cold. Rain started falling. It fell through the lustrous yellow glow of sunlight trapped between brooding clouds and a sombre sea. I'd never seen such a light, nor the way the hound wind drove the rain across the ocean. I felt so bereft I opened my notebook and wrote a poem.

My heart bleeds

A hard rain falling inside me

And I am drowning

In the cold blood

Rising around me

A red tide poisoning the waves.

~

11 November 1984

Dear Anneke,

I'm pretty damned sure Nicky overheard Wheeler and me yesterday, in which case she knows. It's so important to me that she never feels unwanted or unloved, but right now, it's clear she's hurting and I don't have any other explanation.

I've been unbelievably monstrous in sticking to that promise. I should have followed my intuition, not prioritised our agreement, because each year we failed to tell her, it got harder to find the words.

We've all of us betrayed her, traumatised her, and damaged her sense of identity. And now I don't know the words to say sorry for something of this magnitude, don't know how to answer the inevitable questions. We need you to tell us who her father is. She will ask. For now, all I know is that my misery is nothing compared to hers. Wheeler, he's upset with me too, but he's almost as guilty. You, too, Anneke. We must heal our broken bonds, for our daughter's sake. You must write to her. And you must come home.

Love,

Freya

~

Guilt, Promises, and Betrayals

From Wheeler's notebook, Friday 12 November –

Nicky has moved out of the house 'for good'. Doesn't leave her tent. Perhaps just as well. The mood in the house is terrible.

This crazy thing Freya has about sticking to promises. Grabbed my guitar and retreated to the lighthouse. A grey sky, a confused sea and me strumming C# Minor over and over.

32

Bass Strait (Verloren Island) 1984

The Gaslight Flickering

SLEEPING. THAT'S HOW I spent the first three days of the rest of my life. At night I went walking out along the beaches with Kes, confused and angry, trying to reshape a sense of identity, wondering about my real parents and why they didn't keep me, and how old I was when Freya and Wheeler took me on – or! Maybe I was actually abducted. I went stumbling around in the recesses of my brain for a clue, a memory. That story about my birth. So cruel.

They'd made a fool of me. And they'd stolen my real identity.

How many people have deceived me by not telling me? Nan must have known. Probably Sally too. I didn't ever want to see them again.

Eventually, Wheeler came down to my tent and sat beside it while I lay inside, cocooned, exhausted by overthinking. He tried to make small talk and failed and then he wanted to discuss 'a wee misunderstanding, lassie, something you may have overheard.'

I said it wasn't little and he could only talk to me if he was going to be honest, and as I didn't believe that was possible, he could f-off.

There was silence. Then he cleared his throat and told me that *Anneke* is my mother. Yeah, right! I listened with scepticism because I knew by now that parents couldn't be trusted. And who would want Anneke as their mother? She couldn't be more absent if she tried. If she was my mother surely she'd have cared enough to stay in touch beyond the odd measly birthday present.

He told me when Anneke arrived in Armidale, she was having huge mood swings and was about seven months pregnant. She disappeared for a while and when she returned she said she couldn't keep me because she didn't have the means, but Freya wanted me 'desperately' although she was studying and not earning much from waitressing. He said this happened when he and Freya had only known each other about five months but he 'already knew she was the one.'

'So Nicky, we moved in together and together we took you on. The story about the wild fig tree is true, honest, Nicky. Anneke didn't realise she was so advanced – look, your aunt asked that we promise not to tell. It wasn't right. We can't defend it, and it made it so awkward with your nan that frankly, we avoided her as much as we could – but hey, Nicky, look at you! We couldn't love you more if we tried.'

I gave a small snort of disbelief.

'Travel and babies don't go together, that's another reason she couldn't keep you.'

But it didn't stop them!

'Anneke named you. But you know, our silly arguments aside, your mum is quite something. Her generosity is remarkable.'

I see a horrible sister with endometriosis who saw me as her only chance for a child.

'Please say you're glad we wanted you so badly that you didn't have to be adopted out of the family.'

I will not.

'It's natural to feel angry and confused. But when all is said and done, don't blame Freya for an act of love. Lodge those feelings in me.'

I'll lodge them in all of you lying people.

'Anneke wanted you to be brought up to believe she was your aunt, didn't want your nan to know. A lot of hurt there. Even between your mum and Celeste, at that time. It was hard for us to make a promise we didn't believe in, but it was important to Freya that she kept it, given the immensity of Anneke's gesture. Nicky, I stayed well clear of this issue. It was one for the sisters.'

I lay with closed eyes, barely breathing, reluctantly curious, completely hating him.

'Anneke's thinking was pretty confused, and we didn't want a confrontation. Didn't want her to change her mind and you know what your mum's like about keeping her word …'

That would be no! Neither of them has ever kept their word with me. They'd promised we wouldn't move. But here I was, stuck on the island. And sure as anything, we wouldn't be returning to Hobart. I wasn't as important to them as Anneke was, that much was clear.

'We thought she'd be a presence in your life, but we suspect she feels too … I suppose – conflicted.' He paused and the pause was filled with the sounds of wind and birds. 'You know, your mum worried that if she broke her promise, Anneke would break with us all completely. She does everything to keep a bond there, even if it's ridiculously tenuous. It's for you, Nicky. It's mainly for you.'

He hadn't told me who my father was. My wondering was loud as a shout. My mouth stayed zipped.

'It was a horrible way to find out, but we're so relieved you know,' he said, putting their feelings ahead of mine again. 'So very relieved. And we both love you so very, very much.'

He left me to think about what he'd said, but he was too late. I was leaving the island as soon as I could. I'd live with Nan. She'd been duped too. And she would not be impressed.

33

Peramangk and Kaurna Country (Adelaide Hills) 2000

Bass Strait (Verloren Island) 1984

Thwarted

I UNFOLD FREYA'S LETTER dated 26 November 1984, wondering what this one will teach me. It feels uncomfortable reading this beside her while she sleeps, so many conflicting emotions seeking balance within my unsettled mind.

26 November 1984

Dear Anneke,

We have a crisis and I feel for Nicky so deeply, but it's only Celeste she'll turn to. You have no idea how much that hurts and how frustrated I feel with you.

I sent Mum a message, hoping she'll come and support us, although I dread confessing.

Again, we need details about Nicky's father. Again, I'm asking you to send her a letter. Please. We're desperate.

Freya

~

216

The *Rosy Wrasse* was a small dot on the far side of the turquoise ocean. I knew it was her because I'd sneaked into the kitchen to grab supplies and Bert had come over the radio, trying to get Wheeler. I decided I'd stow away below decks.

I gathered up essential gear, then hid my pack among the rocks behind the jetty, and shortly afterwards Wheeler and Freya came along with the cart. There was a large snake on Whale Rock, so my bad luck, we were all on the jetty together, Kes barking exuberantly, his tail looking set to break loose.

Waving to us from the foredeck was a person in a black hat and a tangerine shirt.

'*Nan!*' She had come to me in my hour of greatest need.

'*Dear hearts!*' shouted Nan, waving madly.

Freya's hair was whipping around her tanned face. Here on the jetty in her prettiest dress, my hatred for her dissolved briefly, and then settled right back into place, firmer than ever.

Bert tossed Wheeler the spring line, then I made ready the bow and Freya the stern, and soon Nan was on the jetty.

I couldn't stop hugging her.

There was chat about her trip to France, then, 'Women, give us a hand,' said Wheeler, getting to work with the provisions. He gave me a wink, assuming a relationship we don't have anymore. With my arm tight around Nan, I ignored him and led her up the hill. Before I'd even warned her to be careful of snakes – there had been one curled up on a chair on the veranda the other day – I told her that at the first opportunity I needed time alone with her to tell her important stuff that would completely shock her.

But Freya knew my intentions. She whisked Nan away.

By the time Wheeler and Bert hauled the bouncing cart over the ridge and along the bumpy ground to offload, I was leaning, abandoned, against a boulder.

Bert looked over at South Verloren and asked if any boats had called in recently.

'She's been an empty stretch of ocean,' said Wheeler.

'Been a bit of abalone poachin' going on around here.'

Wheeler rubbed his chin thoughtfully, and Bert turned to Freya, who'd appeared at the door. 'Haven't had a bite to eat since sunup,' he said, and soon she had a meal organised.

'And a cold one for me, if you could be bothered, Wheeler mate.'

He was looking past us. 'G'day, mate. Wondered when you'd pitch.'

Len was standing in the shadows cast by the eaves.

My stomach flipflopped.

'One of my old mates,' Bert said, while I tried to stop smiling.

'Howdy,' said Dad and he went off to grab drinks.

Len didn't move.

'You're going to net a fly standing there like that,' Bert drawled.

A swift grin crossed Len's face as I looked away, but when I glanced back at him, he was expressionless.

Freya followed Wheeler into the house and Nan leaned forward and asked Len if he lived on the island.

'Off and on,' he said.

'Well, this is heaven. I wouldn't be surprised if my family decide never to return to Hobart. Can you hear a car, my dear?' she asked me, but when I told her it was the generator, she said, 'I mean, where's the traffic? Where's the smell of fuel? This is clean air. This is serenity.'

Len caught Bert's eye. Bert, feeling for a cigarette, gave a small snort.

After he'd finished his drink, Len went down to the *Rosy* to load his gear, disappearing over the rise with a long, angular gait, his head upturned, his rucksack bouncing on his back. We waited for an explanation from Bert but, given that the moon was full and the spring low can make for an alarming exit from the gulch, all he said was, 'We'll be holing up here tonight. Move off about three a.m. when the tide's right.'

The surf boomed and an eagle hovered above the isthmus. We lolled around eating Freya's sandwiches and some stale, sad-looking biscuits I'd made before my existential crisis. Nan hadn't realised the island was so big. She hadn't realised it was so far away. I looked at Bert and saw that he had dozed off, and Wheeler had also pulled his hat over his head and was settling back into his chair. Nan and Freya went inside 'to consider sleeping arrangements.' She was working hard to keep us apart.

I lay beside Kes watching his feet run dream marathons, listening to Bert's sporadic snoring. A small cloud lodged itself on the mountain. Geese honked. I got up and walked through the tussocks and past the boulders, down to the gulch. The *Rosy Wrasse* was rocking peacefully against the jetty. There were two pelicans and a couple of gulls down there but no sign of Len.

I hopped over to my next favourite flat boulder because the snake was still on Whale Rock and I lay down to drowse, listening for a change in the intensity of the waves, only opening my eyes when a cloud shadow fell over me. Out of the corner of my eye I saw the pale suckered tentacle of an octopus flicker and disappear.

'It came from under the jetty,' Len said.

I jumped.

'You scare easy.' He flicked a pebble into the water, then came to sit beside me.

'I don't.'

He flicked more pebbles and I watched him surreptitiously, looking at the little notch on his knee. He glanced at me before throwing another one and said, 'You seem different.'

'I just found out something terrible, but I don't want to talk about it.' And I hid my face so he couldn't see my watery eyes.

He rested his arm across his knee then probed in his pocket for another pebble, tumbling it from one hand to the other. It was white, with a patterned intrusion of a darker rock in jagged lines.

'Oystercatchers,' he said. A pair had landed on a boulder nearby.

I stayed face-down.

'Whatever's bothering you, it'll pass, Nicky.' And he put his hand briefly on my back.

'Why are you leaving?'

'Heading home for a while, but I'll be back.'

'For the birding?'

'Before that.'

'How long have you been here this time?'

'Not so long.' He looked beyond me to where the waves turned the corner and moved as swell up the gulch.

'Well, I'm going back to Hobart as soon as I can. I was going to stow away today.'

I peeked at him. His brow was furrowed.

'I love the island. I don't like *them*.'

'Your parents?'

'They're not my parents.'

'What do you mean?'

'I think they stole me. Also, it's lonely here.'

We saw Bert walking down the hill to the jetty. 'Stole,' said Len. 'Well, that's something we know a whole lot about, my mob.'

'It's a horrible feeling.'

'It eats people up. It lasts longer than a lifetime.'

I thought about this. I realised there were stolen people all over this country, all hollowed out by unmanageable grief.

He took my hand and folded it around his pebble, then gave it a gentle squeeze.

'For you, Nicky.' And he went leaping across the boulders towards Bert and then they were on the *Rosy* and I lay on my boulder and looked across at them. Len knew Bert better than I did. He knew the island better than me too. I felt quite thirsty-lonely staring over at them. I didn't belong. Not in this family. Not on this island. Not in the world.

Not in my own skin either. And in the face of his grief, mine seemed petulant.

But I still clung to it.

I trudged up the sandy path with my retrieved rucksack. I looked back once, and they were still standing on deck. Len was eating an orange.

That day was 30 November, St Andrews Day. Wheeler put on his kilt after dinner and stood on the lighthouse steps and sang 'The Road to the Isles', 'Scotland the Brave', and 'Wild Mountain Thyme'. I knew it was for me, but I'm not won over that easily, so it was a party of two, Wheeler and his not so wee dram of whisky, Freya and Nan having used his sudden patriotism to slip away to the beach to talk about me. I hoped Bert and Len hadn't heard him.

Checkmated by Freya, disappointed with Wheeler, I called Kes to heel and slunk away to my tent, hoping Len would wander by.

He didn't. And by the next morning they were gone.

34

Peramangk and Kaurna Country (Adelaide Hills) 2000

Bass Strait (Verloren Island) 1984

Tangled Web

'TAKE SOME TIME TO explore Adelaide,' they've both been saying, and so I borrow Freya's car and head for the Central Market. First brunch, then a wander. My basket is stacked with delicacies by the time I leave.

It's 30 degrees. Air conditioner on, I drive home wondering what keeps stopping me from contacting Sally, agonising over my gamophobia – that's really what I have; a total fear of commitment. A consequence, I suppose, of that argument beneath the window and its trajectory down the years. I've steadfastly believed the blame lay primarily with Freya, but, well, life experience, creating this memoir, and time spent in Adelaide is giving me a more nuanced perspective.

Freya is reading on the couch and smiles as I plonk myself down in a chair and display my booty. This is the perfect opportunity to chat about 'the promise', but first a cold shower and a change into something cooler.

And then I hear Steve putting on Chopin. The sound of the kettle. The clink of mugs. They're deep in conversation when I walk back in.

Opportunity lost, but cooler now, I take a book out to the garden, and loll in the elm tree's shade, made sleepy by the soporific sounds of tennis being played in a neighbouring garden. Sudden bleating makes me start. Giles is creating havoc in the flowerbeds. He surveys me with his yellow eyes and resists when I tug at his collar, so I lure him away with an apple. He looks betrayed when I close the gate, as though all he was seeking was acceptance. I scratch his rough head, gaze into his beautiful eyes, accept his nudges, then watch as he walks away, his little tail flicking at half-mast.

The tennis must have affected Steve and Freya too. They're both napping. Deciding that I might as well finish in the cellar, I've come back out with a glass of iced water.

Two boxes to go. I dawdle, watching a pair of rainbow lorikeets, and chat over the gate to a neighbour who inquires after Freya, and then updates me on the cricket. When I finally escape, I drag a box up and find talismans of Wheeler – his harmonica, and the broken remnants of the mobile made of feathers and shells that he gave Freya that last Christmas. It's so weird to find them here.

'Dad,' I whisper, and the breeze streaming through the foliage provides, just for a perfect moment, a faint resonance of his deep voice singing. This handful of items, freshly exposed to the light, remind me of Nan's first full day on the island, back in December 1984. On that day Freya wrote to herself: *My letters are officially my journal now. I am done with my sister.*

And on that day I was lying in the deep shade of the hideaway crevice of my favourite big boulders on Sunlit when I heard Nan and Freya come down to the beach. They set up in the shade close by. Nan sounded teary. 'I feel so humiliated,' I heard her say, before she broke into some furious French I couldn't follow. 'I want you to go over everything you told me before. In detail!'

I had no qualms about listening.

'I've been carrying this burden for so long,' said Freya. 'It's been exhausting.'

'Give me a moment.' Nan walked towards the water. Through a tiny crack I could see her standing ankle-deep, her back to the beach, her hands on her hips.

When she returned she said, 'Why didn't you come to me at the beginning? Can you even begin to imagine what it's been like to have two daughters who had no interest in keeping in touch? And how much time I've spent wondering why you both avoided me? The pain has been indescribable!'

'I'm *so* sorry, Mum. Honestly, the guilt has been excruciating.'

'I can't believe you didn't feel you could trust me, after we'd been through so much together, the two of us. It makes no sense – unless Wheeler was behind this?'

'He stayed right out of it. It was because of the promise to Anneke. You know honesty is important to me. I hated that every time I saw you I was concealing a lie. It became unbearable.'

'So … I missed out on Nicky, and she missed out on me.' I had never heard Nan sound so bitter, or so hurt.

An oystercatcher's lone call cut across the sound of the breeze and the slack tide's murmurings.

Then, 'You know, Freya, to prioritise a flawed promise over Nicky's wellbeing was unfathomable, nonsensical and damaging in the extreme.'

'Mum, please forgive me!'

'And let's consider Anneke for a moment. Over-sensitive doesn't begin to describe her. She'd wail if I happened to dig through an earthworm or accidentally crushed a snail. You know very well what she was like – I mean, Nicky is rather like her, no? I know my relationship with her was … difficult … but that doesn't mean I was blind to her virtues or didn't love her.'

'Mum …'

'No, listen to me for a moment, Freya. Giving up Nicky would have been unbearable for her and I want to know what suggestions you made to help her keep her child. Did you suggest she come home, even if just for a little while?'

'Mum, she didn't want to.'

'I could have helped her financially.'

Freya grunted her disbelief.

'I would have helped her.'

'She wouldn't have accepted it.'

'I'm not so sure. I received a letter from her about that time saying she was returning to Australia, that she might visit. I've had so few letters from her,' Nan's voice broke, 'that I do reread them from time to time, and there was enough in that letter for me to hope. Something closed the door on that.'

'I can't explain that.'

'You have explained that.' She sighed. 'Well, I suppose it's reassuring to know that it's not solely because of me that she's kept the barriers up.'

'Despite all the effort I've put into bringing them down.'

'Well, no doubt she profoundly feels she betrayed Nicky.'

'Mum! We've been good parents!'

'You don't need to be defensive with me. In all other respects yes, completely.'

'I don't like the way you're questioning my motives, Mum. Seriously, it was never about me.'

'Mm …' A silence. 'Well … do you mind if I ask how much your endometriosis affected your motivation?'

'That's so unfair!'

'No judgement, Freya. Endometriosis is such a tough call. Your suffering has been my suffering. You can safely be honest with me.'

'You weren't there. You can't understand the chaos. Nicky's interests had to come first.'

I lay face-down, barely daring to breathe.

'I'm going to have a swim.' I heard Freya stand up.

'Well, my darling, tell me this then. Who's the father?'

'She said there was no point telling me; it was just a name with no substance. And when I asked Wheeler – because they were in the same share house, you know – he said she had a bit of a – he said—'

'He said she slept around,' Nan said icily. She got up and started packing up her things. 'I think that's as much as I can endure for now.'

'Mum! I repeat! Anneke came to Armidale so happy and then

her mood just went haywire, like around the time of the pink fish episode. Wheeler stayed right out of the picture. She was so hostile towards all my friends except for one, who fortunately happened to be a nurse. Thank God because I don't know how we'd have delivered Nicky without her.'

'Camping that pregnant. Poor Anneke.'

'We were young and stupid. We thought being near the sea would relax a volatile situation.'

'What puzzles me,' said Nan, 'is that of the three of us, she's the most decisive. She started helming her life at a very young age, remember?'

'But you also know how she could lose the plot.' Freya sounded as though she was about to cry. 'After the birth, after she'd had a sleep, she went and sat on the beach with Nicky, and Wheeler went to talk to her. Her mood was much quieter. When they came back, she handed Nicky to me. It was that simple in the end.'

'That simple.'

'Yes! It was.'

'And then Anneke went straight back to Europe?'

'Yes. We helped her buy a ticket.' Freya was getting up. She was walking towards the water, subject closed.

'Hmm,' said Nan, heading off towards the path.

Freya, gathering up her gear a while later, trailed Nan home. 'For someone who is always trying to do their best, I seem to be forever stuffing things up,' she muttered to herself as she passed by.

~

Nan came to find me at my tent, and we took a walk to Sam's Soak, pausing often along the way. She listened to me while I told her everything: the loneliness, the overheard argument, the fears I'd been having about Freya and the uni guy, and she said she was 'devastated beyond words' to discover that both her daughters had deceived her. She felt in turmoil.

'So excluded,' she said.

'So angry!'

'And hurt, and humiliated.'

'And confused and, and – fragmented!'

She drew me into a long hug.

'Shocked,' she said.

'Unwanted and betrayed.'

'I cannot begin to imagine, *ma chérie*, how much this hurts. But your parents *do* love you and I believe Anneke keeps her distance because this has caused her great suffering. I expect she's entangled in big, conflicting emotions. To give up a child, this is overwhelming. This is the sort of suffering that lasts a lifetime. But Nicky, you can always count on me. Love without beginning or end.' She kissed me. 'To the Seven Sisters and back.' And then she held me while I cried into her birdlike shoulder beside that dark tannin water.

I was comforted by her warmth until, as we climbed Mount Aeolian, she said, 'Don't judge people at their worst, though, Nicky. We're not going to be adept at meeting every challenge life throws at us either. It's what becomes of the human heart that matters.'

I pulled a face, not ready to hear that then. I was hard at work transforming my heart into a tough little carapace, determined never to show anyone my vulnerabilities or allow them close enough to hurt me ever again.

35

Peramangk and Kaurna Country (Adelaide Hills) 2000

Bass Strait (Verloren Island) 1984

———————

Lighthouse Privileges

FREYA IS MISERABLE. SHE coughed all night. Her breathing is laboured. To distract her, I share random memories.

'Remember how easily Nan adapted to living by the sun, the moon and the tides? How she'd explore the wrack line looking for driftwood and cuttlebones—'

'Those balls of seagrass that ran along the beaches when the wind was blowing ...'

'She loved those.'

'She hadn't forgiven me,' Freya whispers. 'I've never managed to get over how much I hurt her. You. Anneke.'

I squeeze her hand. 'She forgave you.' And quickly add, 'Or she'd sit in the shade of the boulders painting, and I'd read beside her ...' I broke off, remembering how we'd laze at Sunlit, and how Nan once said of the Dominican gulls, 'When I come back I'll be a seagull.'

'Nan, why? They're so raucous!'

231

'But elegant in flight.'

'They feed at tips then spread contamination.'

'Well,' she shrugged, breathing in the perfume on her wrists. 'The cleaner we are, the dirtier we make the planet. Dispersion is its nature. Not even the poles are fixed.'

These days I see Nan in every gull.

We'd also explored the tiny fern-rimmed streams that cascaded down through the eucalypts and tree ferns on the mountain's slopes. 'She filled pages of her nature journal with peppermint gums and casuarinas, even while we talked,' I said.

'You'd never tell me what you discussed. It was always top secret.'

'Because it was usually about you,' I laugh. 'And likewise, you and Nan – you had secret conversations too.'

We share a smile. 'But you were talking to me again,' she says. 'That made me happy.'

She's exhausted, so I open my journal and am reminded that the moonbirds returned during the last week of November after their weeks-long feeding spree at sea, ready to lay their large, single eggs. Len hadn't returned, and so I'd watched them with Nan, feeling more sad than exultant.

Freya's eyes are closed, but she peeps at me. 'Len,' she says. 'Lovely boy.'

Wheeler wanted to complete the lessons in the curriculum we'd failed to reach, but I was avoiding him and so schoolwork faded into holiday and beneath symphonic skies, Nan and I would sit together on the rocks in a state of semi-consciousness, gazing into the tidal pools on South Verloren. Occasionally one of us would make a statement, like:

'Sponge.'

And the waves roared towards the beach.

'Blenny … Neptune's necklace.'

An eagle flying heavily by, its catch in its claws, would barely disrupt us, we were so engrossed with the beautiful sentient beings, filtering water, or rasping away at rock, seaweed or shell. Nan made the days peaceful, as though she was conducting them by just being there. Our voices had the ocean and the breeze in them but as soon as words were spoken, they dispersed back into the wild sky. Wheeler and Freya laughed and teased each other more. His singing, guitar and harmonica coloured the air, and Shostakovich was back in his box. Outside the sun went on shining, the wind blew gently from the north and the clouds were cumulus humilis, placid and plump as cows knee-deep in a summer paddock.

The cadence of time was sweet, except that I couldn't forgive.

When Nan and Freya went walking, I'd followed them. I could tell more about their walk if the tide was ebbing – the way their footsteps made a braided pattern, how they'd walked higher when a wave came in and how they'd return to the swash. I could see where they'd stopped to examine shells, or where Freya had bent to pick up a stick and walked on with it, carving a line in the sand before throwing it for Kes.

They seemed to have a lot to talk about. I supposed, correctly, that it was all about me.

~

And then, when I least expected it, Rob came back.

The morning was overcast and cool. Small, eerie white clouds hung beneath a purple sky. We all went walking to Squally Cove, doing a detour over Alveolar Ridge, up to Sam's Soak. There were fresh animal tracks in the damp sand around the lake. An echidna had been by. Some birds had idled there. The Cape Barren geese and the wallabies had left fresh scats. As we walked home along Restless, we were surprised to see two people standing beneath the distant lighthouse.

They disappeared as we approached, but when we reached the house there were three people making themselves at home in our kitchen. Bert was sitting on the doorstep chatting to a woman with blonde hair scooped back with a hairband, a wide smile, and large brown eyes. Freya said later that she looked like a Barbie doll if you ignored the old cotton shirt, rugged shorts, and scuffed work boots.

Rob introduced Christa as a zoologist working on shearwaters, and he greeted Nan, reaching his arm across the table. As he had volunteered to make the tea, Nan said, 'Make mine strong, young man. That was quite a walk I did.'

I sat back and listened to her quizzing him, but she didn't get far.

He said, 'You're a nosy family. Did I ever get a drilling last time I was over.' Then he said he'd be assisting Christa with her shearwater research, and I told him I had lots of data and I'd really like to help.

I wished she'd heard me, but she was still standing in the doorway talking to Bert and Wheeler. Only Freya responded. She said, 'Well, you'd better be quick, or Wheeler will get in ahead of you,' and she smoothed back her hair with both hands. (I used to like that vulnerable gesture before I discovered that she's my aunt and my aunt's my mother and I'm nothing but a burden to them all.) Then she asked if I'd serve up the cake, so I slid it on to one of our old, cracked plates.

Bert was telling Christa the story of the Dead Lady's Gulch and Wheeler, emphasising his accent, was adding asides that made her laugh so that she tilted up her chin and her hair caught the light. She was so pretty it was hard not to stare at her – even Freya and Nan kept looking at her. I suppose you get used to that if you're beautiful. When I offered her some cake she smiled and asked if I'd made it (no), and then I bent down to give Bert a slice. In the little space offering the cake made, she moved inside and took the chair beside Freya.

'This is a beautiful island,' she said, beaming at Nan and Freya as if she were complimenting them on having made it. 'It's a pity we're only over for a few days. Apparently there's a shearwater rookery beneath the lighthouse? If it's all right with you, we'll camp here tonight, and tomorrow we'll go and check out the South Verloren rookeries.'

'Not a problem. I'd offer you a bed if we had one,' said Freya.

'We've got tents. But your husband has kindly offered to show us the lighthouse.' She bent down to scratch her leg. It was red and blotchy where sandflies had attacked it.

I noticed that Freya didn't say anything. She played with the handle of her mug, and when Christa asked if we'd come too, she said, 'I don't think so,' and got up to do something about lunch.

'After you've poured me a little something I might have the strength to help you,' Nan said to Freya. 'But Nicky will be happy to go up the lighthouse, won't you, my darling?'

'I'm sure Wheeler would just *love* your company,' said Freya.

~

In the late afternoon I went over to Christa's tent. She'd placed it near Rob's, some distance from the house where it was sheltered by booby-alla bushes. They could lie in their tents, gaze along the isthmus to the mountain and see the coastline curving away on either side.

She was on her knees arranging her sleeping bag, but she came and sat at the entrance so we could talk.

'Have you brought your shearwater notes?' she asked. I waved a fly away from my face and explained that they were observations and I'd leave them with her if she liked. I treasured them, but I acted like it wasn't a big deal.

'Great.' She flicked through some pages, then said as I was such a keen birdwatcher I could help them at the big colony, and a blush spread up my face because I was so pleased.

Then Wheeler came loping towards us. He said he had a free moment if she still wanted to go up the lighthouse. His time is always free, but I didn't say so. 'What d'ya reckon, eh, Christa?' he said, in a particular tone, as though she was the only person on Mount Aeolian.

I was almost annoyed on Freya's behalf before I remembered that I don't care about either of them any more.

'Rob wants to come too,' Christa said. 'Can we wait?'

He pulled her up. 'You'll tell him where we are when he pitches, won't you, Nicky?'

I raised my eyebrows and stared at the grass.

Christa looked uncertain but she slowly followed him across the pigface, then turned around.

'Come with us, Nicky?'

'Sure!'

'Nicky gets sick of all those steps, don't you, lassie?'

I stood there, stupid with disbelief and tight with rage, and watched them disappear into the lighthouse. I could see Rob on Restless as I trudged back to the house avoiding goose scats.

Shadows were lengthening along the grass and the one cast by the lighthouse stretched towards the cliff and disappeared over the edge. A low light reflected off the kitchen windows. Inside Nan and Freya were making pasta at the kitchen table. A seagull circled the lighthouse then swept down into the gulch on perfectly controlled wings.

As I walked through the door, Freya moved to hug me, but I avoided her and went upstairs.

~

In summer it stays light until late, so after tea, Christa, Rob and I went to Sapphire City. Wheeler had suddenly become madly fascinated by moonbirds so he joined us. Rob was narked off because he'd missed the lighthouse trip and Wheeler was still hogging Christa's company.

The sea was still, as though it was listening. Stars were beginning to appear and the moon had a silver halo around it.

'That means rain,' Rob said.

When the birds began arriving, Wheeler kept flicking on his torch. I could tell it spooked the birds, but he took no notice when Rob and I both asked him to stop, so I walked home and went to bed.

The window was open and a breeze was swaying the curtains. The beam of light probed the darkness and my mind also started to probe around, digging up lots of little problems that I hadn't realised were bugging me, like the way Wheeler couldn't be bothered to come and see the moonbirds with me, but with Christa it's another story. When I'd told him that I'd been invited to help down at Beagle Bay, he'd said I'd have to drag birds out of burrows and risk snakes biting and birds nipping, and that I'd probably be better off doing my own thing. But I've put so much time into finding out about them, and he, my so-called teacher, ought to have been encouraging. And as if snakes worry me! Some days I meet up to five of them between the lighthouse and the rookeries. If you wait long enough they unfurl themselves and slither out of your way. (Actually, confession: the idea of a snake in my sleeping bag *is* another reason why I've moved back to my bedroom.)

I held my pebble and longed for Len to come back. I heard good-nights said and lights switched off. Outside the ocean embraced the rocks, surreptitiously weathering them, and my thoughts were a sour sea rising and falling within me, weathering me too. Time gathered in the darkness. The beams reached across the sky, and above that the stars rode out across the celestial landscape.

When I slept, I dreamed of the tides rising and the sea breaking over the dunes, colonising the hollows of the island and banking up in the burrows of the moonbirds. Gunther was a convict attacking Mr Napper at Beagle Bay and there were feathers floating on the still, black sea. Christa pushed Freya out of the rubber ducky just off the Dead Lady's Gulch. The foot visible above the waterline was Freya's foot, and the lighthouse was a rocket Wheeler had built for our escape; only when he said 'lift off', it teetered slowly and fell over the cliff.

~

I added more rocks to the corners of my tent, which I've left at Sapphire City as a hide, and I was sitting inside it when Christa and Rob came by. They said they needed to work swiftly.

When Rob hauled a bird out of her burrow a little roughly and got bitten, he swore at it. I went for a walk along the beach and scratched zoology off my list of future careers.

They were on Sunlit when I returned, and Christa called me over. We sat together and chatted. Rob was still in the water. He wasn't the world's best swimmer.

She said, 'These poor birds. More than half die before their first birthday. Maybe bad parenting or if food is scarce when they fly north, the easterly winds can blow them off course, or, you know, low plankton levels in the Tasman Sea.' She counted on her fingers. 'Then snakes, water rats, feral cats. People take about three hundred thousand birds a year. We are a huge predator. The gillnet fisheries and pollution are terrible problems. Also, they can get limey disease. Sometimes the burrows get flooded.

'Poor birds.'

'The explorer Matthew Flinders saw about one hundred million in a single flock, back in the 1700s. We can't begin to imagine that now.'

Rob came running up the beach and shook water all over us and we both escaped in different directions. I stood on the dune, laughing, then, 'Tell Wheeler to come down,' she called after me as I headed home.

'Christa!' said Rob. 'Don't impose.'

I didn't turn around. The waves were despondent now and a gloomy wind was bothering the tussocks, and I walked a little faster, keen to put distance between us.

36

Peramangk and Kaurna Country (Adelaide Hills) 2000

Bass Strait (Verloren Island) 1984

Silly Adult Games

I'M DOING SOME PRUNING in the soft evening light when Steve comes by to suggest that I spend some time with Freya. He likes to take a walk towards nightfall and as he's usually gone for an hour, I choose some contemplative Bach and settle into the chair beside her bed. There are days when she's devoid of energy, and today is one of those. But as soon as I sit, she wants to talk about the promise, its impact on her and its impact on me.

'You should have grown up knowing from the start. When you love someone as much as I loved you, Nicky, you don't want a secret lying between you.'

'But it did, so, I don't want this to sound harsh, but I'm left wondering how much was about love and how much about possession. You prioritised Anneke, even though as far as I know, she never repeated her request, and she made it when her feelings must have been pretty raw.'

'Honestly, I plead guilty. It was unforgivably stupid of me. I'm not the world's best decision maker.'

That's the gist of our long and rambling conversation. And it's not as though that's the only grievance, but a painful bout of coughing means we cut it short.

When Steve returns, he tells me he saw a tawny frogmouth perching motionless on a paling near the gate, beak pointing at the moon. Because he says the night is beautiful, I pour myself a wine and sit on the boulder, enjoying the fragrant breeze and the small night noises. I close my eyes and there I am, a teenager again, rambling along tracks made by cattle, notebook in my pocket, ink on my fingertips walking the beaches at night, moonlight on the quiet ocean, a raging fire in my chest.

It's difficult to steady my thoughts or even put to one side a different discord that starts to weave around this. The notion that I should leave my job has become a conviction that won't leave me alone. As I turn on the kettle, as I feed Amber, in the music Steve plays, it's there. It makes me want to scream.

Getting up, I walk out across the paddock, past Giles with his knowing eyes, to where the trees begin. There's a rising moon and the breeze is strengthening. Freya's window is a tiny glow in the darkness under a moon that keeps disappearing behind wispy clouds. With only the goat to hear me, I put my hands over my ears and scream, and as the last traces of pain disintegrate into the emptiness, I feel a sense of catharsis. The wind pauses to gather itself. Everything stills and in the quietude of the moment I feel utterly haunted by the island, the present and the past co-mingled in my life, dreams, imagination, and memory. Walking back, pausing a moment with Giles, I remember Yolla saying the island inspired a new sense of direction for her, and then, an owl sweeping low overhead, I recall the day Rob and Christa packed their rucksacks and disappeared down Mount Aeolian, heading for Beagle Bay. I'd watched them through the kitchen window and, overwhelmed by a complex sadness, had gone with Kes to Sunlit Cove, where I'd mooched on the beach thinking about the sort of man who might appeal to Anneke, and how the next morning Wheeler disappeared before I was up and came home after the moonbirds had returned to their burrows. The same thing happened the following day. I didn't say anything to Freya because I knew he was shaming her.

We were sitting at Sunlit after a swim when Freya said, 'You knew, didn't you, that Wheeler sits up there,' and she prodded the air with her finger to indicate the lighthouse, 'with a stash of *boating* magazines and dreams about starting up a yacht charter tourism operation around here? A *charter* service!' There were tears in her eyes.

Storm's beacon, I thought, looking up at that not-so-innocent structure. *He's a drongo, they both are.* Kes was barking and jumping on my feet to get me to throw a stick, so I did, and he shot away, causing seagulls to rise in an undulating wave above us.

Nan looked at her thoughtfully.

'He needs to think about *us* for a change.' Freya dried her hair vigorously with the towel.

'I think I'll take myself over to that boulder and do a sketch that includes that rather fine yacht that seems to be heading our way,' said Nan.

Freya dropped her towel and walked over to the rocks to get a better view.

'Oh, God,' she said. Then, 'You two,' she called. 'Can you go home *now* and put a picnic together for us?'

We ignored her.

It was certainly heading our way and if they didn't watch out, they were going to lodge themselves on Misfortune.

Once in its lee, they dropped their sails. We watched them lower the anchor and then their tender. From time to time they waved, and we waved back, but three people too many for me climbed into it. Freya was agitated. Kes was standing in the water barking at the interlopers and my suspicions were growing as she gave another tentative wave in response to their vigorous ones.

They were almost on the beach.

She waded into the water as the small swells carried the tender forward. There were two men in the boat and one woman, and they were acting as though Freya was a long-lost friend. One man leapt out and kissed her! And she stood there like a moron looking pleased and embarrassed at the same time. Nan and I were exchanging 'what the hell' looks, but I knew who he was.

The uni guy, Steve.

Her *boyfriend*.

He shook my hand firmly and told us about a southern right whale that had come precariously close to the yacht. (Not close enough, I thought.) Meanwhile, the two other people dragged the tender up the beach. Nan didn't move. She sat on her boulder, eyebrows raised, paintbrush poised.

I waited until Freya looked at me and then I indicated Nan with my eyes. So rather awkwardly they all shuffled over to the rocks and stood below her boulder and Freya introduced them: Steve, Tracey and Mark, her top-secret, extremely ordinary university friends. They reached up to shake her hand as though she was a queen on a high throne. Kes ran around offering his stick and Tracey obliged until his yapping began to drive everyone crazy.

Nan decided to go up to the house 'for a little nap'. Mark and Tracey said they had work to do. A lie, because Freya has the island covered, but she suggested I help them, and I took them up the slope (grumpily) to show them the lay of the land. I asked them what they were doing, and they looked at each other and laughed, and Tracey said, 'An archaeological survey of the Furneaux,' and Mark said, 'A survey of the cultural heritage,' and talked too long about how it 'kind of ties in with your mother's work,' probably another lie. They couldn't stay long.

Well, good!

I pointed out certain landmarks while I tried to keep my eye on Freya, and I said that as they were in a hurry, we wouldn't invite them up to the house. I thought they'd got the message because I certainly got theirs – they kept trying to persuade me to go with them: 'It will only be a little walk down to the farm and it would be nice to have your company.' Tracey, hands on hips, kept smiling at me. On the beach, Freya was sitting on the tender gazing up at her boyfriend. Tracey looked at them, then turned and asked yet again if I'd go with them.

No, I wouldn't. I watched them head off. Then I sat down exactly where I was, determined to be inconvenient. I watched Steve and Freya get in the tender and row out to the yacht. I watched them tie it off then clamber onboard. I watched them, right in front of me, go below. If a snake hadn't come cruising along I'd have stayed sitting there. As it was, she betrayed her husband before my very eyes and all I could think was *I am glad she's not my mother.*

~

Before they left, they did a last, unbelievable thing. They all came up to the house as if nothing had happened.

It was hot. The boulders steamed. They sat in the shade of the veranda and Freya brought out the blue bowl piled high with orange quarters and placed it on the old, bleached floorboards. They were talking about Verloren's archaeology and the wreck the sand had covered up again, and Freya mentioned Len and the issue of ethics, but she and Steve couldn't take their eyes off each other. It drove me mad, and Nan too. We went for a walk and she was sighing a lot, but all she said was, 'I'm not very fit,' and I thought that as Freya has nothing to do with me, it might be tactless to talk to Nan about her daughter's pathetic behaviour. We walked a long way, and their yacht was a speck on the sea by the time we turned around.

I hoped they'd never come back.

That evening Freya was in a restless mood. She put on Joni Mitchell, and then she swapped it and put on Gene Ammons' version of 'Play Me' and sang along to his lovely sax, swaying her hips, out on the veranda, spoiling it for me forever. Sometimes she is so inane, so stupidly *stupid.* I stomped upstairs and Nan thought she was ridiculous too, because she poured herself a whisky and came upstairs after me. All she wanted to do, she said, was to lie down, finish her drink, and go to sleep.

But later I sat at the back door with Kes, wondering where Freya had gone (the gulch apparently) and when Wheeler would come back. The cement was still warm. A few stars were floating in the black rivers between the clouds and a gentle northerly nuzzled me. There was a wallaby browsing on the rise of the hill, silhouetted against the sky, and the moonbirds and penguins were deafening.

Finally, Wheeler appeared over the ridge and came and sat beside me on the step and told me that they'd seen whales. He was going to Beagle Bay the next day and as he didn't want me to come along, I didn't tell him about the yacht.

I'm keeping right out of their silly adult games.

37

A Different Perspective

FREYA HAS MANAGED TO make it to the garden bench. She's had a rally after a few listless bedbound days. Despite her coughing, she's keen to talk, and soon we meander into a conversation about Wheeler.

'You know, when I needed to adopt you, he couldn't have backed me more.'

'Needed?'

'For your sake. For all our sakes. Nobody does something like that unless they're all in. But you know how it is. Sometimes the things that attract are the things that become problematic. Carefree became irresponsible.'

I take a sip of my tea, noncommittal.

'On the island I finally realised I couldn't make him change to suit me.'

Her hand, when she sips her tea, when she strokes Amber wedged between us, has a tremor.

'Secondly, I'd been a fool for being cajoled onto Verloren. A week or two would've been fine. I felt increasingly trapped, too separated from uni. Your education was falling behind.'

I raise my eyebrows.

'I remember watching through the window that day your dad offered Christa his hand and took her up the lighthouse. You didn't like it. Neither did I. And your nan was standing beside me! For me, that was jealousy's last death throe.'

'And Nan's thoughts about that?' As though I didn't know.

'Oh, she was acutely aware that the dynamics had shifted. Her opinion of me at that time might have been at an all-time low, but whereas she'd thought Wheeler was a lovable rogue, I'd noticed she'd abandoned the "lovable".'

'I mean, it was a reprieve, actually, that he was down at Beagle Bay trying to capture Christa's heart while she captured moonbirds.' She smiled. 'Look, I felt at that point I could walk away knowing that I had given him every chance, because Nicky, this was a pattern of behaviour that had been going on for years.'

I turn away, unable to defend him.

'I don't want to speak ill of your dad, I really don't, but you were hurting on top of the pain we'd already inflicted on you. Nan did a lot of beach therapy,' she said touching my knee, 'trying to cheer you up.'

'So that's what it was.'

'It was an awkward period.' She tries to laugh, but coughs instead.

'If she hadn't arrived I'd have run away.'

'I was well aware.'

'So Steve arriving on the island?'

'He'd written to say that his archaeological survey was going ahead. In theory I loved the idea. The reality of a visit – not so much. I had a lot of scenarios running through my head. The worst was that Wheeler would encounter him and the whole situation would explode in my face. Thankfully your father was at Beagle Bay, but when I looked up and saw the yacht bearing down on us, honestly Nicky, I could only think *Not here! Not now!*

'I don't know how I got through that – on autopilot, I guess. When everyone else had departed from the beach, there you were – every time I looked up. It took ages for you to disappear. I know you don't want to hear this but when Steve and I were finally able to go out to the yacht, I felt such a sense of liberation, you know?'

Amber purrs. Freya smiles. I look up at the sunlit greens of the foliage while she's remembering their descent to the cabin, the sensation of everything else falling away.

She can stop right now!

A shadow of doubt replaces her smile. 'It wasn't so simple, moving on,' she says. 'I can honestly say that even after Wheeler bought that damned dinghy, my teetering loyalty still lay with him. And as much as being with Steve again was so—' she pauses, gives me a mischievous smile, 'so effortless and easy, there was still the queasy pooling of guilt, and a sort of desperation. Nicky, I hope love is a lot easier for you. The circumstances for us were jarring. I feared with good reason the effect it would have on you.' She leans briefly against my arm. 'And I feared for Wheeler. That's the truth. So that day with Steve was complicated. The thought of the consequences sickened me. For a person who values her integrity, somehow I've ended up bound by betrayals.'

I sit posture-perfect, critically assessing everything she's saying.

'He wanted me to join the survey but obviously I couldn't. He was so understanding.'

Yep, I thought. You talked about how he could help you retreat from your marriage, you must have.

'I had never felt more certain. I have such a clear image of being in that cabin with Steve …'

'Whoa!'

She gives a fragile hoot of laughter that segues into a series of coughs. She's looking past me. She's heard the car in the drive. 'The silence,' she says. 'The water lapping on the hull. It felt such a safe and tender thing being there with Steve but I knew as I said "yes" to him, when I said my marriage was over, that this choice would be both right and wrong. So I wept.' She looks at me defiantly. 'In Steve's arms I wept because loving him was frightening in terms of the changes I had to make, and because I hadn't wanted my marriage to your dad to fail, and because I knew how hard this transition would be for me and *especially* for you.' She reaches for my hand. 'I give you my word. I never wanted to hurt you, Nicky.'

I'm looking away, wondering if it's her medication that has caused her boundaries to disintegrate. 'You know,' she continues, 'I did weep, but as I watched the light dancing up the side of the cabin, so alive, so free, and heard myself telling Steve my marriage was over, this terrible tension broke inside me. I felt such relief, and disbelief – a happiness and power I hadn't experienced for a long, long time. There was no going back.' And she smiles at Steve, ambling across the lawn towards us. His smile could not be broader. He's shaking his head. 'Look at you,' he says to her, his voice full of wonder. 'Still here beneath the apple tree.'

This conversation might have animated her, but it has also tired her out. I watch them slowly walk together towards the house, blossoms gathered by a miniature whirly-whirly swirling around them, his arm around her back, Amber slinking along behind them, tail held high like a middle finger, and I wonder at all the fear and loneliness Freya had carried when to me she'd seemed so strong.

38

Peramangk and Kaurna Country (Adelaide Hills) 2000

Bass Strait (Verloren Island) 1984

Beneath the Aurora, Phosphorescence

IT'S A HOT NIGHT. I can hear Steve reading *The Upanishads* to Freya while I lie in bed unable to sleep, thoughts about work giving way to recollections about the day Bert arrived to take Rob and Christa away.

I turn on the bedside light, reach for my editing, and return to the island, to where I was standing on the path to the gulch, when they walked past.

'You keep your eye on those birds,' Christa said, 'and we'll talk shearwaters when you're back in Hobart.'

I nodded, but I hoped I'd never see them again.

The next afternoon, Nan went fishing with Wheeler. She doesn't like fishing, but there she was, sitting near the stern of the *Cosmopolitan Leatherjacket* holding on to both sides with a fierce grip while the engine spluttered.

Wheeler dropped the anchor and their voices drifted over the water. I saw him messing around with bait and hooking up. She was getting to hear more about fishing than she'd ever want to know.

He demonstrated a cast. She chose a handline. I scanned the high cirrus and thought about how that boat hardly gets used because the sight of it throws Freya into a wobbly and how it would really be beginner's luck if Nan caught a fish. I knew she was only out there to talk about me.

Geese were honking far away, and when a butterfly settled on my book, I waited for it to preen itself and fly off before taking an amble past the vegie patch.

Freya was kneeling beside a pile of weeds and the skinks lay tumbled together, soaking up sunshine. I hadn't been alone with her since I'd found out that she's not my mother. It must have been listlessness or the soporific day that made me agree to lend a hand because I crouched down beside Kes and enjoyed the satisfaction of pulling out the little tussocks coming up among the silverbeet. The sun was hot on my back, his head was on my foot, and skinks wriggled away from my approaching hand.

At one point I sighed, and she said, 'What's up?' and because it wouldn't pay to say I was imagining I lived with Anneke and my unknown father, I simply said, 'I *wish* Sally would arrive. It's taking forever.'

She blurted out in a pained voice, 'I'm sorry we've made such a mess of everything. I wish I'd told you the truth long ago.' Then she looked at the ground and I saw that her stupid face was red and teary.

The sun fell on her hand where it wasn't shadowed by her skirt, and

I stared at the fine wrinkles on it. Then, from not feeling anything as she said those insincere words, anger rose inside me, and I flung down my trowel with such force that she had to spring away.

My fury disintegrated into a feeling of non-existence and all the while she asked me questions – trying to check out my mental state as though I was about to have a breakdown. I went and examined the tomatoes, my back towards her, and out of nowhere a giant fear smashed through my guts and a thin voice said, 'What's going to happen?'

It was my voice. Just for a moment I was back on a cliff edge, wobbling over a raging river.

I don't know where that question came from, but along with it came the pressure on my chest that crunches me when I'm worried, and snatches my breath away.

Freya looked across at me.

'Nicky, you need to know we love you, and that whatever happens, we will both always try to put your interests first.'

'You – are – *impossible!*'

I stormed off, now wised up to the fact that my parents were untrustworthy. I knew that flabby answer meant trouble was rapidly coming my way.

Sunday, 23 December 1984

... Yesterday Wheeler helped me map an unusual site on the lower slopes of the mountain. Thick wire cable, large pieces of twisted metal and a great, contorted anchor lie scattered around, the remnants of the Merilyn, wrecked with her cargo of explosives in 1958.

What could be salvaged was. The rest was blown up. It must have been a forceful explosion. These mutilated objects create, just there, an ominous atmosphere.

Wheeler was trying to make up for his bad behaviour, not knowing about mine. It could have been an opportunity to discuss Nicky but he wanted to talk about his novel. His hero, a Straitsman, is inspired by the men who once lived on Guncarriage Island away from colonial authority. Like them, they'll have thriving gardens and whaleboats for hunting and trading. Wheeler says he wants to explore Gunther's metamorphosis from East End criminal to hermit-naturalist, and the diverse range of nationalities living on the islands in the 1800s, how a new culture was forged on this watery frontier. I suggested he consider why the women bartered from the North East tribe mostly thrived in these new communities, when not far away, on Flinders Island, people placed by the colonial government at Wybelenna, grew demoralised and died.

Welcome swallows were playing on the breeze when Nicky and I were at the vegie patch the other day and when I said I'm coming back as one of those, I actually got a gentle response. I was gazing wistfully at the beautiful curve of her cheekbone and the tender hollow at the base of her throat, wishing I could smooth away her pain the way I used to but she does not trust me now, I fear she hates me, and yet, in the quiet, as we remained together in the vegie patch above the sea, waves breaking ceaselessly against the rocks below, the moment simply hung until she asked me what was going to happen. I think I said I didn't know or not to worry, but I was at a loss, cringing at the platitudes coming out of my mouth. I suggested we'd have done better to have stayed in Hobart, but she exploded. Navigating this new trajectory is going to require enormous skill and understanding on my part, but I'm cautiously optimistic. I've been there. I know the dangers to avoid …

~

One night, Nan grabbed me for a walk. We chose Restless and wandered up and down, and then we went to Whale Rock. Nan talked and I cried, and 'the big blue mystery' (Nan's term for the sea) swished around us as though we were of no consequence. The moon was nearly full, and the odd star hung in the black gaps between the clouds.

She wanted to talk about Freya and Wheeler and about me feeling responsible – wrongly, she says – for the mess they're in. For the longest time there was only the sound of me sniffing and the little night waves lapping around us, then she gave me a hug. 'What do you *really* want?' she asked.

'I want to be dead,' I howled.

She stroked my hair. 'For now, let's concentrate on having a happy Christmas. Freya said Sally's arriving the day I leave. That will be fun, and I don't think you'll be on the island much longer after that.'

'I won't. When Sally leaves, I'm leaving too.'

~

The next day I set off on a walk down the coastline. Usually I tried to be alert to every nuance of the island but that day Verloren felt dead to me.

At Possum Boat Harbour I saw Len but I don't think he saw me. Good. Because he clearly wasn't my friend.

When I finally turned around at Hannah's Hope Bay, I realised my dilemma. If he was still at the reef, it was going to be harder to block him out because I'd be walking along Boat Harbour towards him. This problem seeped steadily into my consciousness and then began to dominate it, and he was still on the rocks. I focused on the pipits, the geese, the opalesque sea, the cirrus clouds, and the shoulder of mountain to my right, but I could not stop stealing glances at him. Mind links two people when they are the only figures in a landscape, and, worse, he had started walking towards me.

He was tossing his pebble from hand to hand. 'Long way from home,' he said.

I tried moving around him. I hoped he couldn't see I'd been crying. 'I'll walk with you.'

He was carrying an old bag. 'Tonight's tucker,' he said.

I nodded and he didn't say anything more. He just swung along the swash while I strode apart from him, my face set towards the declining sun. The last rays were level with my eyes. It was going to be a long walk home in the dark.

Yeah, and I hoped they'd worry!

We walked, and we didn't share a word. When we both had to slow down to negotiate our way over the tussocky slope of a headland, I broke my silence.

'Are you camping at Beagle Bay?' That was well behind us now. 'Always.'

On we walked. There were more tricky spots to climb over. By the time we reached Honeymoon Cove the sun had set and a big yellow moon was gliding up the sky. Plovers, conversing loudly, headed for Hannah's Hope Bay. Every now and then we stopped. He was considering the stars.

If his camp was back there, I thought, scrambling over the boulders and on up the slope to flatter land beneath the casuarina trees, *there's no point in him walking with me.* But he was, and in the private dark, with the night breeze flitting around my legs, it was much easier to allow myself to feel glad to have his company. The lighthouse beam still looked far away.

Along Emita Beach, penguins were coming in from the sea. We stopped to watch; I shrugged off my bag and we shared an orange. The silence between us had softened. We stood beneath a river of stars, and the full moon laid down a path of light that reached for us across the quiet ocean. Then Len pointed at the sky.

Solar winds were pulsating across the celestial reaches in long slow waves of electrical fluidity. Furls of light transformed into flares and fans and plumes, a soundless dance of luminous turquoise, subtle blue, green hues. With slow grace the aurora transformed the night sky.

We watched it, transfixed, then walked on, heads tilted skywards.

I thought to ask, over and over, how far he planned to walk with me, and over and over I did not. Halfway across Restless, we walked into the sea, up to our knees, and phosphorescence swirled around us. Under that magical night sky and in all that quietude, a small wave broke and swept a line of iridescent purple along the length of the bay.

It was like a dream, being on the beach that night. Voices didn't belong there at all, but I could feel his smile in the darkness.

'Saw you in a dream once,' Len said. 'Your red hair like ochre.'

'You've been in my dreams too.'

We were silent for a while.

'Might turn around.'

I looked up at the lighthouse. I'd felt awed but now I felt drained. The beach ahead of me looked a lonely traverse. 'Thanks for the company,' I said. And then, as he turned away, 'It's a long way back. You can sleep in my tent if you like.'

'It's a good night for walking.'

I watched him go. But then he stopped and turned back.

'I know you're sad, but tonight's so beautiful. Nicky, can I kiss you?'

Yes, he could, and it felt so much more than comforting. Freya and Wheeler, the zoologists and the archaeologists vanished from my mind and the absence I'd felt inside myself filled with a kind of hyper-presence finely focussed on Len and what he was doing.

He kissed me once, and I made him kiss me more. We lay down on the sand, and forgot about the aurora until we got up. Tiny waves were sweeping up the swash. The tide had turned. It was coming in.

'So I'm going to go now,' he said, and kissed me again. And then he walked away, and when I called out, 'thank you for walking back with me and all that,' he raised his arm and kept on walking.

It was a different girl who walked up Mount Aeolian that night but everyone still thought I was just the same.

Freya was in the kitchen. She was dusting, which was ominous at that time of night. Luckily for me, Kes distracted her by leaping up and making a fuss, rolling over and presenting me with his belly to scratch and his loving eyes to stare into.

She glared at me through her narrowed ones. 'Nan and I have just got in,' she said, through clenched teeth. I saw that the bottom of her skirt was wet. 'We have been down to the gulch, over to your tent, along Sunlit and the isthmus. In fact, we walked all the way to Beagle Bay looking for you and my voice is hoarse. What the *hell* have you been up to?'

'None of your business.' I started making myself a sandwich, thinking how remarkable it was they'd missed us.

'Your father said you'd be fine. He said you'd be with Len.'

I paused, knife poised, wondering how he knew that. I steadied the bread.

'Don't you *ever* do that again. I was petrified you'd had an accident.'

I gave her my coldest look. 'You can't tell me what to do any more.'

Her face crumpled. I took the unbuttered bread and flounced outside, along the slope to where the grass gives way to pigface and tussock, and you can look down the island to the mountain. The moon was high, the aurora gone. The mountain and the islands in the distance were dark, hunched shapes in the moonlight, powerfully full of their own secret selves. I thought of the cave and its deep earthy floor covering Ice Age bones. When I whispered goodnight to the mountain, I could almost see the words float across the isthmus and gather in its stone ear. Len was walking the path back to Beagle Bay, it was my secret knowledge, and the night had been so amazing – an enormous cliché really – that I wanted to live it all over again.

The lighthouse door shut quietly. Wheeler came down the steps. I watched him walk over to the house and go inside, and I wondered if I'd be ready to be civil in the morning.

39

Gadigal Country (The Rocks, Sydney) 2000

Peramangk and Kaurna Country (Adelaide Hills) 2000

Beneath the Apple Tree

I'm with colleagues at a pub in The Rocks when Arno walks in. We see each other at the same moment, and he signals me over to the counter.

'How've you been?' he asks, with the same old intensity, kissing me on both cheeks.

'Not bad, although travelling to Adelaide so frequently means that every time I'm back in Sydney I feel less at home.'

'I can imagine. Your mother, how's she?'

'Last time I was there, Arno, she had this amazing rally. We got to sit outside and talk, and I was hoping it was a turning point, but her husband keeps me up to date and the news isn't good.'

He squeezes my hand.

'Her decline has been so rapid. I wish she'd acted faster at the beginning.'

'You'll never regret giving her your time.'

'I'm flying back on Friday. I've told work I don't know when I'll be back.'

He puts his arm around my shoulder, his mouth to my ear, and murmurs something in Italian that sounds like a blessing.

'Thank you, for whatever that was.' I shift away a little. 'And you? How have you been?'

He tells me about a kayaking trip, a marathon he's run, and a woman he's been out with who he doesn't think he'll see again.

'Too much information. I don't need to know about that side of your life.'

He shakes his head at me. 'You break up with me and yet you're still jealous.'

'Oh, I am not,' I insist, as Max barges up.

'Keep in touch, *cara*,' he says as I'm hauled away.

~

Carla has been. It's something to do with her radiant presence – the music Steve plays when she's here has a joyous quality and after her departure the air still rings with energy that slowly depletes through the course of the day. This morning she washed Freya with such compassion and respect that it seemed as though the essence of what matters most in the world had been distilled and was present in the bedroom. I am full of admiration for her dedication. I can't avoid a notion that she works because she cares. I work to be busy.

Her voice has Italian cadences. Sometimes she counsels my mother behind closed doors and Steve and I, standing at a loss in the kitchen, can hear their voices but not the words, can trail the silences as well as the laughter. The emotion in this house is sometimes so intense it's like breathing fire.

There are times when we dread her arrival. We dread it when we suspect she's going to tell us what we already sense – that Freya, who has been on a plateau, has weakened. The days when her medication is increased are difficult for all of us. Her pain is expressed in peevish demands. We feel rudderless. A subdued hush fills the house. Death, powerful and unpredictable, marks up a notch in her favour.

Mostly, we long for Carla to arrive. The muscles in Steve's face relax when she knocks, and he always walks her to the gate when she leaves. Watching them confer in the shadows, I'm conscious of being the outsider. I feel wistful; Carla, through circumstance, has a more intimate connection than I've ever achieved. At moments like this I go hollow with longing for a sibling to confide in. No one else shares my past. No one else can confirm my beliefs and perceptions.

At first Freya said that the only pain relief she needed was Amber's company, but for a long time now that's not been enough, and because of her difficulty breathing, her doctor has provided oxygen. Yet she still seems to spend a great deal of time dwelling on our shared past.

'When I think of your childhood, Nicky, it's hard to see you without your pen, your notebook, and that tattered dictionary.'

I remind her that she needs to conserve energy for a friend's visit in the afternoon.

'Nicky ...'

I wait, knowing exactly what she's going to say. 'The promise. I'm so sorry about all that. I'm *so* sorry, and about Wheeler. My guilt, it's dominated my life. For a person who simply wants to be kind I've made so many catastrophic mistakes.'

I swallow, meet her gaze, feel for her hand. 'Don't be. You're *totally* forgiven.' We share a mutual smile, hers of gratitude, mine a confirmation to myself that I am not without compassion. Mine is a big grievance. It's not just about Wheeler. It's Kes too. I look at my feet, eager to escape to the boulder because my words still don't leave me feeling full-hearted. And Freya knows that. Forgiveness is a process. It comes and goes, but in that moment it had briefly enveloped us.

I make myself stay. 'How do you feel about dying?' I ask.

She gives a wry smile. 'If you look on my bookshelves you'll see I've got several versions of the *Tao te Ching*, but at the time of my diagnosis it had been ages since I'd read one.' She glances at the copy on her bedside table and I reach for it. 'I suppose I regard death as a moment of transition, of renewal and rebirth, of change yet no-change,' she says. 'I find Lao Tzu wise and comforting.'

'Nan gave me a copy years ago.' I slowly turn the pages of hers. 'She was the person who explained the Tao to me and I saw how it complemented the quantum physics Wheeler taught me on the island.'

She nods.

'We were walking along Emita and I'd hinted at an experience I'd had on Mount Aeolian.'

She raises her eyebrows.

'I didn't know how to interpret it.'

'And now you do?'

I smile. 'I both understand and don't understand,' and we laugh. 'She also told me about Indra's jeweled net of being. That explained so much, but for all the profundity of interconnectedness—' and then I stop myself from adding that it is my life after she's gone that still frightens me.

'What?'

I give an almost imperceptible shrug and look away.

'Nicky.' She waits for me to look back at her. 'You will be fine.'

'When I think about death I feel the need to personify it. I suppose it makes it feel more human somehow, and not so vast.'

She looks out the window. 'I think it's no gender and every possible gender but I relate to it as if it were female. I'm trusting her to come and enfold me back into timelessness and formlessness at the right moment.' She turns to look at me. 'How do you see it?'

'I probably need to contemplate that,' I say, and look up and smile as Steve enters the room. 'I guess as a goddess, holding together all the opposites in the universe, sweeping in on a high tide.'

She smiles. 'I rather like that,' she says. 'As long as she's kind.'

'Sorry to be so prosaic,' says Steve, 'but I need to know what you want from the supermarket.'

~

The following morning, Steve calls me to join them. Freya is sitting up in bed. She's looking stronger.

'My darling,' he says to her. 'Nicky. Some surprising news for the two of you. I've tracked down Anneke. We talked on the phone. She'll be here tomorrow for a short visit. I've assured her she will be greeted with love and that there will be no recriminations.'

We are stunned, full of questions and trepidation. I notice there are tears in Freya's eyes, but I feel nothing except, briefly, the cold curiosity I thought I'd long ago buried forever.

~

There's a firm knock at the front door and there she stands, about Freya's height, wearing an Akubra over short greying hair, oversized sunglasses, a white linen tunic and white linen pants. Her long earrings shimmer, the silver bangles on her left arm clink, and her big chunky amber necklace is a statement piece. She is nothing like I expected. I'm overwhelmed by a sense of familiarity.

'Nicky,' she says, with a warm but cautious smile. 'Steve?'

It's an almost out-of-body experience and I'm grateful when he steps forward, takes her by the arm and makes small talk in the hallway. We share quick glances and tentative smiles, and then he calmly guides her in to see Freya.

I wait beneath the apple tree, my heart unsteady, wondering whether it's something in her features or her mannerisms that's driving my strong sense of reconnection, until, after close to an hour, she comes into the garden bearing cups of coffee. They create a little adjustment space for us as she puts them on the bench and then we stand, holding hands, looking at each other, tuning in to each other's presence, the unanticipated sense of familiarity, before we step into a hug.

'I am so looking forward to getting to know you, Nicky. I want you to know, I've thought about you every day.'

Bullshit, but whatever. 'Freya really tried to keep you well informed.'

She considers me carefully. 'She said so too. You guys moved around a lot. Me too. I'm pretty sure we both still have letters at post offices across Europe and Australia.'

I offer her space on the bench, and we sit with our drinks beside us.

'It's a little sad,' she continues, 'because when there's no letter waiting for you, and you're feeling lonely, you read rejection into the silence.'

'There was never rejection. She always had a letter on the go to you.'

She looks away. 'I'm dyslexic, you know. The moment I pick up a pen I feel an anxiety that borders on terror. And she writes so well.'

'I didn't know that.'

'She never said? You know, I really wasn't difficult to find. Steve says he went to the library to search the phone directories. He started with Sydney. It took five minutes.'

'We all thought you lived overseas.'

'You were seven when I moved back. I wrote to Freya to let her know.'

'I'm positive she had no idea.'

We regard each other. I'm wondering how different things might have been if not for their misaligned correspondence.

'Well, nothing we can do about the past but I will say it was so good to hear from Steve, even though his news about Freya was distressing.'

'Anneke, you always knew Nan's address though.'

'I did, but I didn't know how to tear down the wall we all seemed to be maintaining. I twice came to Hobart. Made it to Sandy Bay. Couldn't make myself take those final steps.'

I started to say, *so you clearly weren't interested in me*, then stopped myself.

'My whole life I've felt burdened by the need to forgive Freya for things that had been plaguing us both, it turns out. I felt terribly hurt. I held on to resentment for such a long time.'

'It will have meant everything to her, this visit. She's missed your presence in her life massively.'

'She told me. Nicky, honestly, for the longest time imaginable I've felt trapped in an awkward situation. I've felt shunned. I lacked the courage to act.' She shrugs. 'But you! I've imagined getting to know you better endlessly, although it was never here, nor under these circumstances.'

'I'd hoped you'd come to Nan's funeral. I kept looking around for someone who might be you.'

'I was in Paris when I heard.'

'So you did know.'

'A dear friend – a friend who has always urged me to make contact – let me know. There was an article in the paper.'

'It's because of Nan that I'm still standing.'

'For that I owe her everything. It might comfort you to know that I went to the Sainte-Chapelle because I knew she loved it. No crowds. I lit a candle and the light falling through the stained-glass windows was—' she grapples for a word. 'I made my peace with her and walked out lighter.' She nods emphatically and for a while we are silent, sitting beneath the tree, our tea grown cold, our postures perfect.

We talk about Freya and her prognosis, and she explains that she can't spend more than tomorrow here because of a travel commitment. I'm holding so much of myself back and she clearly is too.

'I have so many questions and I feel as though we're avoiding the big topics.'

She nods. 'Me too, there's a lot I want to ask you. But there's a time and place, and I don't think that's now, do you?'

But I might never see you again!

She intuits my thoughts. 'Now that I've found you, you've unfortunately got me for life.'

I discover she owns a small studio in Rushcutters Bay, not that far away from me, so we agree it's feasible we've passed on the street.

'And home?'

'My yacht. No fixed address. But I have a phone at the studio.'

I take down the number and later she says, 'You know, my worst trait is that I've been unforgiving. The cost was missing out on you. At a particular point, returning seemed blocked by the passage of time and the pain that had built up. To see you regularly would have meant everything, but it would also have been the most traumatic thing I could have done to myself and to you – I think I might have made your complicated situation worse. I'm not good at confessions. Worse at apologies. But I'm here. I'm telling it like it is and I'm apologising to you, Nicky, with everything I've got.'

I accept this with a cautious nod.

'Because it was all my fault. A huge loss of courage.'

'There's been a lot of turmoil in this family. There was a time when your presence might have been helpful.'

'I do know that. It was tempting to intervene, but like I said, it could have made a bad situation worse.'

That she knew is confusing; she must have received some letters, but I let it pass. 'I've spent years feeling betrayed by both you and Freya. Less so by Wheeler.'

'Oh, the men, how they always get off lightly!' She picks up a gum leaf, magenta and purple, and gives it to me, turning away to touch her fingers to her eyes. 'I deserve every complaint you have against me.'

I glance at her. She and Freya have the same nose, yet in her gestures she reminds me of Nan.

'Do you have a significant other in your life?' she asks me, after a small silence.

I shake my head. 'I don't know how to commit. Have you?'

'I hope *you* will become increasingly significant, Nicky.'

I gather our mugs to cover my confusion. She looks at her watch, and Steve appears to say her taxi has arrived.

After all the intensity, she's gone. Needing space, I go to see Giles, to consider my thoughts before talking to Freya, filled with amazement that I have finally met my aunt, my other mother, and uncertain how I feel.

~

'How is she?' whispers Steve, touching Freya's cheek with the back of his hand. I gesture with mine: *cosi cosi*, like Carla does: so so. He's come home from his evening walk looking so miserable that I pour glasses of wine, which we drink in his study. He puts on the 'Moonlight Sonata', and we sit in companionable silence, listening to the music and the night noises emanating from the garden.

I want to ask him how he thinks it went, Anneke and Freya's reunion, but, 'Oh, Nicky,' he sighs. 'How I'm going to miss your mother!' Had she not fallen ill, he tells me, she would've taken up a professorship in Vancouver. They'd both been looking forward to exploring the Americas. But that's of no consequence now. What he'll most miss is seeing her out in the garden, standing with her head to one side considering a particular planting; or strolling with her in the evening, wine glass in hand, idly weeding. Who will he go to the theatre with now? Who will he turn to when he wants to exclaim over a piece of music? Who will he go cruising with? 'I might as well sell the boat,' he says, looking bereft.

'It's the little things, isn't it, that are the hardest to deal with?' And perhaps it's the music, but we both feel increasingly maudlin.

'And you're leaving so soon. You won't consider extending your stay?'

I give a tiny shrug and he an understanding smile.

'I've been so lucky to have found Freya. The kindest person! I often wonder what she saw in me.'

I shift in my chair, remembering my conversation with Sally about Steve the night she came for dinner. 'Shared passion for archaeology? Dependable and intellectual? You both like the finer things in life?' I sweep my gaze around the room, but I'm put off by the way he's regarding me, a curious half-smile on his face. 'She says you're a good listener. You are. And you're kind to her too, so thank you for being kind to my mother,' I add, because it seems to be the day for apologies and forgiveness.

He chuckles. 'Thank you, but that was a rhetorical question. The answer must have cost you a lot.'

'The price has dropped dramatically.'

He squeezes my shoulder as he gets up to turn off the gramophone. 'And I apologise to you, Nicky, for my part in stuffing up your childhood.'

'That was long ago. But thanks anyway. And for getting Anneke here. I suppose it should have been me who tried, but, you know, too much baggage.'

He won't be drawn. He stands there stroking his chin, staring out over the garden. Just standing, and there's no music. There's just Steve and the silence.

I could have told him that he's affable, with a wry sense of humour, and that I've never seen him lose his equanimity, but Anneke is on my mind. She's left me feeling confused. I need someone to discuss this with but he's too absorbed in supporting Freya. Later, preparing for bed, I rest my gaze on the bird-girl, reach for my touchstone and will her to strengthen me.

Peramangk and Kaurna Country (Adelaide Hills) 2000

Finding the Map

IT'S MID-MORNING WHEN I wake. The sky is an unsullied blue. It takes a moment for me to realise that for the first time in years I've dreamed – dreamed I was lost without a map in a foreign city, my disoriented wanderings leading me into a dispirited business zone. The traffic made my head ache. My feet were tired. I sat down at a bus stop, alienated by a language I didn't understand.

Late afternoon shadows darkened the office blocks across the road, and my attention was drawn to a window where a woman was shuffling papers. Soon she emerged from a doorway wearing a short black dress and high heels, clutching a folder in her arms. She strode towards me but when our eyes met she veered away, her head bobbing through the crowd then disappearing. Ready to leave, I realised that the road was covered by a swash of water and seagrass grew on the bitumen.

~

Freya's eyes well when I ask her what it was like to see Anneke again. 'All those wasted years.'

'You *tried*. So hard!'

'Not hard enough. And you? What was it like for you?'

I shrug. I'm not ready for this conversation and she's not well enough. And then I tell her today's the day I resign, and assure her that with no commitments I don't need to rush back to Sydney.

'So happy,' she manages, before exhaustion sets in, and with that I send off my resignation email.

Steve looks visibly relieved when I tell him I'll stay on. We never mention Freya's downward slides and the ever-diminishing plateaus. We never share the thought we both must have each evening – that perhaps this has been her last day, will be her final night. We always wait for Carla to voice our concerns or defuse our worsening fears. I can't dispel this fear of death. I don't want to see Freya go. I don't know how close we'd have grown with more future ahead of us, but I'm missing the opportunity I might have had to find out.

When Anneke arrives, we join Freya and I fill her in on my change of status to unemployed. 'Impulse! I love it,' she says.

'Hardly. It's taken a dream to make me act.' And she smiles at me as though I've said something marvellous.

Steve brings us glasses of chilled rosé and lunchtime snacks, and we raise our glasses. 'To Freya, and you,' Anneke says.

'And to Nan,' I add and it feels complete, the three of us in the room, Steve standing in the doorway, taking a photo.

Freya, struggling to talk, manages to say how much she hopes we three will develop a strong relationship. We assure her we will, and she and Steve share a smile, as though they're alone in the room.

She's tired, so we go out to the veranda and Anneke says she feels sad that on both occasions she and Freya have been able to do little more than reassure each other of forgiveness for past misunderstandings and hurtful acts, largely through hand squeezes. 'And, you know, with our eyes,' she adds.

Steve stares soberly at the cockatoos flying overhead and then he and Anneke engage in a chat about yachts.

As he walks away, I ask for her version of why she left home when she was a teenager.

'So many reasons. I was hopeless at school. My relationship with Celeste was stressful; I'm so sorry to have to tell you that, Nicky; I realise she mellowed.'

'She was so mellow.'

'We had art in common. It was a slight bond and my happy place, but she started drinking heavily after my father left – perfectly understandable – but it made her critical, about me, about my art, this one thing I felt good at. I ended up burning my canvases.'

'I feel like you're talking about a different person. She kept your photo on the sideboard and lit a candle for you every evening. She saved some of your art. It was on her walls. I never heard her speak a word against you.'

Anneke stares at the ground. 'I can't imagine,' she says slowly. 'Except, she *adored* my father, so the loss, the grief, the pain and uncertainty, as well as two girls to raise – it seems my mother changed considerably.'

She's reluctant to continue. I can see her wrestling with doubt.

'Maybe losing you started her off on a trajectory of personal growth and I was the lucky recipient?'

'Maybe. Anyway, when he left I lost my best friend.'

'That I understand.'

'The Sydney to Hobart Yacht Race had just finished and Marti and I volunteered to help deliver a yacht back to Sydney. It's not like I was deliberately running away; I simply got the opportunity to carry on sailing, and so I did because it was far and away the best option. I was able to sail across the Pacific. Then I kept going.'

'We've always wondered what happened to your father.'

'He was living in London. I visited him, but he had a new wife who had two kids much younger than me. She didn't want me there. When the door closed on me, that was it. I don't know if he's still alive, quite frankly.'

'That's really tough. I'm sorry that happened to you.' I saw a pattern of abandonment that kept repeating and was about to ask about my own father when she said, 'After that I went back to sailing. In winter I'd find a base on land and I'd paint, pose, busk, work as a waitress – anything and everything.' She taps her lips thoughtfully. 'But crewing was always my fallback option. It seldom let me down. Not that it paid anything.'

It's like she knows the question I most want to ask. She keeps deflecting. 'It's different now. Now, mostly painting but also photography.'

Giles arrives at the gate, and we wander over to greet him. Anneke sings to him while she scratches his ears. She has a great voice; it draws me into the lyrics:

Silence at noon, sun trembling above

earth burning beneath the casuarina trees.

There off the boulders of Honeymoon Cove

I cast my gold net in the silver seas.

Fresh abalone and warrener

and fish that dazzle in the azure blue.

All that I want is the freedom to be

out there on the island, white sand, silver sea.

'What's that song called?'

She shrugs. 'It's by an a cappella group.'

She has the cassette with her, and back inside I peruse the tracks and the group members. 'We have to put it on!'

'I don't think …' says Steve.

'Listen to the lyrics,' I beg Freya. '*Sally wrote those words*. It says so – here!'

She smiles, but doesn't open her eyes.

'It's my friend, Sally, Anneke. She's singing about Verloren Island!'

'That's called synchronicity, Nicky. It happens to me all the time.'

In the living room I give in to a moment of overwhelm.

'She's going to die.' My whisper is shaky. 'There are so many things I need to talk to her about and I've left it too late.'

Anneke passes me a tissue, her face softening.

'You know, Anneke, when we were kids, Sally said she'd always be my sister, but I let that friendship go. We drifted apart during the years I spent with Nan.'

'If ever you needed a sister, it's now. Have you got her number?'

I don't, but we find the Joneses' details in Freya's address book.

'Marti's daughter,' she marvels. 'My first boyfriend. So, he ended up being Freya's friend? It was ever thus.'

'We rented a house from them in Hobart.'

'I see.' She taps her lips with her finger, a Nan gesture, and I go into the garden while she phones him. When she comes out, waving a piece of paper, there is triumph spread across her face. 'I have her number for you, and I just got to speak to Marti for the first time in decades. Lots to reminisce about!'

Not only is Sally here, but when I phone her – immediately, because Anneke is insistent – she's eager to meet up and shocked to hear about Freya.

By the time Anneke leaves, there are still so many questions unanswered. 'When all this is over,' she says, 'We're going to meet up, you and I. We will not lose touch.' And she passes me an address on Flinders Island. 'Now you have two places you can contact me, if I don't get in touch with you first.'

'Flinders? Really?'

She nods. 'I love the islands, and you and I, we have mutual friends.'

'We do?'

She kisses Freya goodbye tremulously, thanks Steve, and as we hug at the gate, she whispers light and fast, 'I met you once, Nicky, on a day long ago …'

I laugh. 'Beneath a wild fig tree, beside a creek, in the pouring rain. I know.'

And I stand there waving as the taxi carries her away, wishing I'd asked her the most important question of all.

'Did she tell you who my father was?' I ask Freya.

She shakes her head.

'Must feel frustrating,' says Steve.

'You have no idea. She is so enigmatic.'

41

Peramangk and Kaurna Country (Adelaide Hills) 2000

The Gadfly

THE DOCTOR CAME WITH Carla today. She said Freya is to have no more visitors and, after an emotional discussion, she agreed to increase the morphine one last time. Freya's finding breathing too painful. She's utterly exhausted.

There's a hushed atmosphere. A painful countdown.

Which is why Sally makes her visit short. We sit on the bench and the intensity of the situation dissolves the distance I'd allowed to develop.

'Give your relationship with Anneke time,' she urges, once I've blurted out my confusion, which hasn't been helped by the fact that in this family stories seem wildly off-kilter, depending on the teller. I want crisp layers of shared experience. What I get is a fuzzy focus.

She writes down her address. 'I'm around for you.' She's wearing silver Hopi earrings and her clothes remind me of Freya's a long time ago.

'You know, those shorts and bare feet – much more you than the Ms Corporate Lawyer look.'

'Thanks *a lot!*'

'I'm your sister, remember? I'm allowed to be honest.'

We laugh, but I'm desperate to get back to Freya. 'I'll let you know how things go, I promise.' I walk with her to her van. 'My love to Mr and Mrs Jones.'

She hugs me, climbs into her dilapidated Kombi, starts to drive away, then brakes. 'By the way, you were lucky to catch me – I'm moving back to Hobart next month.'

'Might see you there.' I stand for a moment watching her go, her hand out the window waving, and then I walk inside to be with Freya.

~

Death comes visiting.

Eyes closed, Freya lies sunk in her bed, very still. She looks asleep but she and Death are sizing each other up. Occasionally Death – dark, divine and diabolical, wildly capricious yet gentle – makes her intentions known, then drifts away, leaving behind a presence – a colour, a temperature, an odour in the air.

I kiss her brow and we gaze into each other's eyes.

'Love you, Mum.' Saying that is like walking barefoot over barnacles.

'Love you too, Nicky.'

I pass her water and support her while she drinks.

Steve is standing in the lounge staring out over the garden to the hills. A Beethoven concerto is playing quietly in the background, tender notes that fall like a quiet rain. When he turns I notice that his eyes are damp.

'Freya wants you.' I walk over and hug him and am startled by the relief with which he returns this impulsive embrace.

~

Later, in a brief interlude away from her bedside, he sits in the worn leather chair in the corner of the study, and I sit on the Chesterfield that she will not reach again. The shelves sag with archaeological texts. He leans forward and talks about the painfully slow recognition of traditional ownership, the rich sophistication of culturally held knowledge, and a concept called the Anthropocene he'd come across that day.

He evidently doesn't want to talk about Freya.

'Fire management and climate change,' he says. 'We need to listen to Indigenous people if we aren't to head in a perilous direction.' I wonder what Len would make of what he's saying.

'We gave ourselves the wrong moniker when we labelled ourselves "sapiens". Wise we are not. Hubris we have in full measure. The colonial project – disastrous.'

The telephone rings. We don't move. The answering machine captures a call from a friend, enquiring after Freya, as we cradle our drinks and listen to Gregorian chants flowing from the speakers. I steal a glance at him, pleased that at the end of her life she has someone so caring. Small touches, like the way he brings her a single bloom first thing in the morning.

We both smile carefully as he gets up to select another recording.

He puts on Shostakovich's *The Gadfly*, the volume just loud enough for Freya to hear. 'One of our favourites,' he says.

He doesn't realise the connotation Shostakovich has for me, a less than subtle semaphore. For once, I stay put. And this time it makes me want to cry.

42

Bass Strait (Verloren Island) 1984

Fat Turkey Cove

SEARCHING THROUGH MY JOURNAL for Christmas 1984, memories of our bleary-eyed breakfast, of opening our presents under a melaleuca branch Freya had decorated for the occasion, the mobile Wheeler made me from shells, feathers, and driftwood, and the carvings he'd made for Nan and Freya flood back.

Freya gave me a fountain pen and, still angry, I gave them nothing. Nan gave me my Parisian journals and I gave her a tiny nautilus shell, one of several that had recently washed in on the tide. Wheeler cracked open a bottle of champagne and made a toast to the following year, declaring it would be our best yet. He smiled warmly at Freya, but she stared down at the table, a little frown lodged between her eyebrows.

Fat Turkey Cove, our picnic spot, was a tiny pocket of sand north of Squally Cove. It only emerged on a spring low tide so it didn't have a name – Wheeler made it up for the occasion, even though we didn't have a turkey with us. 'We are the turkeys,' he said.

It was probably the truest announcement he'd ever made.

Nan found a shady spot and proceeded to paint. Freya read and Wheeler and I dived for abalone. Suspended upside-down in a timeless limbo, I stared at the delicate finery of tubeworm feelers and zebra fish half-hidden by the slow sway of seaweed, and watched a colourful nudibranch graze. And what I discovered was that you could cry in the water without anyone knowing. We weren't a family anymore and this didn't feel like Christmas.

Lunch was seafood.

'This is the life!' Wheeler munched a cray leg, the juice dribbling down his chin. 'A small Christmas on a small island.'

'Wipe your face, Wheeler,' said Freya.

Nan was drinking her third glass of champagne.

'I'm going to have a swim and I'll have dessert after that,' she said, and ran unsteadily into the little waves.

'Not bad for an old turkey,' said Wheeler. 'Come to think of it,' he added, turning to Freya, 'you haven't been in yet! Come on Nicky! Let's sacrifice this beautiful goddess to Neptune!'

I rolled my eyes. She ran into the poa and over the ridge, and the sound of her laughter drifted back to us on the breeze.

'Well, time for some more diving. Come on, you.'

Later, Nan and Wheeler both fell asleep in the shade, and I took Kes for a walk. There was a yacht off Honeymoon Cove, but no sign of Freya. Once I'd have worried. That day I didn't give a damn.

Wheeler woke when the wind turned to the south and the waves got up. 'If we want to use the boat we're going to have to get cracking,' he said. He was annoyed with Freya, which wasn't fair, given his habit of disappearing.

Nan took one look at the developing chop and said she'd walk, thank you very much, and she set off at once. But Kes and I went with Wheeler and we all got drenched by the slop on the way home.

Friday, 28 December 1984

… On Christmas Day I behaved despicably, even though, opening gifts, I'd looked at Nicky and Wheeler and felt heartsore. I longed for the simplicity of those days when he was my everything and she was our delight.

We idled a couple of hours away over a picnic but when Wheeler decided to dump me into the sea (a rather annoying habit of his), I escaped, and approaching Honeymoon I spotted a familiar yacht.

Although I'd been longing for this, I was thrown by the timing. So was Tracey. She said we were fools – that she and Mark didn't like being involved in our duplicity. Mark tried to excuse her by saying she was uptight because he'd nearly installed the yacht on The Dagger and whatever we did was our business; all he wanted was some Christmas celebrating. Meanwhile Steve was overly apologetic ('I'm crazy, but I couldn't stop myself,' that sort of thing.)

They'd chosen to anchor off Honeymoon because they didn't want to approach the lighthouse, although they'd apparently sailed close in, hoping to attract my attention. Tracey kept asking where 'they' were and was I sure this was safe because she certainly didn't want to meet Wheeler, so we decided to cruise towards Lone Egg

Island. Honestly, while there were moments of that afternoon that felt quite blissful, each time I visualised my family sitting on that tiny beach wondering where I was, I loathed myself.

Short sail. We returned to Honeymoon ahead of the southerly and I had to run home, arriving well after everyone had eaten tea, and receiving – quite justifiably – a stony welcome. I said I'd found a new site and would work down the coast the following day. All this they believed. I'm torn between relief and self-hatred.

43

Bass Strait (Verloren Island) 1985

Arrivals and Departures

THERE WAS ALREADY AN atmosphere of arrival and departure when Dorothy buzzed us. Carrying bits of luggage, we headed down to Emita Beach and sat among the correa and pigface as the plane headed straight towards us and taxied to a halt.

Sally leapt out, 'overexcited' according to Nan, and I was so busy catching up on all the gossip that I didn't notice Len until he climbed out and looked across at me.

I followed him around to the other side of the plane to find out how long he'd be staying, but all he said was, 'Gunna camp down south,' and our hands touched briefly, then flew apart as Dorothy came over and hugged him goodbye.

He hoisted his pack on to his shoulders. 'Be going then,' he mumbled, and he glanced at me briefly with his amazing eyes and walked away.

Wheeler yelled, 'Len! My man! Come and have some tucker up at the house first,' but Len raised his arm in the air and kept right on walking.

'*Weird* boy,' said Sally.

But Dorothy, manoeuvring Nan's luggage into the plane's hold, told her he was smart, independent and resourceful, and that he knew Verloren better than anyone else in the Furneaux. 'I've got a lot of time for young Leonard,' she said.

~

Dorothy wanted a quick swim before leaving, so we left Freya and Nan in deep conversation on the beach and Sally and I went to the gulch with her while Wheeler carted gear to the house.

We sat on Whale Rock and Dorothy said, 'I hear Arthur Mahoney's some kind of relative of yours,' and she laughed when Sally rolled her eyes.

'Once when Yolla was here, he came to check up on the place, and caught her meditating here on this rock, in her birthday suit. Bert reckons your uncle was calling forth fire and brimstone and before they'd even made fast to the jetty, he was shaking his fist and accusing her of satanic acts, claiming that he wouldn't have "no pagans" on his island.'

'Sounds like my uncle.'

'What happened then?' I asked.

'She stood on the boulder and sang 'I Shall Not Be Moved' before jumping down to give Bert a hand. She's got a beautiful voice. You should hear her sing the blues. Your uncle was blessed.'

I hoped she'd put her clothes on by then. 'Did she tell you we met?' I asked.

'She raved about you, Nicky. It was hard to shut her up.'

'Why?'

Sally laughed. 'Yes, why? She's my best friend – you are, Nicky – but I'm not going to rave about you!'

'Well!' Dorothy shrugged. 'I know she wished she'd had more time with you. It seems you had a good conversation.'

'I suppose.'

'You can always get in touch through me.'

But why would I? It was just one conversation. The water sloshed around us. The boulder radiated heat. We were silent, watching terns work the damp sand with their feet, then when they'd flown away Sally and Dorothy jumped in, but I stayed on the boulder, thinking about Yolla. She seemed to spend a lot of time wandering around in the nude.

~

Sadness lumped in my throat as we said goodbye to Nan. The engine started up, the propellor turned, and we waved as Dorothy brought the plane around into the breeze. We watched it gather itself, change stride to a gallop, leap lightly into the air and begin its climb, heading out over the ocean, over the deeps and the seagrass meadows and the shifting sands of the ancient Bassian Plain. And we saw its shadow racing after it over the surface of the water, and then Nan was gone.

After she left, Wheeler and Freya appeared more relaxed, but they were dissembling, so her letters and Wheeler's ledger were pivotal to helping me understand exactly how things unfolded. She'd written:

… Since Sally arrived Wheeler doesn't disappear as much. Sometimes I look at him fooling with his guitar or scaling fish, apparently oblivious to the guillotine poised above his head, and I can see exactly why I loved him.

Sally is a helpful buffer between Nicky and me. She's also interested in plants and learns names quickly. As we all sat on the dunes watching raindrops falling, listening to the frogs starting up, she noticed a small seedling bending under the weight of tiny splashes and remarked how much like people they are, in that they can be destroyed by lots of little blows. Indeed, and relationships too. I hurriedly changed the subject because she's such a perceptive girl and I don't know how much she may have heard from Janet. Still, since she arrived, it's rare to find that clenched-up look on Nicky's face. For that, I'm grateful, and grateful too because before she left, my mother agreed that Nicky and I can move in with her. She made it clear that this is for Nicky's sake. I don't feel I've been entirely forgiven …

Right on cue at the start of January, the moonbird chicks tumbled out of their eggs in the sandy burrows. The breadwinner parents spent their days skimming the ocean hunting for krill while their partners bunkered down to preen and coddle their plump offspring. We all agreed the moulting penguins looked scruffy. They were the ones that either hadn't bred, or their babies had already taken to the sea, so they were fasting.

With Sally here, I didn't watch the birds as much, except when she and Wheeler were jamming. That's when I went to the rookeries, hoping Len would find me there, but he never did. Mostly we'd go to Sunlit, Sal and I, to read and talk in the shade of the boulders.

Once, Freya and Wheeler wandered by, Kes sniffing along the wrack ahead of them. Wheeler reached for Freya and waltzed her towards the waves. She broke away when they were ankle-deep, and started to jog, looking back at him over her shoulder; they were both laughing, and he chased her, but she was too quick for him.

Sally said, 'Mr and Mrs Jones are *never* romantic.'

Hope caught in my throat. 'They often do things like that.' I wished saying it could make it true. I hadn't even told Sally I was adopted. Whenever I tried to, my throat tightened. That's what happened then. I opened my mouth and my throat clamped shut.

That night a huge, luminous moon edged into view and Albinoni's 'Adagio in G Minor' was playing in the lounge. Outside, the beaches were pale, cold reaches of dream. On Emita the gastropods and crabs would be creating tiny crisscrossing paths and flounder would be vacating their resting places, leaving hollows in the sand.

'Let's all go midnight walking,' I suggested. So we did. And somewhere on the island was Len, but his somewhere wasn't the same as ours because even though I looked, I didn't see his footprints.

~

I find the moment everything was torn asunder in Wheeler's ledger entry for 31 January 1985 and here it is in his own words:

Freya cornered me at Honeymoon Cove in the late afternoon. Had a line out; didn't hear her coming. She was suddenly there, and I could tell from the look of her that I was in for a battering.

Time to talk, she said, sitting on a boulder some distance away. Looked at the sand clinging to her feet. She has broad feet – not her best feature.

Reeled in, playing for time. Was feeling subdued, a battle the last thing I felt like. And then the line hooked on a submerged boulder. Tried coaxing it, manoeuvring it this way and that. The thing was so snared I couldn't work it free.

Just break it, she said irritably.

Yanked the line and as it snapped something oppressive lifted. Head felt clear at last. I'd had enough. If she wanted out, she could damn well have out.

Turned to face her. Looked at those large brown eyes, that beautiful face, and was not moved. The curve of her cheekbone and her mouth, once so generous in every respect, were ordinary beyond measure. Looked at that body I'd always found magnificent and discovered that I was impervious to its attractions. This was the woman who had lain down beside me night after night – I looked, and in that moment I did not care anymore for what I saw.

She said my name, but even her voice got lost in the sound of the surf. She sat there grappling for words, so I said it for her. There's bugger all left, is that it?

Yes, she said. Just, yes.

I told her she was free to leave. She did not move. I bent down and fiddled with some sinkers and when she asked what I planned to do, I told her it wasn't her business any longer.

She had the gall to tell me she still cared. Don't give me that crap, I said.

The bond between us had snapped. We didn't know the new rules. I stood up, faced the sea, the clarity gone. She quietly picked her way through the casuarinas and left me alone.

The meaninglessness. That word repeated in my head on the long walk home. This relationship had been my life, had been more than the sum of us. Buggered if I understand how it could have ended so pathetically.

Sitting here in the darkness, barely seeing the words I'm writing, barely holding the glass steady, wishing today had never happened. Just want to lie down spread-eagled on Mr Napper's cold stone floor.

I reread this entry several times. There's a lump in my throat. It takes a while before I wonder where Sally and I were at this moment when my life irreparably fell apart. It doesn't take me long to find this entry from Freya:

The conversation has been had. When I got home I lay down, wondering how we'll keep up appearances until we leave. There was a shell beside our bed, one Nicky had given me when we first arrived. I held it up to the light, turning it over slowly. I'd considered it ordinary, but when I looked at it closely, exquisite details emerged. There was dignity in its weathering. The tiny creases of its hinge entranced me. It had been washed by the sea, touched by fish, covered by sand, and tumbled by waves. And yet it had endured.

I held it in my hands, and in that moment felt peace settle on me.

That day, according to my journal, Sally and I were hatching a plan to circumnavigate the island. Wheeler could carry our gear in the *Cosmopolitan Leatherjacket.* We'd camp somewhere overnight. Great plan. She wanted to see the island. I wanted to see Len.

So, two days later, just before sunrise, with the night chill still emanating off the beach, we set off along Restless with Kes, walking barefoot down the sand, while hooded plovers on their flimsy little legs ran before the breeze, and when the sun rose the beaches stretched away from us in hues of silver and blue, across the isthmus and around Mount Naturaliste. The mountain and the islands were sharply defined against the morning light. The sky was mirrored in the swash.

We loped overland. Wheeler was on the water, and Freya was back at the house, writing this letter:

Dear Anneke,

I wasn't going to write again, but you need to know that this family you in effect created is over. I had imagined I'd feel free and elated, but I sat at the gulch and wept – for Wheeler, Nicky, and Kes; for Alison Blair, the Dead Lady of the Gulch; and those in the graves marked and unmarked, the First People and us, the latest. I wept because with the best of intentions things sometimes fall apart and because we had something so special once, and in breaking my promise to provide Nicky with love and security, I feel I've failed you, even though you, too, failed me.

I'm dreading telling Nicky. Wheeler is chaperoning the girls around the island while I pack up and steel myself.

Can't wait to get back to Hobart.

With love,

Freya

44

Bass Strait (Verloren Island) 1985

———————

Circumnavigation

WE WALKED ALONG EMITA and over Alveolar Ridge to Sam's Soak and then we took the Squally Cove route. I was looking out for Len, loitering on boulders and checking tidal pools.

'They're boring,' said Sally.

But by now I'd learned that everything on Verloren shimmers with beauty. I showed her some Neptune's necklace and explained how you often find warreners grazing on it and how their shells are everywhere in what Freya calls middens, but Len says are the places where the Old People loved gathering to eat.

We looked around for an easy route through the tussocks to Squally Cove. It was hot. We'd already had to wait for two tiger snakes to slither off our path.

At the cove we encountered a pair of seals. They lumbered into the water the moment they saw us, and on the high headland on the far side of Squally we sat down to regain our breath after the steep climb. The *Rising Moon* out of Whitemark cut her engine beneath the headland

and the men started setting their pots. Sometimes they'd shout something jokey up at us, and we'd try to be witty back. A small white dog ran along the deck barking at Kes.

Wheeler was a small dot south off the isthmus. We rolled over to eat our apples while the gulls hung on the breeze and the sea eagles soared on the morning thermals. 'I'm coming back as an eagle,' said Sally.

'Freya wants to be a swallow.' After a moment's reflection I added, 'I'm coming back as the wind.'

'You're a strange girl, but I like you,' said Sally. 'You can be my sister.'

'Really?'

'Why not? We both need one.'

'Sisters forever,' we vowed, and immediately the atmosphere shifted. Sally said quietly, 'If you're my sister you have to tell me what's upsetting you.'

I stared fixedly at the fishing boat, which had long ago started up its engine and was moving slowly down the coast.

'Nothing.' My throat tightened.

She gave my arm a little shake. 'There is though. You're moody and keep disappearing. Wheeler's not his usual happy self and Freya is over-friendly. You've been calling them by their first names. I feel like an intruder. It's uncomfortable.'

'I'm sorry.' I rubbed my throat.

She took a deep breath. 'Nicky, what's going on?'

A tear slid down my face.

'Remember how I said there were lots of reasons why you were coming to Verloren?'

I nodded.

'Your folks were having one last stab at getting things together again. *Everyone* knows that. It's all to do with Freya and her supervisor. You *had* to have known.'

I wanted to block my ears, squeeze my eyes shut. I saw Freya down on Sunlit again, smiling at him. I pressed my hands against my eyes, but it didn't stop me from crying.

She hugged me. 'Things will get better.' But the gulping noises I was making wouldn't stop.

'It's not just Freya,' she said. I turned to look at her. She was nibbling her lips. 'Wheeler flirts too much. He's fun, but he does.'

She saw my look of horror and hurriedly started joking about Kes, who was giving anxious little whines. He'd make as though he was getting up and then he'd sit down again and look at me, his head on one side. And she joked about Wheeler, who didn't seem to be getting any closer, probably because he was checking every metre of the coastline for potential diving spots.

'Parents are the pits,' said Sally. 'Even if you're not adopted. But who needs parents if they've got a sister? Cheer up, Nicky. Let's have some fun.'

'Who told you I'm adopted?' I said slowly.

'Freya,' said Sally. 'That day I went learning about plants with her because you weren't in the mood to do anything. I've been waiting for you to tell me yourself but apparently you were never going to. Freya only told me because she's so worried about you and thought I needed to know.'

'I *hate* her!'

'Well, at least she's got a brain,' said Sally. 'Not like Mrs Jones.'

Sally always knows more about my business than I do. And as I stomped off ahead of her, what I thought was, *Freya's betrayed me again. Parents should never be trusted.*

~

Wheeler caught up with us as we came over the dunes at Beagle Bay. Sally, not at all concerned about trespassing, had taken a good look at the birding hut. Len was nowhere to be seen.

Wheeler and Sally got stuck into some tucker, but I wasn't hungry. Then they had a swim, but I stayed lying on the sand. When he looked at me suspiciously, Sally covered up for me. Having a sister, even a tactless one, can be helpful. It deflects attention.

Pretty soon the effect of the sun overwhelmed Wheeler and he had a little snooze. Sally gave a sly smile and pulled a bottle of crimson nail polish out of her backpack, and pointing at the nail polish, and then at his toes, she passed me the bottle.

Painting his toenails red gave me a vindictive pleasure.

We wrote him a note in the sand and then we went around to the arch in Stumpy's Bay where we sat absorbing the secluded serenity of the cove and the pungent breath of the dark, wet cave.

'I could stay here forever.' Sally sang fragments of song as we carried on walking along the cool, blue swash.

In Nautilus Bay there's a series of granite boulders that look like gigantic misshapen buns, rather like at the gulch. We began clambering over them. Sally was ahead of me. When she reached the top, she gave a loud gasp. I looked up and saw her wobble. When I reached her, she clutched my arm tightly.

'A *corpse!*'

A body floated on the surface of the water.

'It's floating, Sally.'

'A *bloated* corpse!' She put her hand to her heart.

'You idiot. It's not bloated. It's Len.'

My sister recovered fast. She pulled me down behind a boulder and said, 'Those pebbles you've been filling your pockets with – let's throw them at him!'

She dug in my pocket, then threw one while I crouched behind a boulder.

He dived and stayed underwater a long time.

We waited. Again, he floated face-down.

Sally gave me a prod. I threw half-heartedly. I heard the patter of my tiny stones hitting water.

'Did you see his daggy bathers?'

'They're okay.'

The patter had barely ceased when a pebble pinged off our boulder. When we looked, he seemed not to have moved, but the water patterns had changed. Sally threw again.

Len turned around slowly and hurled another pebble at our boulder. Then he flipped over and did some lazy freestyle.

'Let's go down and say hello,' she said.

Kes was still on the sand behind us, sniffing at a dead penguin.

We dropped down onto the beach and she shouted, 'What's the water like?' as he turned and swam a lazy breaststroke back in.

He gave a thumbs-up. I thought he smiled at me, but Sally said, 'Time to get convivial. See the smile he flashed me?' which was disappointing. On the beach, in the sunlight, with Sally's company, the seabirds gliding and diving, and geese honking away in the distant tussocks, it felt very different from the night on the beach. All I could think was that before the day was done, he'd be kissing Sally.

She walked into the water, flicking back her long blonde hair, and then she swam out into the deep water where Len was doing some show-off bursts of different strokes. I could see immediately that she would dazzle him.

I waded into the water and Len and Sally broke off talking.

'You've got sharp eyes,' I said to Len when I reached them. A truly, pathetically unimaginative comment.

'You've got loud voices.'

I looked past him, as though deeply fascinated by something way out at sea and we all trod water, bobbing over the incoming swells, while Sally chatted. Then she swam back towards the beach to where Kes was lying with our daypacks.

'You melt into the island,' I said. 'I thought we'd bump into you once in a while.'

'I've been around.'

'Like where?'

'About. Seen you plenty.'

I sank beneath the waves to cool down my face. I hoped he hadn't seen me dancing on the beach when I thought seabirds were my only audience.

'Sounds like your boat,' said Len, so I told him about our circumnavigation.

We bobbed over a swell and he dived again. When he came up he blew out a great arc of water. 'This beach is getting crowded. Might leave youse to it.' So disappointing. I said we wouldn't be hanging around, we just needed to catch up with Wheeler, then Sally, swimming back towards us, asked where he was camping.

He pointed with his chin. 'Beagle Bay.'

Wheeler cut back the motor and as he puttered up to us, Sally and I grabbed the sides and hitched a ride up to the beach.

There were some crayfish in a bucket. 'Good blokes, those fishers,' he said.

He invited Len to have a barbie with us that evening. Len shook the water out of his hair, cast a critical eye over the crays and said, 'Might get some abalone.'

Water slopped in the bottom of the boat and the smell of fuel hung in the air as we dragged the dinghy up the beach. 'Where's a good place for us to camp tonight, d'ya reckon?' Wheeler asked.

Len scratched at a mozzie bite on his cheek and shrugged. 'Good spot about an hour's walk from here.'

Wheeler told us he'd brought a bat and ball and that it was time for a quick game-and-picnic stop.

We played. We ate. Len kept darting looks at Wheeler's toenails and Wheeler kept giving him puzzled little glances. I thought Len would disappear at the first opportunity, but he didn't. He and Wheeler went diving and came back with abalone, and Len was talking about the island, telling him how his family came birding here every year. I heard him say, 'My mum was birding when I was born,' and he pointed back towards Beagle Bay. Then Wheeler said, 'That's why you like coming here?' and, shifting uncomfortably, Len said, 'Just so happens I've time on my hands.'

'How come?' Wheeler asked.

'Thought I'd give school a miss, didn't I?'

'Hey, mate,' said Wheeler. 'I did the same thing. Tossed it in for a bit of this and that. Next thing I know, I'm back doing my A levels.'

'Can't see the point. I'd rather do a bit of fishing for my keep.'

'Mate!' He scuffed the sand with his foot – and *that's* when he noticed his toes. He said, 'Well, that explains a lot! I'll get you for this, young ladies! You'll have cost me my reputation around these islands.' Then he turned to Len and said, 'It pays to stay on the alert around your local sheilas. Their sense of humour isn't exactly profound,' and after that he carried on talking to him about why he should hang in at school and the dodgy future of the fishing industry. He didn't know that I was never going back to school again either.

Sally sat down beside Len and started asking him questions. I could tell he was uncomfortable. I saw that he'd reached into his pocket and was rolling a pebble in his hands. It looked a lot like the one he'd given me.

Wheeler squinted at the sun and said, 'We're going to have to make tracks, comrades. Last chance to say *yes* to a boat ride,' and when Sally said, 'Let's camp here,' he shook his head. 'On we go,' he said, getting up. Then he told Len there'd be room in the boat; maybe they could do more diving.

Len looked at his feet. 'Yeah, why not?' he said.

Kes was also keen on a ride. He stood in the bow, nose held high, sniffing the breeze, mouth a huge grin of delight, his tail charting circles. We watched them disappear and then we set off.

'Wheeler's not quite himself,' said Sally.

It was true. I'd also caught him with a sombre look on his face when he thought he wasn't being observed. Another argument, I supposed, but I didn't share that with Sally.

We were tired and grumpy by the time we came upon them at Hannah's Hope Bay. We'd walked fast, determined to do it quickly and we did, but the tide had been in, which had meant headland climbing, bush bashing and tussock leaping, and our arms and legs were scratched from fighting antagonistic vegetation.

Hannah's Hope has a tiny freshwater creek and a delicious curve of perfectly white sand. Bluebottles, kelp and cuttlebones dotted the wrack line. Wheeler and Len were on a reef at the far end, and we couldn't see Kes anywhere.

'Probably fell out the boat.' Sally threw her pack down beside it.

'That's not funny.' I opened my water bottle. 'And I don't think we need more abalone, if that's what they're doing,' but what I was thinking was that from the moment we'd declared ourselves sisters, Sally had become incredibly annoying.

~

We sat around the fire in the dark. Len relaxed. He talked about the islands while I stroked Kes and stared up at the stars. He knew a bit about them, it turned out, and explained how some indicate the changing seasons, others foretell the weather and still others are navigational. He said his people call the Southern Cross the Stingray. I could feel the mountain at my back and the steady stillness of the casuarinas silently communicating, their roots entangled and descending by tiny increments down through the soil and around the subterranean rocks.

Sally and Wheeler spread music out into the night. He pulled out his harmonica and sang Eric Clapton's 'Promises' three times, but the third time there was a little crack in his voice. 'Sore throat,' he said, and left the singing to Sally.

The breeze was sweeping lightly over the beach. The waves were breaking quietly as the tide went out. I closed my eyes, already missing Verloren. No more Bert, no more Len, although, the more I watched him watching Sally, the more I realised that I probably didn't care about him after all. Mostly, I sat there aching, because of Freya and that stupid Steve. I wanted to cry suddenly, looking across the flames at Wheeler smiling at Sally as they made music, the fire lighting up his face and the darkness casting shadows on it. How, exactly, could Freya prefer that idiot to the idiot she already had?

By the time we reached the lighthouse the next day, I felt as though Len might as well have been Wheeler's son. Even Kes had been all over him because he threw good sticks, and he'd obviously fallen for Sally. I felt like a shadow on the sand, there but not there, just walking, aware subconsciously that our days as a family were over.

45

Peramangk and Kaurna Country (Adelaide Hills) 2000

Bass Strait (Verloren Island) 1985

____

Bittersweet

EACH TIME I ENTER Freya's room there seems less of her there. The presence of the oxygen, the shadows closing in around us, imbue her room with finality. Amber demands some attention, but mostly I sit, absorbing Freya's face, committing it to memory.

Steve enters with a cup of tea. 'It's drizzling, but I'm going for a walk anyway,' he whispers, touching her lightly on the hand.

I start to read, then realise Freya is gazing at me.

'Are you all right?'

'I'm going to die soon,' she whispers.

'Do you feel ready?' I reach for her hand.

'Resigned to it.' I watch her drop back into sleep.

There are frogs chorusing outside. Giles bleats. I can't decide what's stronger – the palpable presence of death or the sense of myself as a child, ghosting the present, but I feel a sudden urge to phone Arno.

'I've got a bad case of cognitive dissonance. I need your advice.'

'You really don't, Nicky.'

'I'm scared to be here.'

'Does Freya need you?'

'I promised I'd stay.'

'So?'

'I step up?'

'Anything else?'

'I sent my resignation email.'

'Excellent! Let's catch up for a celebratory drink when you're back in Sydney.'

'*Ciao*, Arno. *Baci.*'

~

Later, after doing some editing, I collapse into bed, allowing memories of the past to carry me into sleep, considering different angles of the day on the island when Freya cornered me at the kitchen table for a 'little chat', playing with her coffee mug, saying that they'd decided it was important I returned to school. I had a rolled-up magazine in my hand and my eye was following a fly that was droning around the kitchen. I began leaping around, trying to kill it.

'This is important! Listen! You, Sally, and I will be leaving the day after tomorrow. We'll be staying with Nan and we'll take things from there.'

As usual, I hadn't been consulted. I wanted to go, but not with her. And what did she mean, *we'll take things from there?* The fly landed on the edge of the table, and I thwacked it with every iota of strength I had.

Maggots spilled out. I leaned over and flicked some off the table with my finger.

'That's *disgusting!*' Her teeth were clenched.

I slowly flicked off the rest. She was obviously waiting for me to ask about Wheeler. *You can suffer*, I thought. *I'm not doing you any favours.*

She told me anyway. She said he wanted to stay on Verloren, but she knew he'd soon return to Hobart. She said mean things about his 'grandiose plans'. I wanted to block my ears. Instead, I stared at the stain the fly had left and wished I hadn't killed it.

She cleared her throat. I couldn't see her face. I was only conscious of her red skirt and her hand, clutching her stomach. I hoped she was in pain. Out of the corner of my eye I saw Kes quietly slink outside with a worried expression.

In a little rush she told me that she and Wheeler were separating. I didn't want to care, but for a few moments, all I was aware of was the gurgling river noise the fridge was making as the rest of the world retreated and then I heard myself say in a casual voice that sounded far away, 'Well, I've decided I'm not going back to school.'

'You love school and you are.'

'I prefer learning *independently*, especially after having such a *fantastic* teacher. And in any case, all my friends will have forgotten me by now.'

She sighed down her nose.

'Besides, you're not my parent.' And I stalked outside.

Kes was anxious, his body hunched. I hugged him and took him to the gulch and we sat on Whale Rock. I had one arm around him, one hand holding my pebble. 'I'll make my own decisions,' I told him. 'They've got *no right* to boss me.'

The sea blurred. I wished I didn't have to suffer those two heinous adults any longer, I wished I'd brought a tissue, and I hated the pain that was ripping through the centre of my heart.

~

Sally was all tact as usual: 'Can't you be happy', and, 'Honestly, you're so morbid, I don't know why I came here'. (She was definitely not my kind of sister.)

We stormed off in opposite directions and when I returned she was sickly sweet, which meant that Freya had filled her in. I *hated* the world. I *hated* everyone. I especially *hated* Freya and her horrible boyfriend.

That evening Sally played bridge with her, but I went to the light-house to find Wheeler.

He was standing with a whisky, listening to 'How's the World Treating You?' It made me want to cry.

'Got nothing up here to offer you, Nicky old thing.'

I perched on the table and he patted my knee, and I told him about the conversation I'd had with Freya that morning. The more I talked the more choked up I got. When he squeezed my knee I started to sniff, so he passed me his hanky. It was still light outside and there were alto-cumulus clouds tessellating a corner of the sky where a crescent moon was waning.

'Nicky,' he said, staring into his glass, and my heart fell. 'Freya wants the best for you and so do I,' and when I interrupted, he put his hand across my mouth. It stank of bait.

He went on about how I couldn't leave school yet. 'That's not us telling you that; that's the law and common sense. You're not sixteen yet and you're far too bright to pack it in because you're upset with us.' He said that he'd like me to stay on the island; he wished we both could, but that even though schooling me had been fun, I needed friends and Freya had 'doubts that were reasonable'.

I'd expected more support from him. 'Another thing,' he said, but I turned my face away. He turned it back so that I had to look at him.

'She's tired of me, Nicky. She's sick of being shacked up with an old bum.'

'Don't call yourself that!' I said, looking down. I noticed that on his toes, the polish was still gleaming.

'Aye, but you know what I mean. I'd be happy to spend the rest of my days fishing and reading, but Freya wants to carve a little niche for herself in the academic world.'

He drained the last of his whisky and I noticed that his hand was shaking. He went on talking about how she couldn't turn him into something he's not, and he said, 'I'd rather sit down with blokes like Bert or your friend Len and have a yarn.'

'Len's not my friend.'

'He's your friend, Nicky, believe me.'

How did he know that? I didn't ask.

Then he said, 'Sun's beginning to set.' The horizon was pink.

A small cloud floated alone near the mountain peak and the valleys and gullies were deep purple. There were swans flying over the isthmus.

He patted me on the back. 'You'll pull through, Nicky. I've got faith in you. You won't let me down.'

Everything seemed loud and crashing, so I went to bed early, and I tried to sleep through the terrible pain of it all, my pebble in one hand, the bird-girl looking down at me, her wings wide open, and the breeze blowing through the open window.

~

When Sally and I took our last island swim, Len appeared over the dunes. I shared the shade of a boulder with him, watching her swim lengths along the beach.

'I'll look after your old man while you're away. He can come and do some birding with me and my mates.' His feet were touching my feet and Sally was right – his bathers were daggy, but every time I saw him he looked more handsome.

'I hope he doesn't. I hate birding.'

'You seen it?'

'You don't have to see it to know you don't like it.'

'Does that mean you don't like me either?'

'Because you're a birder?'

'Yeah.'

I took a deep breath. 'I *really* like you, Len,' I said slowly. 'It's just a pity you like birding.'

He grinned at me, and his finger trailed along the sweaty underside of my leg and then he leaned over and kissed me. 'If I'm here when you come back,' he said. 'I'll show you another cave on the mountain.'

'Thank you,' I said primly. 'That would be extremely nice.'

Sally would have thought up a slick comment – especially if she'd noticed what Len had just done, but she was still face-down, powering through the water.

I was kind of relieved about that.

46

Bass Strait (Verloren Island) 1985

Mouheneenner Country (Hobart) 1985

Too Much to Bear

SALLY WAS FIRST INTO the plane. Kes intuited the situation. He jumped on me, pushing me backwards.

'Please let him come too,' I begged, teary-eyed, but they were adamant. I hugged him, inhaling the scent of his coat, savouring his generous licks, and when Dad kissed Freya goodbye it was the saddest I'd ever seen him look. *Her* mood frustrated me. She gave Kes a quick cuddle and couldn't climb into the plane fast enough, but I held Dad's hand until Dorothy started up the plane and he closed the door. And then I kept my eyes on the two of them – Kes, whining with anxiety and Wheeler's hair fiercely salted together, his scuffed clothes, his sad, dimpled smile. My complex feelings for Wheeler and concern for Kes got drawn into my love for Verloren and its animals, plants, and rocks and as the island streamed past, the lump in my throat was a boulder. Within minutes the island fell away, transforming Mount Naturaliste into something oddly diminutive – and then it slipped completely out

316

of sight, along with the communities of animals that we had shared that little space with. All the way to Launceston, I was still on Verloren in spirit, so that in the plane, with its engine making a loud and steady hum, I felt the same sense of dislocation and emptiness I'd felt when we'd arrived. As I looked down at other tussocky islands passing beneath us, sadness enveloped me. In all that time we hadn't visited any of them and now the opportunity was probably gone forever.

I saw the Tasmanian mainland differently as we flew over it, as if a skin had been peeled off my eyes. The land was wounded and there were monstrous scars where forests had recently been. All the disconnected individual actions of people had coalesced into a terrible mutilation and I understood that we were a gigantic parasite killing the beauty that nourished and sustained us. A tiredness overcame me as we walked across the airstrip to Marti's car and when we joined the rush of traffic, of people hurtling along in pursuit of materialistic goals, I longed to be back there, away from the mania.

We stayed at Nan's and I retreated to my bedroom. The world seemed full of anxious overactivity and ignorant destruction. The damage that we, a so-called family, had inflicted upon each other, and the damage I'd seen inflicted on the land seemed pretty much the same thing, and I felt *so* unexpectedly homesick for Verloren. I'd lie in the hammock dreaming I was there again or I stayed in bed and didn't get up at all.

47

Mouheneenner Country (Hobart) 1985

—————

Headwinds

BACK IN HOBART, FREYA'S happiness depressed me. I was convinced she was lying every time she left the house. Once when I was peeling oranges in the kitchen, she poked her head around the door. 'I'm just going out,' she said.

'You're always "just going out",' I snapped, and so she invited me around to Steve's house. 'There's Wheeler alone on Verloren,' I hissed, 'and you're wasting your time with that *creep*!' I gripped the fruit so tightly the juice ran down my arm and the temptation to throw it at her was huge. I was upstairs when the front door slammed. I opened my window and screamed, 'I hope you *never* come back!'

Old Mr Gromsky next door looked up from his gardening, open-mouthed. I flopped down on my bed, put a pillow over my face and wept.

Sally kept coaxing me to go to the beach with her, and Sam Doody asked me out. I knew he wouldn't ask me again because I hardly spoke in response. At school even Mrs Porter had turned her attention to some

318

other little star. I rarely went to school anyway.

Wheeler sent me reports on the wildlife. He'd been seeing great rafts of moonbirds and there'd been a snake in the house. He sent Freya a driftwood carving. He'd included a small wooden sculpture for me, a Bert creation.

'He has a poetic soul,' I told her, and she agreed.

~

I was not the only one doing it tough. Wheeler's ledgers were testimony to his state of mind during February and March, and it seems appropriate to let him speak for himself.

They've gone. Watched the plane until it disappeared. Path back up felt like Bein Nibheis. Dog every bit as miserable. Came around the front of the house and there on the steps sat Len.

Took the boat and went fishing. Polish still clinging to my nails. Dog looked sideways whenever our eyes threatened to meet.

Bad luck to fish when you're downhearted. Didn't catch a thing, but Len came up to the house and we shared the last of Freya's bread. Never eaten so slowly, lingered over every crumb …

… Dorothy drops letters from Nicky, never anything from Freya. She wants to know when she can return, wants me back in Hobart. Mentioned some Doody bloke; had the grace not to tell Len. Sat on the veranda with pen and paper. Don't know what to say, I told him.

Tell her about the whale, he says.

But Gunther can have the baby whale. Can find it strolling the beach with his daughter. Instead, I write about the dolphins surfing.

Keep forgetting to feed the dog. Len brings fish heads. Kes would starve rather than complain, but I watch him nudge Len's ankle then look up at me mournfully …

Been sitting on the front veranda, day in and day out, looking at the mountain, indifferent to my suffering. These days I'm haunted by Freya's smile, her hips when she danced, the way she threw back her head and laughed so deep you'd swear it began somewhere down around her pelvis.

Len drops by in the afternoon. Sometimes we set a pot. Sometimes he brings me fish and Bert has dropped off supplies. Suggested I join him on his service run to the outer islands. Considered a weekend in Whitemark would do me good, so that's where we've been, the dog and I; getting to know the region and living the fast life on Flinders Island.

Asked him to try and rustle up some interest in my tourism venture, see if one of the better-heeled farmers will come in as a backer, but Flinders isn't exactly a metropolis of big spenders.

I haven't the motivation to write. Have half a mind to drown my manuscript or donate the pages to the birds.

Saw a stranger on Emita the other day. Mind's playing tricks – for a moment I thought it was Anneke. She crops up when I least expect her to, claiming to have known me in another life when I was the Pope and she St. Joan, accusing me of stealing her dreams, disrupting my sleep with strange poetry. Wild dreams I've been having, and always Anneke in them, squatting in a smoky cave like Pythia …

… Woke to a strong northerly, this morning of the 14ᵗʰ March. About midday we noticed smoke behind the mountain. Len figured it was coming from his old campsite and went off to investigate. Was sitting on the veranda come ten p.m. and Len hadn't shown. Next day – no smoke, no Len. Returned this evening. Said the penguin colony near Boat Harbour has been burnt out. Some men were loitering. Waved tinnies at him.

Better not tell Nicky, said Len. He's been sleeping in her room. Says it makes a change from his tent. Says I need the company, that the dog needs him. Dog is getting somewhat lean.

Should we climb that mountain? I suggest.

Sure, says Len.

Maybe tomorrow.

~

When I returned to Verloren for the Easter holidays, it could have been Gunther Berg greeting me on Emita, and I noticed Dorothy's uncertainty about leaving me there. Wheeler's clothes were a mess, and his hair was long and wind-tangled. He'd talk but conclude mid-sentence, his accent more pronounced. He'd look past me, as if at images impressed against the sky, and he spent much of his time in the lighthouse, drinking. Len told me Uncle Arthur had come over and hadn't appreciated the mess around the house.

'The solitude's no good for him,' Len said.

Wheeler seemed to have run out of cash. He had barely any food and tussocks had reclaimed the vegie patch.

'I eat like Gunther eats,' he said. 'I'm working on my self-sufficiency.'

But it was *less* than the Straitsmen ate because they'd had pigs and chooks, successful gardens and a more bountiful sea.

He'd ask occasional questions about Freya but couldn't bring himself to mention Steve's name, which was fine by me. It bothered him that we were feuding, and her absence was a presence in itself. She might as well have been sitting in the room with us.

'He needs to leave,' Len repeated like a mantra, and like a mantra Wheeler insisted that he was there for the long haul.

But it wasn't all bad. He'd sold an article to a magazine. He let me cut his hair and he promised me he'd stop drinking. He said his novel had taken a direction he hadn't anticipated and was more about a woman and her child now – Gunther was fading out of the plot.

We played card games and scrabble, went walking out to fishing spots so he could get us dinner. When it rained, Len and I retreated to my room, the rain slamming against the windows, the fire consuming too much wood, while we explored the geographies of each other's bodies. We were two school absconders wondering how to move forward in a world that seemed careless of our interests. Once, though, sitting in the kitchen, he saw the map of the island and took the pen I was holding.

'*No*, Len! Don't cross out all the names!' We scuffled to grab possession of the map and it ripped.

'This island was once full of different names. The true names. Many, many more names,' he said, fending me off, swiftly replacing them with the names his family knew the island's features by. Then he said something like, '*You* know what it's like to feel stolen. So does the island. You whitefellas look at the land and see beauty. We look at Country and feel its pain. You wonder why I come here? Because Country and I need each other to heal, so let's put respect back on it and give it names that mean something.'

He thinks we are a culture of thieves and ticked off why on his fingers – the murders and massacres, stolen women and children, stolen and broken Country, lost and broken language, lost and broken cultural knowledge, stolen bones, stolen health and happiness, so much that was known about Country – Sea Country and Sky Country too – gone.

'I'm sorry,' I said, but words felt inane against the accumulation of all that agony that made my own seem pitiful.

The next day, in better weather, we went walking with the map, Len telling me about the island from his perspective. Listening to the island, I was learning, was like being in conversation with someone you thought you knew only to discover that was just their public face.

A boatload of birders – Len's family and friends – had arrived shortly after me. It meant I didn't see much of him. When he packed his gear and said he'd be heading down to the shed, we walked with him, but only as far as Squally Cove.

The adult moonbirds had left to fly north to the Arctic in April, before I'd arrived. There only seemed to be bewildered-looking chicks left at the rookeries, as betrayed as I felt I'd been by Freya, Wheeler, and Anneke.

As for the Beagle Bay rookery, the closest I got was the headland, a place I could never go without remembering Wheeler and Christa cavorting in the waves. This was where I'd meet Len, but it was also close enough to see people silhouetted against the sky and the small, dark bodies of the juvenile birds dangling from poles carried horizontally across their shoulders.

'Come up and say hello,' Len invited, but I declined.

The birders worked Sapphire City too, but I kept away. I went alone to watch the chicks emerge from their burrows after dark. They wandered around, stretching their wings. Some entered the cold night water. Much hungrier now they weren't being fed, they were preparing to depart on the next following breeze, kicking off their first northward migration. I hoped an adult or two had stayed behind to guide them.

At Honeymoon Cove, Len and I sat beneath the casuarinas trading life stories. He told me that most of his family were from the Bay of Fires area, now mostly living on Cape Barren Island; and in between talking we fooled around in the sea.

My passion for Len gave the holiday a fierce intensity that only a visit from Bert disrupted. He was keeping a weather eye out on Wheeler too, and one magnificent day he'd dropped by to offer us a Furneaux cruise.

On Goose Island we found a huge container of fabric, balancing on top of a massive boulder, hurled up by stormy seas. On Badger Island Len showed me graves and on Vansittart, he showed me the rusting hulk of the *Farsund* stuck high and dry on a reef. We didn't put foot on

Babel Island. There were too many snakes watching us from the rocks and bushes.

Len came to say goodbye the day I left for Hobart. I said I'd be back in June and he promised to visit but by then I'd come to understand that it was less painful to have no expectations at all. When Dad assured me that next time I'd have his undivided attention, I laughed.

A cold front arrived. We weren't sure Dorothy would be able to land because of the wind, but she enjoyed the challenge. Dad held me tightly. He cupped my face in his hands and made me promise three times to return in June. I was keen. It's when the young moonbirds finally follow the adults north, on a following southwesterly wind.

'None of your acrobatics,' he said to Dorothy, who was keen to get going, and when he gave me a final hug he whispered in my ear, 'Give my love to Freya,' while slipping a note in my pocket. His eyes were damp – 'must be coming down with the flu,' he said.

As we veered away for Launceston in that big, bumpy wind, Dad stood beneath us, slowly waving his hat, a small dark figure on a pale beach on an island at the edge of the world. When I could no longer see him, I opened the note. It was the first verse of the old Irish blessing he often used to sing to me, the one that begins, 'may the road rise to meet you, may the wind be always at your back'.

I keep it in my wallet still.

~

Freya met me at Launceston airport. A few hours later, as we drove across the bridge into Hobart, she told me that she'd moved in with

Steve and she'd decorated one of the rooms especially for me. Bitter words were spoken. I stayed on with Nan, declined to see Freya on any account and buried myself in books, wrote long letters to my dad and Len, and avoided school, almost completely.

48

Peramangk and Kaurna Country (Adelaide Hills) 2000

Suffused With Light

OUTSIDE, THE ELM TREE is suffused with light, the leaves shimmering in the breeze. The flowers in the vase rustle. There is pollen on the tabletop and a play of light and shadow across the carpet; patterns forming and falling apart. In the distance, I can hear the swish of wheels on bitumen as they speed purposefully along other people's lifelines.

Time has stilled in the bedroom. Amber is curled up beside my mother, emitting small snores. I'm not always sure when Freya is sleeping. I think she sometimes closes her eyes to be alone with her thoughts. It gives me time to observe her and reflect. Sometimes I can do this with serenity. At other times the anticipation of death frightens me. I grew up a scrawny child in the shadow of her beauty. Now the delicate wrinkles etched on her face are storylines marking the passage of time. She has grandeur. Her eyes have grace.

Until the shock of her diagnosis, I'd abhorred her touch. Now, with our hands joined, there is a feeling I have not encountered before – that the past, the present and the future are poised in equilibrium in this room.

It lies beyond the reach of language, dwarfing us. For far too long I've failed to imagine the world from her viewpoint. I need to *deeply* apologise for judging her so harshly, for all the many ways in which I've let her down. But it doesn't feel like the right time when I help her tackle a tiny dinner, and later, that dinner rejected, I simply sit beside her, conscious that she is receding from us into small, tentative dances with Death.

Steve is playing 'Deep Peace', the Irish blessing that Wheeler used to occasionally sing to us under the stars and it returns Verloren to me, so that the waves and breeze, the midnight constellations and the quiet earth feel present in this room, potent with departure.

The whole day has felt impregnated with a sense of Freya's decline, intensifying our foreboding. Each time this happens we brace ourselves for death's high tide, but she will not let go.

In my pocket I can feel my touchstone's steady weight. I get up to write her a note beneath the apple tree, watching the flowers lean into the sunlight, before putting pen to paper. When I finally do, it's simple to admit regret for holding her responsible for problems I should have been able to sort out sooner myself.

'I've forgiven you both completely,' I write. 'And I apologise for years of self-centred behaviour. I love you.'

And then I seal the envelope and ask Steve to read it to her when she wakes, adding that the note is for him as well.

~

As afternoon softens into evening I go back out into the garden. Voices drift on the breeze. Swallows flit above a neighbour's dam, but the lorikeets are uncannily quiet, and there's an unusual stillness as I pick the fragrant flowers Mum loves best – jasmine and the deep red roses that grow against the stone wall, and vibrant bottlebrush for their colour. I pause beside the apple tree listening for Giles, but he doesn't bleat.

Inside, Amber has moved progressively up the bed to nestle near Mum's pillow, and Steve, never a superstitious man, has chosen to read a sign into that.

Later we light the bedroom with candles and Steve holds one of her hands and I hold the other, and Carla is with us. There's a changed mood in the quiet room. Mum has decided not to wait for tomorrow's morphine. She wants to go before the doctor arrives in the morning. She's quite clear that she will. We know it. Death knows too. Her presence in the room is tangible, but she's no longer frightening; she feels like a protector.

As the night progresses Mum draws into herself and appears to be sleeping. We watch the colour fade from her face and her cheeks slowly sink. We hear her breathing slow. Each breath becomes compelling. Steve gets up briefly to put on, quietly, 'The Gadfly', and when he returns he comments on how cold her fingers have become. Her feet are cold too, and the coldness climbs in her through the night as we sit and listen to her breathing grow fainter. Later, it's as if Barber himself is conducting his 'Adagio for Strings' very softly and with immense feeling. The violins soar and soar, high and pure, and the music, though quiet, is ethereal and all around us like warm sunlight. Looking at the pearl ring on Mum's finger I remember that drowned violin. We slip her rings off, stroke her fingers.

Freya probably can't hear the music, Carla says. More likely she'll feel caught up in a wild wind. For a while her breathing is raspy, and then it seems almost to cease. 'I love you,' I murmur. 'I love you.' And it's of no concern to me that she can't hear, or that tears roll down my face unabated because Steve and Carla are equally moved. As the music dies away, so does Mum, peacefully. Three long exhalations, and then I hear Carla say quietly, 'She's passed away now, but she's still here with us,' and I know that Death and my mother are in an embrace, slowly dancing down a dark river on the outgoing tide. Like sublime notes that have faded yet still seem suspended in the air, a certain presence fills the room. We sit there, the three of us, our faces shining with tears, recalling Mum, talking to her, stroking her, until we are quite sure that she is with us no more but has taken flight, leaving her body behind her like a peeled skin, Amber curled upon her breast.

~

The fabric of reality has ripped, leaving a vast space that Mum once filled. Everything feels precarious, fragile and untethered. Together Steve and I navigate the new terrain the days lay out before us – terrain that looks the same but feels substantially altered. And somehow we cope.

After the funeral, after their friends have left, we sit in his study reminiscing. He puts on Rachmaninov's 'Rhapsody on a Theme of Paganini', and it adds a searing quality to our sense of loss, and a fragile and exquisite cohesiveness to the world about me as he quietly emphasises how he, too, regretted our paths didn't cross more, but they both understood my antagonism, especially regarding Wheeler. 'So I can't thank you enough for the kindness of your note,' he says.

Our eyes are damp when we smile at each other. Freya's death has filled me with a nostalgic lethargy, dislocating me in some subtle way from the world around me, leaving me feeling that I'm staring at Death the hunter, across an empty expanse, no elders standing before me as protection.

49

Mouheneenner Country (Hobart) 1985

Low Tide

IT WAS ONLY A month after my trip to Verloren that the phone rang in Nan's hallway late one night. I paid it no attention. It was in retrospect that I recalled her sombre tone and the long pause before she dialled a number (Freya's) and spoke in a hushed voice.

They didn't tell me until the next day that there'd been a tragedy on Verloren. Freya came to the house. They sat me down and told me Dad was missing; that he might still be found.

But as I lay on my bed and wept, I heard her telling Mr Gromsky that they'd found a flipper at the Tinman's Teeth reef. Nan couldn't calm me down. A doctor had to sedate me, and while I slept, Freya and Steve flew to Verloren.

As well as being overwhelmed by grief, my anger at Freya and Steve became an all-consuming rage. *If it hadn't been for them, none of this would have happened*, was the way I rationalised it. And, *he had no right to go with her to Verloren; I should have. I'm the one who knew best where he dived.* I castigated myself for having kept quiet about the changes I'd noticed in Dad. I'd thought he was improving. He had talked about building a yacht again and sailing the world. He was thinking about his future. I'd persuaded myself to believe him.

This secret crippled me. My emotions made me unbearable. I don't know how Nan coped, but she remained patient and loving, absolutely.

Talking to Steve about this period, he told me that Freya had lived with the concern that it might not have been an accident. But given Wheeler dived alone, he thought it most likely he had drowned, perhaps by putting himself in a more dangerous situation than usual. This was the simplest explanation and therefore the most likely. He opened his hand, palm up. 'It's no clearer today than it was back then.'

I was silent, twisting the pearl ring I'd slipped onto my finger, wishing I'd had the opportunity to talk it over with Len.

Steve said, 'I did feel quite terrible about your father, you know. And you mustn't underestimate how difficult that time was for Freya. She blamed herself for his death and for your pain and she was acutely conscious of the difficulties the two of you were encountering getting along.'

'But as a child you're only conscious of loss. It takes time to develop a mature perspective, to understand the imperfections of life.' As I defended myself, the memory of abandonment rushed in on me, the sound of feet running down a dark road, a river close beside me.

'Of course. It was traumatic. These things can hold you back.'

What lay unspoken between Steve and me was the move they'd made to Canberra, and as though reading my thoughts, he cleared his throat and said, 'You know, when we were offered positions on the mainland, she felt she had to leave if she was to put everything behind her. More importantly, she believed that her presence was hampering your recovery. You might not know this, but your grandmother thought so too.'

They'd left Hobart a year after Dad's accident, if that's what it was. My hostile behaviour, I'd believed, had chased Freya away and I'd hated her for not persevering with me, for not meeting the challenge of loving me. I'd hated her for being happy with Steve when I felt emotionally ripped apart. I was glad to see them gone. I didn't say goodbye and each night, for months to come, I had visions of Dad's body entangled in kelp, rolling in the sea, beached on rocks, a flippered foot above the waves. Once I dreamed he'd been found washed up in Gullet Cove, but although I waited for news, none ever came.

Sometimes I was convinced I glimpsed him on the street – crossing the road, disappearing around a corner – and I'd rush to catch up with him, only to find it was a stranger. I made up stories to explain his disappearance – he'd sailed away and one day he'd write, or I might bump into him somewhere out in the world.

His disappearance haunts me still. I like to think that these alternatives are possible.

'Life sometimes feels like an endless pathway of mistakes,' Steve murmured. 'Looking back, you see how much better you could have handled things.' He began talking about Mum again and I gave a brief smile. I was watching welcome swallows at play in the sky above the elm tree, and remembering her standing beneath the lighthouse, her long dress whipping around her legs while they dipped and dived.

~

Without a sense of direction, I could do with Dad's compass right now. I cross my legs and listen to a bronzewing's mournful call. A little while ago, finally getting through to Arno, I'd launched into a discourse on my state of mind and all the delving into the past I'd been doing – 'mostly thanks to you,' I'd acknowledged.

I take an afternoon drive to Glenelg Beach and walk the swash, thinking about the grand sweep of Emita – the abundant birds and crustacea, how Freya jogged it, Kes raced it, and Dorothy landed her plane on it and I'm struck by one of those small moments of clarity – I'm going to ask Sally to go back to Verloren with me. I need to close that circle.

50

Mouheneenner Country (Hobart) 1984

Bass Strait (Flinders and Verloren Islands) 2000

Jewels and Binoculars

As we begin our descent into Hobart, the porthole fills with the greens and purples of the Tasmanian landscape, yellow fingers of land interleaved with magical sea, and rising above the curves and contours of the island and the city, the dark, snow-flecked bulk of the mountain. A glimpse of the river, that drowned and rifted valley that I'd walked with Mum, exploring beaches and smuggling coves. I can vividly hear Freya telling me how so much of the island was carved and scraped by glaciers, about the little mountain streams that still flow off Mount Nelson and the mountain, but are buried alive beneath suburban streets now, all but forgotten yet ever present.

It's a magnificent day and a handful of hours after landing, after a meal with Marti and Janet, Sally and I go to Nan's house. Strangers live there now. They rent from me.

'But their lease is nearly up,' I tell Sally.

'Aha! Perfect timing?'

There's a swing near the apricot tree and a child flying back and forth like a pendulum. The goldfish pond and the birches are still there, and a Burmese cat lies in the middle of the plumbago that cascades over the fence.

We drive up the narrow, winding mountain road, through rain-forest, alongside small waterfalls and then through the low alpine forest of sculptural snow gums to the summit and linger in the freezing cold to absorb the place we both love most – this city, this mountain, the estuary and Ralphs Bay, the peninsulas, hills, Betsey Island and Storm Bay – agreeing that there can be no more beautiful city on the planet. We reminisce about sailing with her parents and wonder where friends are now as we run towards the warmth of the car.

'I met Len again, recently,' I tell Sally, and as we both laugh at the improbability, I explain how in May friends and I had walked with hundreds of thousands of others across the Sydney Harbour Bridge, the wave of goodwill breaking across the waterway a resounding 'yes' to reconciliation, in one of those rare moments when living felt enriched by an upwelling of cohesion, inclusion and the possibility of a more open-hearted Australia.

As we'd walked off the bridge, swept up by a surge of exhilaration, someone said my name, and there was Len. We shared an incredulous laugh before we were swept in different directions, but our meeting left me elated because in all the world there was no-one more fitting to see that day than the friend who'd taught me what it means to have roots, thousands upon thousands of years deep, in the soil of this country, and the generational trauma our ignorance had unleashed on the people who had loved and cared for it, known its every little nuance before we, the barbarians, arrived.

'Amazing,' says Sally, as we emerge from the forest. 'He's sometimes in the newspapers. Speaks out on land rights, the return of ancestral remains from overseas, cultural belongings from museums, matters like that.'

'I didn't know.' We turn right onto the old Huon Highway and begin weaving our way down into the valley of the North West River.

Then, 'Don't you ever wonder about your biological father?'

'Of course!'

'Yet you didn't ask Anneke?'

'It wasn't the right time. On Flinders, I'll ask her then.'

~

It's a windy Saturday morning when we land at Flinders Island airport and today it looks to be full of farmers talking loudly.

Sally grabs my arm. 'Look over there. Could that be Len?'

There's a rush of recognition. He's tall and lean and focusing on a conversation, except that every so often he looks around as though he's expecting someone.

'Looks like he's about to go fishing,' says Sally.

He's looking straight at us. I see recognition dawn in his eyes, and I smile as he walks towards us. I've been thrown off balance, too aware of his eyes, of his being there. He is smiling at me, we are smiling, and Sally is saying, 'Well, no introductions needed, I'll go and get the luggage,' and we stand there smiling, Len and I, and I figure someone's set me up.

He says, 'I wondered when you'd be back. Sure took your time. It's good to see you.'

'You too.' I barely notice the crowd dwindling.

'I hear your mum …' and he steps forward and hugs me. It's a big hug; it feels like a harbour, and he smells like a beach and the salty sea breeze, and just momentarily I wonder how he heard that news. Stepping back, he keeps a grip on my shoulders.

'I'm supposed to be meeting a puppy,' he says, and we walk out into boisterous weather.

'This meeting had nothing at all to do with Sally, did it?'

But he simply grins and looks away.

'Thanks a lot, Sal,' I say as she gives me my bag. 'Len's got to pick up a puppy. Any sign of one with the baggage?'

'Didn't notice. Sorry Len. Looks like you got us instead. There certainly wasn't a dog on the plane.'

'He's got to be around here somewhere,' he says, as we walk back inside. A woman says, 'That yours, Len?' and points at a crate partially hidden behind boxes.

We crowd around as he puts his hands in and gently pulls out a whimpering puppy, tan and white. A springer spaniel.

'Gift from a friend,' says Len, stroking him gently behind his floppy ears and along his back. 'You'll do, you little beauty,' he tells him. The puppy is assessing us all, a knowing expression on his speckled face.

'You two need a lift anywhere? I've got a ute out the front,' says Len, tucking his puppy under his arm.

'Dorothy's place, if that's not too far.'

He points to his ute. 'Hop in, I've got a quick phone call to make.'

The puppy ends up on my lap and, phone call made, Len returns, revs up and we're off, through green paddocks, beneath a blue sky, Cape Barren geese flying overhead. Squashed between the two of them, I stroke the puppy's fur, talking, catching up, gazing out at the island. I could sit like this forever, it feels so good. Energy rushes through my veins, skips along my nerves. It's a novel feeling. I can't see Verloren, but looking at Mount Strzelecki, I feel the presence of Mount Naturaliste and it seems to me that today is like the end of all things and the beginning of all things, merged, interweaving, part of the whole; that time's illusions truly play us all.

We bump down the driveway towards Dorothy's weatherboard beach cottage. The two women at the door move towards us.

I turn to Sally. 'Anneke and Dorothy!'

We pull up, hop out. 'Dorothy,' says Len. 'Yolla. Your visitors, collected as requested.' There are warm reunions all round, but I'm confused. I point at her. *Did Len just call you Yolla?*

'Come here,' she says, while the other three, chatting amiably, go inside with our luggage and the puppy.

'Where to start?' she says slowly. 'I've been calling myself Yolla for years, at first as a professional pseudonym for my creative work – but it's increasingly spilled into the rest of my life, at least here, on the islands and with my friends. Do you remember our meeting on Verloren?'

To say I feel taken aback is an understatement.

'Yes, but that was one brief meeting *years* ago. Your hair was dark and long. It's short now, and, you know, grey. You're so *different* and we're all older now.' I laugh incredulously.

'I'd have clarified, but there was too much overwhelm happening in Adelaide. At least for me. I felt vulnerable. I was learning that grudge-holding can wreck lives. Nicky, the year we met – Dorothy had told me about the new tenants on Verloren. To say I was stunned is an understatement.

'You and I, we spent so much time talking that day at Honeymoon, there really wasn't enough time for me to meet up with Freya and Wheeler. And the fact that I was on Verloren at all – Dorothy made me. I was somewhat terrified.'

Disbelief is plastered across my face.

'The situation was *so* complicated. This probably sounds ridiculous to you, but to arrive unannounced when there'd been no contact for so long – fear stopped me. That's why I got no further than Honeymoon Cove.' She pauses.

'Carry on.'

'Well, when you arrived on the beach alone, it was such a gift. Honestly, the best of gifts. The ability to get to know you without disturbing family dynamics – without, in such a little space of time, having to divide my attention between Freya and you and cope with Wheeler, avoid getting caught up in recriminations – well, hanging out with you on Honeymoon was bliss. It got the better of me.'

I straighten my spine, tighten my lips. Questions thunder through my head.

'Come,' she says, and like a mind reader, 'Plenty of time for questions. Let's go inside and join the others.'

There's a laden table and Dorothy has prepared the garden

studio for us, 'unless you'd rather stay on the boat with Yolla,' she says to me.

No, I wouldn't, but I merely shrug.

Over lunch Dorothy tells us about the flight the two of them did to Alaska, following the moonbirds, and Anneke tells us how she bought her boat for a song in Greece, restored it and sailed it with a crew of four friends, including Dorothy, back to Australia. By the dates she provides, I work out she bought it a few years after our wild fig tree arrival and departure. We can see the boat. It's anchored in the bay where it's protected from all but a northerly blow.

'My forever home,' she says, smiling at me. 'And Dorothy and Len are willing crew when I'm here. Sometimes Bert comes along for the ride.'

'*Isibongo* is beautiful,' says Dorothy. 'A Van der Stadt. She sailed in the 1971 Cape to Rio Race.'

'A timber classic,' says Anneke. 'I can't wait to get you on board.'

'Would you be willing to sail us to Verloren?' asks Sally, cuddling the puppy.

'Len's keen to take us all over on his boat,' says Dorothy.

Len nods. 'The forecast is good for tomorrow.'

~

After Len leaves, Dorothy and Sally prepare for a stroll along the beach. Anneke and I change into more suitable gear and row out to the yacht moored in the natural harbour formed by a rockshelf and an island. It's meticulously maintained. There's a chart spread across the navigation table. The bookshelves in the saloon are full of nautical classics.

She pours us drinks and we sit in the cockpit talking about Freya's funeral, then, noticing my ring, she touches the pearl with the tip of a finger. 'I once had a ring exactly like this,' she muses. 'Funny thing. It was Celeste's. I nicked her toiletry bag when I left home and discovered the ring in the bottom of it.'

I slip it off and give it to her. 'Another funny thing. I found it on the island, in a violin case, washed up on the beach.'

'You did not!' She laughs softly, holding it up to the light. 'How serendipitous.' And slips it onto her finger as though it's an old friend.

'It's yours to keep if I can trade it for information.'

'What would that be?'

'My father. Tell me *everything*.'

'Honestly?'

'Honestly.'

'I'm appalled you don't know.' I watch anxiety shift to decisiveness. 'We met in Ullapool,' she begins. 'I knew his sister; we sailed together. The three of us travelled to Europe, to the Greek islands. She sailed home and he and I talked about a shared future. We discussed living on one of the islands long-term but then decided to carry on travelling through Asia to Australia.'

A gust swings the yacht's bow north-easterly. 'About that time I was offered an exhibition; couldn't believe my luck. It was career altering, and so we agreed he'd head to Bali with a mate while I stayed back to put in the work before meeting him in Australia, not understanding that from that point on our plans were doomed. He arrived ahead of me, and well, the rest is history.'

'*Wheeler?* You can't be serious.'

She's watching me carefully.

'I don't believe you.'

She straightens her back, plays with her wine. 'You should have been told a long time ago.'

'Assuming what you say is true, did he know you were pregnant?'

'He didn't need to ask and I didn't need to tell. I'm shocked you don't know.'

'Will you give me a moment?' My hand trembles as I put down my wine and make my way forward to the pulpit. A slow-motion explosion in my head is fragmenting me.

After a while, I hear her footsteps approach and surreptitiously wipe my eyes, staring steadfastly ahead of me. Holding onto the furled headsail, she says to my back, 'Nicky, the distressing two weeks before your birth, and the subsequent consequences to my life and yours – it will take many conversations to settle on an agreed understanding. But what I need you to know is that for me it was always about making the best of a bad situation with your needs foremost in my mind. None of us could offer you much in the way of security – financial or emotional – in our own right, but Freya and Wheeler had more family backing than I had. They had a home. My feelings towards the two of them were beyond conflicted. I couldn't stand the messages I was being fed about myself. I felt sideswiped by betrayal on many fronts. Frankly, I did not want to be anywhere near them and neither did they want to be around me. In a moment of deep despair, I succumbed to their view that I was unfit and unsound. I was so alone, so without resources, but believe me,

I was inconsolable and not in a state of mind where I could consider the options rationally.'

'Did Freya know about the two of you?'

'I was seething but told her nothing. You know better than me how he handled it in the longer term, but I can say with certainty that he didn't tell her while I was around.'

Is it feasible their communication skills were so comprehensively atrocious? That they were so ethically challenged, so disarrayed? I'm listening with considerable suspicion. I have no good reason to trust her, but being sideswiped by betrayal is an all too familiar feeling.

'What did he say to you when you got to Australia?'

'He avoided me until the day we had a raging argument. It was the only time we were ever alone to speak to each other; Freya was always present and he was invariably absent. I had you in my arms on the beach and I had to listen to him playing down our relationship. So hurtful. Just another disappointing man.'

Above us a seagull hangs, steadying itself against a gust.

'Maybe they were being truthful, you know, when they said I wasn't in my right mind. If I was, surely I would have kept you against all odds. I mean, the things they said confused me. Hurt. They lodged deep. Every time I considered getting in touch – and often still, quite randomly – their words loom up and haunt me, lay me low. One of my many unwon battles.'

I watch Sally and Dorothy walk back up to the house.

'I'll take a storm at sea over *ever* letting anyone get too close to me again. Dorothy says I have trust issues. I run from relationships. I run fast.'

There's another silence I make no effort to break.

'That's between you and me,' she says. 'And Dorothy.'

Frankly, the churn in my head is so all-consuming it's hard to pay attention.

'Freya and Wheeler, they enjoyed your childhood. I hope you'll let me share the next however many decades with you.'

I give a small snort of derision. 'What you've told me about Wheeler – it's incomprehensible he'd keep that secret from us.' But an old childish refrain, that parents should never be trusted, is also telling me otherwise. My voice is purple with anger. The solace of believing that the father I knew really was my father coupled with the cruelty of his deception is intolerable. If it weren't for the fact that Dorothy and Len seem to like Anneke and that Sally has challenged me, I wouldn't listen to what she's telling me at all.

She nods. 'Let me give you some space,' and behind me I hear her returning to the galley, and the rising wind in the rigging.

Eventually I follow her down the companionway. I'm thinking how nebulous the truth is. 'The story about the wild fig tree. Was that even true?'

She takes a pen from the chart table. 'Give me your hand, Nicky.'

I proffer it reluctantly. She holds it gently with her left hand and draws a little map.

'It was. The tree still stands, I hope, between a river and the sea. That day on the beach with Wheeler, I'd have caused the sea to rise if I could, I was so angry with him.'

I head up the companionway. Behind me she says, 'One day we

should sail up there, and go and pay our respects to that kind tree.'

She's talking to keep connection, to help me mask the turmoil she knows isn't abating, assuming more trust than there really is, because her comments about my father aren't helping. I feel protective towards him.

'Here,' she says, when we're in the tender, in the lee of the yacht, and she hands me a pill for the headache that is killing me, the pearl a full moon on her finger.

~

'You feel the cold these days, Nicky?' Len says as we reach the Lady Barron wharf. I don't, but engine checks completed, he helps me into wet weather gear that smells of bait and therefore of Wheeler, while Dorothy assumes a position at the bow and Anneke prepares to release the lines.

'Look after that puppy,' he says to Sally, over the thrum of the engine. Anneke clambers aboard the *Rosy Wrasse*, and we pull the fenders on board as he steers her around rusty scallop boats moored at the wharf.

Sally is sitting on a cray pot. I stand beside Len as we pass Little Green Island. Cape Barren Island stretches out serenely ahead of us.

'These islands!' I remark. 'How to tell one from the other?'

He fiddles in his pocket. 'You need this. Your old man lost it a long time ago. Found it in the cave, a flipper down near Tinman's.'

It's Wheeler's compass.

I hold it tightly and he drapes an arm around me. 'Knew you'd come back for it one day,' he says keeping his eye on a cormorant winging by, his face angled to the breeze. 'What kept you?'

'I guess it took me a long time to find the map.'

He laughs. 'Well, the island's a conservation area now. It has a marine park too.'

'That's a massive change!'

'Long time coming. All thanks to Sam's Soak, some critical seabird breeding sites, and sea caves off The Dagger.'

'Did you hear that, Sal?'

She turns to face him. 'Tell me more.'

'Uncle Arthur's cattle are gone.'

'I know that. He was outraged.'

'Some islands are back in Aboriginal hands now,' says Dorothy, coming up the companionway, Anneke behind her. 'Lots to do to heal Verloren.'

'It's happening. There was a Wildcare group here last month,' says Len. 'I brought them out here.'

'And there's talk of making the house an artist's retreat,' says Anneke. 'Bring it on, I say.'

'Or having volunteers mind the lighthouse,' adds Len. 'Forward steps, but climate change, Nicky. If you're sufficiently connected to the land and sea, you can see the signs.'

I lean against the transom, remembering how the island had felt overwhelmingly hostile when we'd arrived in 1984. Today we approach it in silence, Mount Naturaliste half hidden by cloud. There are moonbirds around us and if Wheeler were here he'd be quoting TS Eliot.

Cormorants rise from the jetty as we come alongside. All I see is the beauty. All I feel is a poignant nostalgia tightening my throat.

Lines secured, I stand for a moment on Whale Rock as the sun breaks through the clouds, and nostalgia creates a strong sense of my father's presence. Honking geese, descendants of Phil and Liz, head south over the isthmus as we reach the lighthouse.

A little later Sally, standing on the steps with Anneke and Dorothy, sings the first few lines of 'Auld Lang Syne' to herself as I stand with Len, surveying the island in silence. The mountain is listening; it knows we're here. I search the sky for eagles, but I only see gulls and cormorants. Len is preoccupied with a firestick; gum leaves wrapped in paperbark, bound with river reed.

'Remember how much Kes loved this island?' I'm watching the puppy sniff the scats and feathers then bound back for cuddles.

'You should have seen how he took to Flinders,' Len says. 'Loved a day out fishing on the *Rosy Wrasse*.'

I'm grateful for that. It had hurt intensely when Freya made an ad hoc decision to let Len keep Kes, on account of Nan's cat.

'I buried him in the dunes behind Restless. Always reckoned it was his favourite beach.'

His body and Wheeler's have transformed into the luminous beauty all around me, but while my feelings for Kes involve guilt, my feelings about my father are ambivalent and painful.

A pipit releases a long yearning trill and I pause to watch its quivering dive. There are more tussocks out the front of the house than I remember. The boulders are every bit as atmospheric.

'I do tours out here. Fishing, diving – that sort of thing.'

'Wheeler would be envious.'

'Got Bert to thank for my livelihood. He's a silent partner in this venture. He let me buy a part share in the boat. But you know me, Nicky. It's really all about caring for Country.'

The others join us as he welcomes us to Country, and it feels like all his Ancestors are gathered there with us. The firestick is smoking. He holds it forward to each of us in turn and we fan the smoke towards us. A deep peace settles over me. This island and me. We are one and the same. I have the distinct feeling that if I turn around I'll see Wheeler striding over Mount Aeolian, fishing rod in hand, Kes at heel.

Afterwards, when the others are chatting at a little distance, we talk about our lives and our work and I tell him that I'm deciding what to do next. I scoop up the puppy Len has started calling Skipper and we follow the others down to Sunlit.

'Len, what do *you* think happened to Wheeler?' I ask.

'Bert and me, we puzzled over it.' He looks at me carefully. 'Could be he just went diving once too often.'

As the five of us stand together in silence, watching the waves move towards the shore, I put my hand in my pocket and fold my fingers around the page I'd found loose in his notebook. It's a page I've read so many times that I can recite it from memory and it's quite possible that he wrote it shortly before he died:

Letters come from Nicky, but not a word from Freya. Dream of her constantly. One moment she's Alison Blair, next, a Southern Ocean kelpie. I encounter her at Emita, at Honeymoon, at Gullet Cove. She's out on the Tinman's Teeth and I'm cutting my feet trying to reach her. As I stretch to grasp her, she slips into the sea and never reappears.

Sullen clouds. Bert stopped by to pick up Len. Saw them off, then sat on the cliff below the lighthouse, thinking about a river in New Zealand, the way its roar still repeats in my head, thinking about the way Freya makes that dive down at Tinman's. Sometimes it's not so easy keeping your balance.

There's the mountain and there's the cliff and there's Freya waiting at the Tinman's Teeth. Need to ask Bert to get me off here, A man can't sit about watching his mountain receding, got to get my act together. Time to head down to Hobart. Got to start building a boat.

We walk behind Sapphire City and over to Restless to pay our respects to Kes, making plans to visit Bert. A dead goose lies decaying among the tussocks.

'My god, that stinks!' Sally stumbles clear of it and a wallaby bounds away, stopping to stare back at us from a safe distance. I pause for a moment, thinking about Wheeler's lost manuscript. When I mention it to Len, he shakes his head. 'No idea. I'd forgotten about it, quite honestly, if I ever knew about it at all.'

It means I'll continue to hold in my head the image of pages scattered along the beaches, lining nests, submerged beneath the sea, entangled in branches, blowing out across the island and the ocean, spreading and dispersing, unread, across the strait. Seems to me that epitomises Wheeler. He spread himself too thin. He couldn't reconcile his inner conflicts and endless interests. All those things about him that I'd once easily loved, that drove Freya crazy, that potentially destabilised him so that like Gunther, he faded out of the plot.

~

Early the next morning, while Sally jogs Emita and Len and I amble behind, I look across at the mountain, serene in the distance, and at the islands where I once pretended palms and orange trees grew.

'So,' he says. 'Wheeler, your father in every sense of the word?'

'I still can't get my head around the implications.'

We walk on in silence, Len and I. I'm remembering our trip down to Tinman's at sunset the previous evening when we'd stood together on the reef, arm in arm the five of us, and when I'd got teary Len had let me wipe my face on his sleeve and when I'd talked about parental betrayal, he'd offered it again.

'What do you think you'll do now?' he says, bending down to pick up a cowrie shell lying on the damp kelp at our feet.

'Get to know Anneke, figure out to what extent she's trustworthy, and take time to find clarity.'

'You could do that here – find a place to write on Flinders.'

We turn to face the lighthouse, looking back along the tracks we've written into the sand, and then we go on walking, catching up with Sally at Sam's Soak.

At Sunlit Cove, she and Len decide to swim while I stay on

the warm beach teaching Skipper about sticks while he teaches me patience.

'Fetch,' I urge, but he wags his tail and goes galloping clumsily after a welcome swallow that dips low over the water, circles about us and flies straight back up to Mount Aeolian. I laugh, because the world is sublime, and while seabirds swirl above me, I am struck with wonder, suffused with sudden happiness, for it seems in that moment that the world exists on a current of love. Time stills, it stops. The waves stop and even the wind stops. Illusions of separateness dissolve. And then the moment passes and everything breathes again, together, and the planet continues to turn, rolling through space and time, a small, wondrous planet ablaze with life; with warring life forms all underpinned by love, all jewels in the radiant and infinite web of being.

The End

Author's Note

To you, the reader – I hope the shearwater has been able to lift you effortlessly across these pages and that you've enjoyed the experience as much as I've enjoyed writing my characters into places I love or have imagined.

I had a treasure chest at my disposal while working long ago in the library of what in 2024 is the Department of Natural Resources and Environment (Tasmania) and have threaded tiny jewels I found there through this novel.

Anita Heiss's *Growing up Aboriginal in Australia*, (Black Inc, 2011), Silas Piotrowski's 2021 PhD thesis, *The rights of Indigenous people in archaeology and cultural heritage using a case study from lutruwita / Tasmania* (University of Queensland, 2021) and *Grease and Ochre: The blending of two cultures at the colonial sea frontier* by Aunty Patsy Cameron (Fullers Bookshop, 2011) were found later and proved invaluable. If the chapter titled 'Jewels and Binoculars' has a familiar ring, it's because it's from 'Visions of Johanna' by Bob Dylan. The poem in the novel was first published in Famous Reporter, No. 26 (2002).

Little penguins, part of this novel's supporting cast, are benefitting directly from *Beneath the Wild Fig Tree* via a biomimicry project. Curious? Well, it's beautiful and it's clever. You can find out more at wildmindpublishing.com.au.

Acknowledgements

AUSTRALIA'S NATURAL BEAUTY INSPIRED this novel and so my first acknowledgement is to the land and waters that sustain us, and to the many First People of Australia, who under the guidance of their Elders have cared for them with an understanding far beyond the comprehension of us later arrivals. I hope my novel honours Country, Sea and Stars. I'd particularly like to acknowledge, with heartfelt thanks, Aunty Patsy Cameron, for her warmth and generosity in helping me ensure that this novel respects the values of her people. Deep gratitude, as well, to those members of the pakana/palawa community who have shared their understanding of Country with me. If I've made errors stumbling along cultural boundaries, these are unintended and mine alone.

I'd like to acknowledge the Tasmanian Writers' Centre (now TasWriters), who gave me a mentorship. In addition, I owe huge thanks to Louise Thurtell for a manuscript assessment that became my guiding star while David Owen helped me navigate through shoals of beginner's mistakes. Thanks also go to Gordon Thompson.

Gratitude to Alice Youell for a thoughtful structural edit and to Jocelyn Hungerford for going above and beyond with copy editing, contributing lived insights I hadn't anticipated. Warmest thanks to Hannah Pemberton for an initial sensitivity reading, for gifting me characters, and for her belief and enthusiasm. Thanks, Andy Bridge for reading my novel before designing this beautiful cover and kudos to Ann Dettori and her team for an interior design that far exceeded my expectations. Jessica Perini, my appreciation for your proofreading and help besides. Across the UK, France, and Australia, it's been an enjoyable series of collaborations.

If not for conversations with Peter Nichol, Dave and Leisha Owen and Jayne Walker, I might have stayed forever anchored. A particularly deep bow of gratitude to Ian Terry and Helen Semmler. They, along with Greg Hocking, enabled me to visit many Tasmanian islands. Ian was also my final draft's last reader and his book, *Uninnocent Landscapes*, my final read before preparing this work for publication.

I also owe thanks to Ray Carpenter for scrutinising the last draft, as well as to other friends and family who contributed their opinions, knowledge, showed interest, offered encouragement and read earlier drafts and chapters. For help with one important decision, I thank the following friends and family. In Cape Town: Lois Apter, Maria Pemberton and her family, Helene Tyndall, Diana Judge and my brother, Andrew Preston.

In Hobart, Launceston and Canberra, thanks go to Sue Dilley, Sue Hood, Kay and Peter Hughes, Yeutha May, Claire Nicol, Terese Henning, Jane Bamford, Andrew Wilson, David Pemberton, Rosemary Gales, Ollie Gales, Elsa Gales and Anna Mackintosh. Karmen and John Pemberton - additional thanks for the goat.

In New South Wales, Allan Rudner, Janet Court, Todd and Jayne Walker, Deb and John Schmidt, Jo Brady, her family and David Rapaport also contributed to this decision. Thanks, Geof Fethers in Victoria, and in the UK, Carmen and Niall Bradnick, and Nikki and Sam Reynolds. Thanks also go to Trish and Richard Munday. Gill Mee, in addition, lured me up hills on the homeward stretch, and thanks, Bridget Canham, for supportive conversations on land and water.

This novel endured neglect while I wrote letters to a certain Federal Minister, then opted for sailing. I've named a yacht in memory of Ernest Targett, and with thanks for the good times to the crew. To all those who sailed with me and with whom I sailed, along with my co-boatowner of *Samos*, Eloise Carr – you've all infused a little sailing into this novel.

Many passionate zoologists, botanists, geologists and archaeologists shared stories, knowledge and occasional fieldtrips with me. I'm indebted, because these conversations and a longing to visit some of the remote places they went to played into this work. In many ways, this novel became the fieldtrip I went on when I couldn't leave home.

In addition, Judy van Rooyen, Michelle Seymour, Jacky Tetlow, and Di Forrester in Cape Town have eased the way this year, and to my mother, Kay Preston – thank you for helping me make this possible.

Mike Pemberton read this novel many times over, picked up the slack when the study door was closed and often when it was open, engaged in endless natural history conversations and stood by patiently while my novel took me adventuring. He gets my biggest heartfelt thank you of all, for this reason and so many more.

Finally, sláinte to the animals, both domestic and wild, who accompanied and inspired my writing, and, while I pay respect to the Ancestors who cared for all the Countries on this continent, I also pay respect to my own. My father for igniting my love of the coast and wildlife, as well as Agnes Marshall, chef, writer, entrepreneur and inventor extraordinaire for making this seem possible and for giving me a lifelong passion for ice cream.

Fiona Preston was born in South Africa but has spent most of her life in Tasmania (Lutruwita / Trouwerner), where this novel was substantially written. She has also lived in the Kimberley, Western Australia and in New South Wales. She has blogged about exploring coastlines and has been published in local publications. This novel was completed on Gumbaynggirr Country on the Australian mainland.